DreamLand

by

Ken Reeth

&

Matthew J. Pallamary

Mystic Ink Publishing

KEN REETH & MATTHEW J. PALLAMARY

Mystic Ink Publishing
San Diego, CA
www.mysticinkpublishing.com

ISBN 10: 0692220283 (sc)
ISBN 13: 978-0692220283 (sc)
Printed in the United States of America
San Bernardino, California

This book is printed on acid-free paper made from 30% post-consumer waste recycled material.

Library of Congress Control Number: 2014940813
Mystic Ink Publishing, San Diego, CA

Book Jacket and Page Design: Matthew J. Pallamary/San Diego CA
Author's Photograph: Matthew J. Pallamary -- Gibbs Photo/Malibu CA
Ken Reeth -- Barbara Reeth

DEDICATION

This book is dedicated to Ken Reeth and Colleen Kennedy.

CHAPTER ONE

A fuzzy sensation blurred Tom's thoughts and numbed his body. His vision clouded as a cool gray haze enveloped him, soft and shimmery, like meadow mist, then his surroundings snapped into focus, sharp and clear. He smelled the fresh scent of pine, heard songbirds warbling in the conifer thicket across a sun dappled pond. A dragonfly, fanning crystalline wings, sunned on a twig at the tip of a half-submerged log at the water's edge.

Tom filled his lungs with sweet morning air and grinned at the five-year old beside him. Handsome little guy. Thick, dark hair, like Tom once had. His mom's blue eyes. "This is how you bait a hook, son. If you don't do it just right, the fish'll steal him." He impaled a squirming night crawler on the barb of a fishhook.

"There." Tom held the baited hook up for the boy to admire. "That'll do the job."

The five-year-old giggled, blue eyes twinkling. "This is fun, Dad."

"Sure is, pal. Now, let's get after that fish." Tom tossed the line into the water, rippling the smooth surface. "Here, you hold it." He handed the rod to the boy. "Keep your eye on the bobber. Soon as it dips underwater, tug hard and you'll hook him."

"Okay, Dad." The boy took the rod.

Tears of happiness burned Tom's eyes as he watched the small hands tighten around the grip. "That's the way, son. Attaboy."

"Later, can we go to the park?"

"Okay. We'll play catch. We'll have lots of fun, you and me."

A flash.

Tom's feet flew out from under him. His body tingled, and he floated in a soundless void, then as suddenly as he had gone, he returned to the pond.

"I love you, Dad," the small boy said as if nothing had happened. "I love you too, son," Tom choked. Don't let it end now. Please.

"Let's go to the park and ride the merry-go-round, Dad."

"We will, pal." Tom's voice trembled. His legs felt weak. "We'll do lots of fun things."

Another flash.

Tom turned his face to the sky. "No! I'm not ready!"
Again, the void swallowed him.

"Have mercy!" he shouted as he spiraled into a vortex, tumbling downward. "I need more time. Need to hear him say he loves me again. My little boy! I'm sorry, son. I wanted it to last longer. Tell me you love me, son. Please. Please."

The boy's voice grew faint. "Take me to the zoo, Dad. Wanna fly a kite, walk in the woods, wanna be with you. Please, Dad, take me to a ball-bb-ball-ballgame, ballgame, Dad, Dad, Dad.

The tiny voice echoed into emptiness...

A high-pitched tone pierced the shadows of a dimly lit room and the thin green lifeline on a life support monitor went flat. Rita Cariño's fingers danced over a panel, triggering a series of beeps that silenced the alarm before lines of code flashed onto multiple screens. Did they get enough to verify? Would she have to bring him back? She faced Doctor Jackson with a second syringe primed, thumb on the plunger. "Nineteen seconds. Want me to try again?"

Her heart raced. At this moment, Morgan Jackson represented God and Rita his instrument. She held the power of life or death in her hand.

Morgan shook his head. "We have enough. Let him go." The tall black physician placed Tom's arm at his side. "We'll need the usual reports." He released the bony wrist and fumbled for his pen. "I'll sign the death certificate."

Rita breathed an inner sigh and set the syringe on a tray, then handed Morgan the IPad containing the certificate and stats on Thomas Harley. Stepping around the bed, she removed wires from the temple and extremities of his withered corpse.

Petite and dark-haired, Rita's soft-spoken manner had occasionally been construed as timidity, but her brown eyes flashed and spit fire when she spoke her mind about the things she cared most about. Right now her heart went out to the five-year-old boy with his mother's blue eyes, forced to grow up without a dad. "Harley wasn't much of a man, was he?"

Morgan looked up from his paperwork. "Worthless. This dream was probably the highlight of his miserable life. Spent most of it in prison. Drew his final sentence thirty years ago. Life without parole. First degree murder. Harley told me he thought about his boy every day for the past thirty years. Supplied us with an excellent description. Amazing details."

Rita removed the I.V. "Has anybody talked with his son?"

"I thought you knew." Morgan scribbled his signature on the death certificate. "Thirty years ago, Tom Harley came home drunk and beat his pregnant wife to death. His son was never born."

CHAPTER TWO

Rita watched Morgan moving in the stiff, formal fashion he always assumed after shepherding another soul into the afterlife. As the final gesture, he drew the sheet over the late Thomas Harley's head.

"Almost lost him at eleven," she said.

"You did fine." Morgan glanced at the stop clock. "Terminated at nineteen."

The door whisked open and tall, thin Hodge Michaels breezed into PermaDream, collar open, sandy hair uncombed, and a two day stubble on his face. "What a death!" he said, grinning as if he'd just made his final payment and owned the world. "What a beautiful death!" His voice quivered with excitement as he approached. "Absolutely amazing, the amount of dreaming we can jam into such a short time. Amazing."

"He flat lined at nine seconds." Morgan snapped latex gloves from his slender brown fingers. "Rita brought him back."

"Pumped him with Epinephrine-G," she said.

Morgan nodded toward the covered body. "You kept him going long enough for the initial sequence to play out."

"Nice work, Rita," Hodge said. "Dad'll be proud of you."

Rita handed Morgan an IPad. "Here's the tracking data."

"I saw a sneak preview of the background track," Morgan said. "It was wonderful."

"I saw it too." Rita smiled. "The merry-go-round scene was breathtaking."

"Too bad Harley didn't last long enough to reach it," Morgan added.

"It won't be wasted," Hodge interjected. "We'll use it for others. Maybe a terminal child." He snatched the IPad from Morgan and scanned it. "How does this look?"

"Hey, not so fast." Morgan reached over Hodge's shoulder and took back the IPad. "I'm not finished."

"Sorry, Morg. Don't mind me, I'm just excited." Hodge pounded his palm. "Two hundred successful subjects in less than a year. Two hundred peaceful, pleasant, planned deaths. Two hundred miracles. Nothing can stop PermaDream now. Nothing!"

Hodge took Rita's hand and pumped it. "We worked our butts off and damned if we didn't make it happen." He slapped Morgan on the back. "By God, it's like winning the lottery, Morg. Feels great!"

"Sure does." Morgan rubbed his cheek. "These old smile muscles haven't had much exercise lately."

Hodge looked in the mirror and flexed his facial muscles, then frowned, rubbing his chin. "Jesus, I need a shave." He turned from the mirror. "No time for that now. I can't wait to tell Dad."

"He'll be thrilled." Rita permitted herself a smile, relieved that the year long pressure of nonstop testing, evaluating, and retesting had concluded. She gave Hodge's slender arm a gentle squeeze, aware of the grim truth he faced, knowing that his father, Edgar, would not be with them much longer.

Rita loved, respected and cared for the ailing neuroscientist as if he were her own father. With Edgar Michaels' fragile condition worsening by the day, the past month had been especially intense. Now, Edgar's final dream waited. More than anything, she wanted him to have it. He had hung on until the final test series had been completed. Now PermaDream, the miracle he invented, would assure a happy ending for his life. "I visited Edgar this morning," she said. "He was lucid. Upbeat. Talked about joining your mother."

"Soon," Hodge replied. "The Indiana dream sequences have been ready for weeks."

"Edgar's been fending off the end, waiting for these results," Morgan added as he scanned rows of figures scrolling down a screen. "Such will power. Never saw anything like it."

Hodge pulled a crumpled sheet of paper from his pocket.

"I've been putting together some facts for our press release. Tell me if it's too technical." He unfolded the paper and held it in front of him. "From the beginning, Edgar Michaels' belief in euthanasia, coupled with degrees in computer science, psychology, and neuroscience fueled his interest in synaptic brain wave research. His dream became reality when he developed the concept of using magnetic resonance to stimulate the synapses in an area of the brain known as the pontine tegmentum." He looked up with an expectant expression. "Too far out?"

Rita shook her head. "If the editors think it is, they'll come up with an expert to translate it."

"Sure, that's their job," Morgan said. "Hell, we're talking about a major scientific breakthrough here. It's impressive even if the readers can't fathom it."

"There's more." Hodge resumed reading. "Coupled with the discovery of a harmonic that increased dopamine levels, Michaels devised a method of modulating neurotransmitter and receptor activity across the synapses. The end result is what we refer to as, PermaDream."

"PermaDream." Rita repeated with a sigh. Finally. She always joked that old Edgar would have developed computer generated dreams years earlier, but he had to slow down to allow technology to catch up with him.

She had been with him a good part of the way. Several years before what they called the Kevorkian trials triggered the suicide revolution in the United States, Rita, a Mexican citizen with a degree from San Diego State, had experienced the dismay of seeing loved ones die in misery. First, her beloved grandfather when she was a little girl in Tijuana, then her mother several years ago.

Grandpapa's death had been sudden, something she never talked about, but she couldn't speak enough about her mother's agonizing, yearlong passing. Rita could only watch in helpless horror as her mother suffered, atrophied, and finally died, consumed by inoperable cancer. If only PermaDream had existed for her. If only she could have slipped away, dreaming of happy times, instead of...

"Your dad's going to love the obituary," Morgan said. "You should read it to him."

"Maybe I will." Hodge folded the paper and returned it to his pocket. "He'll want you to put him under as soon as he hears the news, Morg. Can't blame him. It's been hell for him cooped up in that hospital room."

"Like I said, will power." Morgan shook his head in disbelief. "The only reason he's still alive."

"God bless him," Rita said, crossing herself.

Hodge Michaels removed his lab jacket, hung it in a closet and slipped into a sport coat, smoothing the lapel with trembling fingers. Time to bring Dad the news. Time to say good-bye. Time to take charge. His armpits dampened and his heart pounded. The realization that the moment was at hand made breathing difficult. Finger-combing his hair, he headed for the door. Might as well get it over with. He managed a deep, shaky breath, trying to calm himself, but his stomach continued to flip-flop. "See you in Dad's room."

"Hold on, Hodge!" Morgan followed him into the hallway. "I'd better cross-check Harley's stats with Pre-dream. We don't want any discrepancies. Coming, Rita?"

"No. I'll notify the medical examiner's office to pick up Harley and tie things down at this end. See you in Edgar's room." Rita uncradled the wall phone, then glanced up, her dark eyes wet and shiny. "Tell Edgar we did it for him, Hodge."

"I will." Hodge sighed, grateful for the delay. He followed Morgan through a door marked, "PREDREAM", into a large room with pastel pink walls. Muted beeps and soft humming sounds permeated the air and the peaceful strains of Brahm's Lullaby flowed like warm honey from concealed speakers.

Six beds lined one wall. A maze of wires and IV tubes from each bedside streamed into a bank of panels, where dozens of red, green, blue, and amber LED's blinked. Two nurses moved from bed to bed like white shadows, supervising the stabilization and well-being of terminally ill volunteers and monitoring the intravenous drug delivery system, designed by Morgan and controlled by Morpheus, the supercomputer.

Morgan slipped behind a U-shaped console to check a bank of six flickering monitors, each displaying multi-colored waveforms. Rows of geometric and alphanumeric figures and symbols filled a seventh. As he touched each waveform with his long index finger, the display transformed, scrolling fresh information down the screen.

Hodge's stomach churned in anticipation of telling his father the good news and in dread at the thought of bidding him farewell. Pouring himself coffee, he stirred in a spoonful of sugar and watched from inside the doorway. Morg had enough of the old country doctor in him that he would not be satisfied until he personally checked, then rechecked every detail. In Hodge's mind, his lanky African-American friend's ability to heal and sustain life bordered on mythical. He saw Morgan as a modern day healer, descended from a lineage dating back to pre-history shamans.

Hodge felt positive about facing the future without his dad. He had been a key motivator in the creative process all the way, even when away at school, but the old man skillfully managed to avoid any discussion of financial affairs with him. Edgar Michaels had made his fortune as a world-class neuroscientist, headquartered in the United States and had personally funded the venture, rather than bring in outsiders. Moving the project to Mexico served two purposes, cutting expenses and avoiding the inevitable paper-laden government interloping that accompanied federal grants.

For the first time, Hodge would have to delve into the convoluted financial affairs of PermaDream and the idea left him cold. Still, he had decided to accept total responsibility and would do his best to manage the business end. There had to be an attorney and his first mission would be to root him out and pursue the details.

The original staff, created by Edgar Michaels, with shrinking funds and tall promises had stuck together, driven by the old man's glittering vision of PermaDream and a world devoid of the apprehension of lonely, lingering death.

Hodge vowed to maintain his dad's unwavering drive. Now, he fidgeted, as his father suffered and waited. "Hey, Morg, what did you guys do about the data transfer problem?" He asked, making conversation to help the time pass. "Ever get the infra-red working?"

Morgan smiled, mostly with his eyes, as he continued to process information. "Too much crosstalk and reflection. We decided to go with a microwave system. When it's time for the terminal dream, we download vitals from the main console and switch to battery." He tapped another panel. "Unit's plugged in here and hooked up to Morpheus, through radio link. Once Morpheus establishes a connection and verifies the subject's stability, the CPU resumes operations and initiates its subroutines, then we move the patient to the PermaDream facility."

Hodge smothered a grin with the back of his hand as his Dad's closest friend rattled off computer jargon with the fluency of an engineer. The all Georgia high school track star and honor graduate of UCSD Medical School, joined the PermaDream team during the intensive early years of its evolution, while young Hodge was still absorbing the classics and quoting Romeo and Juliet to the coeds at Stamford. Much like Edgar Michaels before him, Morgan Jackson, one of San Diego's most respected physicians, had become a fifty-year-old computer whiz; an electronic shaman.

"Congratulations," a husky voice whispered at Hodge's shoulder. Soft breath brushed his ear and the lush scent of Royal Secret filled his senses.

Denise.

Hodge glanced around and caught his breath as Denise Moore's smoke-gray eyes connected with his and pillow soft lips returned his smile. A surge of carnal heat exploded in the pit of his stomach and raged through his body. After years of platonic friendship and painful longing, the daily eye-jolt of seeing her still weakened his knees. Today, the onrushing specter of his father's death added urgency to his desire.

Denise shook loose chestnut hair that tumbled over her shoulders, then leaned closer and half-whispered, "How'd we do?" The huskiness in her voice added to her aura.

"Looks great," he said. "Morg's wrapping up. Then, I'll give Dad the news."

"What'll I tell the press about Edgar?"

"I need time to think. If they ask, be vague. Tell them he's thrilled with the final results and is resting. Change the subject."

Denise nodded. "I'll handle it." She touched his cheek, sending a shiver of excitement through him, same as the night they met. During his final year at Stamford, Denise had approached Hodge at one of his father's UCSD lectures and introduced herself as former Science Editor of the Baltimore Sun and a devoted follower of the dream-control project.

From the moment he first laid eyes on the tall beauty, with the graceful curves and long legs, Hodge felt a staggering physical attraction toward her. He often wondered if she felt it too, but Denise gave him no clue. After an impromptu midnight dinner of ribs, gnocchi and red wine at the Lido in Lemon Grove, they huddled in a corner booth, sipping Cherry Heering and drinking coffee, while Hodge wowed her with his father's ideas for PermaDream. Soon after, he introduced her to Edgar and she joined the team as Director of Marketing and Operations.

Denise peered past him to the corner work station where Morgan consulted with a team of nurses. "No problems? Morpheus? Data transfer? Drug delivery?"

"Not a hitch." Hodge snapped his fingers. "Harley went out like a light."

"About time." She frowned. "If I was in charge of his dream, the creep wouldn't have had such a fast, happy exit." Her expression hardened. "Imagine, allowing that monster to spend quality time with the son he murdered. Why?"

"Harley was Ollie Daggett's cousin," Hodge answered in a matter-of-fact tone.

"Another Goddamned Daggett!" Denise snapped, her eyes ablaze with sudden fury. "I should have known. Everyone connected to that bastard makes my skin crawl. When I think about Congressman Manzur and his family..." She caught her breath and turned away. "I can still see the pictures of the burning wreckage on the tarmac."

Hodge sighed. "It's never been proven that the crash was anything but an accident."

"Oh, please, Hodge! Manzur calls for a Congressional investigation and the next night his damned plane blows up on the runway. His wife and two sweet little children murdered with him. On Christmas Eve!" Her smoky eyes flashed with seldom seen fury. "Ollie Daggett is a cruel, homicidal piece of shit. Now we're blessed with the repulsive monster he calls a son."

"What are you talking about?"

"I just shared an elevator with that degenerate." She hugged herself. "The way Chazz stared at me made my skin crawl."

Hodge tensed. "Chazz Daggett stared at you?" He felt a twinge of anger at the thought of young Daggett ogling Denise. His Denise.

"Chazz Daggett!" She spit out the name, wrinkling her nose as if smelling something bad. "He was a dream volunteer during the prelims. I'll never forget his ugly, bigoted fantasies."

Hodge nodded. "Morgan turned him down every time. For some reason, Dad overruled the decisions."

"It's that oddball relationship between Edgar and Ollie Daggett," she said. "I wonder if we'll ever find out what's at the bottom of it."

"I keep telling you, they're friends, nothing more."

"Yeah sure, Edgar and Ollie, the Odd Couple." She frowned and shook her head. "Not likely. Remember those rumors about Daggett trying to buy PermaDream?"

"Please, not that again." Hodge rolled his eyes. "It's ridiculous."

"Somebody greased palms at the President's Palace to clear the way for us in Mexico. Probably the same crooks who opened up Daggett's cocaine route to the states. PermaDream would be the perfect legal sideline for that low-life, drug dealing scum."

"Sounds like page one of the Enquirer."

"Chazz strolls around here like he owns the place."

"Not for long." Hodge felt his mood darken. "Ollie Daggett is my Dad's friend, not mine. He frowned at the thought of his father crawling into bed with criminals. No way that could be true no matter how badly Dad needed money. "You've been drawn into believing an obvious pack of lies."

"How can you overlook such persistent rumors?"

"Gossip, not rumors." He made a dismissive gesture. "That bullshit about Daggett killing the Congressman is nothing but hearsay. As far as him being an owner of PermaDream, that's just plain ridiculous. I admit, Dad and I never discussed business, but if a drug dealer was a silent partner, I'd know."

A flicker of warmth returned to Denise's gaze. She squeezed his arm. "Forget it for now."

Hodge smiled, pleased to end the squabbling, confident of his dad's business acumen. "Dad and Ollie Daggett are friends, nothing more," he said.

"You'll lead us in the right direction, Hodge. We all believe in you." She squeezed his arm again. "Especially me."

Morgan approached, brown eyes gleaming with pride, big teeth shiny-white against chocolate skin. "Things couldn't be better. Go share the good news with your dad." His teeth flashed in a wider grin. "Tell him the PermaDream era has begun."

CHAPTER THREE

A mind reeling rush took Edgar Michaels by surprise. Enveloped by soft shadows he seemed to drift off the bed, his mind freed from the prison of withered flesh and brittle bone. Borne aloft, he wafted to and fro, as if captured by a summer breeze.

On the darkened horizon, golden memories, glistening like sunbeams, pierced the dull gray dust of time. A summer morning fingered the murky gloom, brushing Edgar's cold, gray, antiseptic world with pastel shades from a rainbow palette.

He breathed deep, inhaling the honeysuckle morning of long ago when carefree days drifted by like flower petals on the peaceful Wabash. Mid-August in beautiful Indiana. He caught the sweet scent of freshly mown grass, still moist from a pre-dawn thundershower that rumbled in the distance. His senses tingled as he felt the stubby green carpet beneath his feet. He heard the laughter of children. The sweetest sound of all.

A mockingbird warbling from a leafy sycamore brought a smile to his face. He couldn't recall ever hearing a songbird perform so magnificently. In his hospital bed, he had often remained still, barely breathing, vainly trying to hear the chirping of courtyard birds on the other side of the window. Now, as he stood listening to the mockingbird, Edgar felt warmth flowing through his veins.

He smoothed his thick brown hair, marveling at its sudden fullness. His legs felt strong and his heart thumped with excitement. After a few tentative steps, Edgar threw back his shoulders, filled his lungs with the sweet morning and burst into a full run. Skipping curbs, leaping hedges, bounding over fences, he raced toward the white Victorian house, halfway down a familiar tree shaded street, stopping at the edge of the lawn.

Jenny!

She sat on the porch swing, long honey hair shimmering in the morning sun. A lavender hair ribbon matched his favorite dress. His Jenny. So young. So beautiful. He thought he had lost her forever.

"Jenny!" He marveled at his voice, young, strong, vibrant.

She stood and waved. "Hurry, my love." Her smile sweetened the mockingbird's song.

Edgar rejoiced at another wild burst of energy. He felt even younger.

She held out her arms. "Hurry, Edgar. Hurry."

He took the porch steps, two at a time, thanking God for the chance to embrace her again.

"See, Jenny, not even winded." His voice cracked with emotion. His eyes misted. He wanted to laugh and cry. Most of all, he wanted to hold her.

"Edgar." Tears of joy glistened. "Is it really you?"

He stepped closer, took her in his arms, smelled the familiar scent of lilac, felt the softness of her hair brushing his cheek and the sweet warmth of her breath. "Jenny," he whispered. "Darling Jenny." He pressed his lips to hers, closed his eyes, and with a soft "pop", Edgar's world vanished in a wash of milky haze...

Like a diminutive, dark-haired angel, Rita Cariño hovered over the grinning face of Edgar Michaels, her sadness made all the more poignant by stinging memories of her mother's passage without the wonder of PermaDream. The ultimate siege of cancer had climaxed with a painful onslaught of drugs, chemotherapy, and sickness. At the end, death came as a blessing. Fate, it seemed could be kinder to some than others.

She looked up at Hodge, then down at Edgar and glimpsed a vision of the younger Michaels in forty years. Her fingers brushed the dead man's cheek and she smiled in spite of herself. To honor his wife, Edgar had chosen to pass away in the same suit he wore in his dream, but his final illness had caused him to lose a hundred pounds. The suit fit like a deflated Glenn plaid balloon. His scrawny neck stuck out of the starched collar like a bleached stick.

"My mother loved this suit." Hodge said, his voice husky as he smoothed the rumpled lapel. "She urged him to wear it more often, but Dad felt out of place in a collar and tie. This old suit's been in the attic since the night she died."

"He told me he spent his life wishing he'd worn it for her more often." Rita struggled to keep the quiver from her voice, aware that Hodge also hovered on the verge of tears. He seemed so lost. Like a little boy. "We'll all miss Edgar." She darkened the bed area and pulled the sheet over the old man's head. "Want me to contact the undertaker?"

"I'll stop by this afternoon for final arrangements," Hodge said.

"Cremation?" Morgan's deep, rich voice preceded him as he entered from the control booth, toting an IPad.

Rita sensed the formal authority in his tone and the empathetic warmth in his gaze. God's shepherd on autopilot. Doctor Jackson, her dear friend, on the case, prepared to oversee the final details.

"Cremation is what he wanted." Hodge turned from his father's lifeless body. "I'll hire a boat to take me out far enough to scatter his ashes."

Morgan signed the death certificate, then glanced at Hodge. "Want company?"

Hodge shook his head. "Just Dad and me this time."

"I understand. Memorial service?"

"No service, no flowers, no tears! Dad's last words. If we held a service, he'd probably come back and blow out the candles." Rita and Morgan exchanged knowing smiles.

Hodge said, "Ollie Daggett's lawyer left a message. He claims to represent my father and his estate. Wants us to meet with the staff at noon tomorrow in the conference room."

Rita's insides turned cold at the mention of Daggett's attorney. "I'll put out the word." Smiling to cover her sudden uneasiness, she made a mental note to e-mail the others.

"I'm meeting him in Dad's office first," Hodge said. "I never knew we had the same attorney as Daggett."

"I didn't know we had an attorney, period," Rita muttered, unable to dismiss the icy apprehension that gnawed at her.

Morgan said, "If he's Daggett's attorney, he must be pretty sharp.

You'll see, everything'll work out. He probably wants to fill you in on the deal with the Mexican government. Don't be surprised if the in-laws of a few of the top ruling PLC party government officials own a piece of the operation."

"Jesus!"

As much as she resented hearing it, Rita knew Morgan was right. She felt shame. Bribery! A constant temptation for the people in power in her country. So many Mexican people had grown up in poverty. So many remained trapped in its grasp.

She studied Hodge's face. Drawn and pale. Could do with a B-12 shot or something stronger. She eyed Morgan, whose own countenance reflected her anxiety. He reached out and touched the younger man's shoulder. "You okay, Hodge? Need something?"

"Nah. A little shaky, that's all." Hodge let out a nervous, high-pitched laugh. "Guess it's a good thing there is an attorney; somebody to walk me through this transition."

"You'll do fine," Morgan said.

Hodge's eyes met Rita's, then looked away. "How about some coffee, Morg?" he said, turning his back to her. "I need some input."

"That's what friends are for." Morgan draped his arm over Hodge's shoulder and steered him from the room. "Come on, I'll buy." As they left the room, he looked back and winked, assuring Rita that he had things under control.

She watched them leave, heard their footsteps fade.

Only then, did she weep for Edgar.

Flickering neon Cerveza signs adorned the windows of Casa de Sandoval. Embroidered sombreros graced the adobe walls and gaudily painted piñatas dangled from the ceiling of the popular Tijuana restaurant. Mariachi music squawked over tinny speakers and the air hung thick with the aroma of sizzling meats, grilled onions, and pungent jalapénos.

Hodge had no appetite for food, or the atmosphere. The sudden appearance of Ollie Daggett's lawyer made him uneasy. Disregarding the menu, he leaned back in the booth and folded his arms, staring straight ahead, trying to organize his scattered thoughts.

"Let's see." Morgan looked up from his menu to eye the petite Mexican waitress, who returned his amiable big-toothed smile. "Carne asada burrito, with jalapénos, onions, and extra jack cheese. Easy on the sour cream." He touched the girl's arm. "Don't put the guacamole on the burrito. Makes it too gooey. Bring it on the side. A double portion. I'll eat it with chips."

The waitress nodded, then turned to Hodge.

"Just coffee." As the waitress left, Hodge patted his pockets. "I'm dying for a cigarette, Morg. Christ, won't this craving ever go away?"

"Patience."

"It's been two years." Hodge rubbed his palms together, then fanned his fingers on the tabletop. "I'd kill for a Marlboro. Hell, coffee isn't even interesting any more."

Morgan smiled. "That's two lousy habits you've kicked. Eat something. Food can be a great comfort. Y'know, when I was a kid, I thought funerals were great, because the relatives would all bring casseroles and meats and pies. Best food I ever ate. Me and the other kids'd feast like it was Christmas. We usually didn't even have to look at the dead person." He sighed. "That all changed when my mama died and I met the reaper close-up for the first time."

Hodge peered out the restaurant window at the shabby dwellings of the Tijuana side street, his mind on la playa, the clean sandy beach several miles away. Tomorrow morning he would spread his father's ashes on the water and return to take charge of PermaDream. "We're going to do right by Dad's memory. I'm committed to making PermaDream affordable to everyone."

Morgan nodded, his dark brown eyes probing Hodge's. "It's what we all want." He grinned. "Jack Scanlon and some of the others are already jabbering about moving back to the States and reopening the door to Uncle Sam's grants."

"Jack Scanlon knows we'll never go back." Hodge shook his head, blanching at the thought of paper-shuffling Washington officials toying with his father's miracle. "They had their chance. We're in Mexico to stay."

After repeatedly refusing the initial funding, the government had done an about face and tried to ease back into the picture once it became apparent that his dad was, in fact, onto something. The moment Edgar Michaels initiated clinical PermaDream trials, the FDA and the AMA zeroed in, administering pressure from every possible angle. "Dad moved us down here to get away from rules and regulations."

Morgan sighed. "And all that paperwork."

Hodge nodded. "Like I said, as much as he mouths off about it,

Jack Scanlon knows we can never go back. He's a loud-mouthed-horse's ass."

"And the best neural net designer in the business. Maybe you can convince him that it's best for us to stay put."

"Frankly, I don't intend to try." Hodge felt his face pinch into a frown. "There's no way to involve that son-of-a-bitch in a rational conversation. If Jack doesn't like Mexico, he can leave. I won't kiss his ass. I don't care how terrific he is with neural networks, his brain is trapped back in the twentieth century with that archaic, 'Power to the People' crap."

"Comes from growing up in the San Francisco Hippie communes."

"Well, PermaDream is no commune and I'm in charge, not Jack Scanlon. No pun intended, but my bed is made in the present, here in Mexico. If he disagrees with my decisions, he can pack up his neural networks and his Zig-Zag papers and take a hike. Who else would hire that pot smoking social maladroit?"

Morgan nodded. "Attaboy, show him some steel, Hodge. Let him know who's boss." The waitress brought chips, salsa and coffee. Morgan dipped and chewed thoughtfully. "I'm counting on you to be strong."

"I won't let you down."

Morgan shook a tortilla chip at Hodge. "Tell them in no uncertain terms that we're here in Mexico to stay. Look Jack Scanlon square in the eye when you say it."

"I will." Hodge's heart picked up a beat. "By God, I will!" A burgeoning strength surged from deep within. The baton had been exchanged. At long last, Hodge Michaels sat in the driver's seat.

When he spoke again, his voice resonated with a booming depth of tone he had never noticed before. "I'm a private enterprise guy, Morg. Always have been. Too damned many strings attached to government money."

Morgan's dark eyes twinkled. "You sound like your father."

"Damn right I do!" Hodge tapped his chest. "Edgar Michaels is a part of me. Always will be. I inherited Dad's suspicion of all things political. PermaDream stays on this side of the border."

"Now, you're talking!"

"Tomorrow after I meet with the attorney, I'll make an announcement to the group. Strictly low key. Growth plans. Steady hand on the tiller. Stuff like that." He balled his fist. "Make no mistake, the PermaDream miracle will be shared with the world."

"How fast do you think we can go with it?"

Hodge grinned wide, feeling in control for the first time. "Let's shoot for twenty dream terminals. As soon as possible, we can expand to whatever the traffic'll bear."

Morgan flashed a thumbs up.

"Prediction!" Hodge's chest swelled and his heart seemed to pump liquid fire. "PermaDream goes worldwide inside of ten years, within everyone's price range."

Morgan grinned. "Headquartered in Mexico."

"You bet!" Hodge scribbled notes on a napkin as he spoke. "Morpheus will be the main development system, but each facility will have its own CPU with a back up to cover emergencies. We'll beef up the firewall to keep out hackers and run all dream sequences directly from Morpheus, encrypted and transmitted to the others by satellite link."

"You can start by installing those new processors Jack and Cheryl designed."

"And a high-speed memory upgrade. Greater storage capabilities too. Every hard-wired data connection will be made with fiber. As the demand for terminal dreaming grows, we'll adjust the price. Before long, PermaDream will be accessible to everyone."

"Trickle down dreams. I like it."

Hodge folded the napkin and slipped it into his pocket. "Phase one begins tomorrow."

Hodge's mind hummed like a machine, churning out a plethora of ideas, each one clicking into place. Feeling like a newly commissioned general seated at the war table, he leaned forward and unfurled his verbal blueprint like a battle flag. "Rita's top drawer, she stays on as Medical Administrator. Denise keeps her position as Director of Marketing and Operations."

"Good calls."

Hodge bit his lower lip and shook his head slowly, picturing Denise coming to him, face flushed, eyes gleaming with pride, yet burning with desire. He snapped his fingers. "Of course we'll continue to maintain your medical facilities, fully compliant with AMA standards, but without the interference."

"Thank you, sir."

"I'll probably spend the next week or so locked away with the attorney, trying to unravel Dad's bookkeeping. Soon as we free up some money, my number one priority is to fund your needs, so get your budget requests together." He sat back and slapped his hand on the table. "By God, I can't wait!"

"The key to the future's in your hand," Morg said.

"Damn right!" Hodge sat up straight and picked up the menu. "And tomorrow, I unlock the door."

CHAPTER FOUR

Morgan entered the PermaDream Corporation's lunch room, blinking at bright sunlight streaming through the bank of windows on the opposite wall. A stainless steel sink, microwave, and coffee maker lined a Formica counter along a second wall and a large video screen and cabinet full of electronics took up most of the third. A bulletin board covered with notes, comic strips and coupons took up half of the fourth.

At the far end of a long conference table, Jack Scanlon sat balanced on the hind legs of a chair, with sandaled feet on the floor and slender fingers intertwined behind his balding head. A receding hairline exaggerated bushy black eyebrows and intensified the look of concentration in the deep-set brown eyes that stared at the microwave.

On the other side of the table, nearest the door, Jack's collaborator, neuroscientist, Cheryl Martin sat reading a battered paperback romance novel. Her pale blue eyes never welcomed anyone's gaze, but Morgan often noticed her scrutinizing others. Analyzing them, no doubt. He smiled to himself. Always on the job, that Cheryl.

She scorned makeup and pulled her long strawberry-blonde hair back in a tight bun, offering no hint of warmth to her icy demeanor. Morgan assumed she chose the severe hairdo as a practicality. Everything in place. Hell, as far as Morgan was concerned, she could shave her head. Truth was, he stood in awe of her brilliant and ordered mind.

Cheryl's expertise in synaptic modulation and neurotransmitters, coupled with Jack's breakthrough in neural microprocessor design, kindled the flame that made the concept of dream travel a reality. Truly married to her career, she controlled an invisible curtain, drawing it shut in the face of anyone reaching out to befriend her. Morgan had been the only one to ever come close. He understood what it took to give himself completely to his work.

Several years ago, during a stressful period in the development of PermaDream, Cheryl showed up in his office, complaining that she couldn't sleep. For the others, when hypertension interfered with work, Morgan prescribed Tretesterote the latest miracle anti-stress drug from Sweden, but Cheryl patently rejected what she called, mind-altering drugs, so Morgan suggested that she read novels as a form of escape. To his surprise she had taken to romances. It seemed ludicrous, but the brilliant Cheryl had rarely been seen of late without a bookmarked copy within arm's reach.

"Don't fall, Jack," Morgan said, heading for the coffee pot.

Scanlon threw Morgan a lopsided grin. "Fall? Me?" He looked over his shoulder, blinking from beneath scrubby eyebrows. "No sweat, Doc." He held out his arms like a boy pretending to be an airplane. "See, perfect balance. I'm nuking a dish of cheese soup. Be done in one minute and four seconds. Timing's critical with cheese."

"Guess I'll have a cup of this black death." Morgan rinsed his mug and filled it with coffee. "I can always tell when Rita makes coffee. Reminds me of the tonic my mother forced down my throat every spring." He raised the pot. "Coats the glass, like blackstrap on a frosty morning."

"Don't blame Rita," Cheryl said without looking up from her novel. "*I* made that coffee."

Morgan winced. "Only teasing." He joined her at the table.

She nodded, turning a page.

"Well, I knew Cheryl made it." Jack set the front chair legs down and stood, hiking tattered shorts above his knobby knees. "Looks like shit. Smells like tar. Makes Rita's mud taste like a piná colada."

Cheryl's lips pursed and her sapphire eyes narrowed behind thick lenses, but they stayed riveted to the paperback. Pretending not to listen. Morgan knew better.

Jack scratched the back of his neck. "Truth is, no woman ever lived who could brew a good pot of coffee." He sighed. "Guess that goes for my mother too, God rest her. She'd cook her fanny off, but couldn't put together the proper blend of grounds and water to make decent coffee."

He popped open the microwave door and wiped a hand across the front of his T-shirt. "Magic time." Removing the bowl, he stuck a finger in the soup and licked it. "Perfecto! Cheese soup should be warm, not hot."

Sitting beside Cheryl, he dipped his finger again and held it in front of her. "Lick?"

She adjusted her glasses, pulled at her collar and frowned at her counterpart.

Jack snorted. "You had your chance baby, now watch Jacko." He smeared cheese soup across his tongue.

Cheryl eyed him with the intensity of an entomologist inspecting an ant farm. "Surely you don't intend to eat that whole bowl of soup with your index finger, Jack. That's the finger you use to pick your nose."

Jack's ears reddened.

Morgan felt a warm burst of satisfaction at Jack's discomfort. By God, look at him blush. Good for you, girl. Good for you.

Cheryl seldom responded to Jack's taunts, but when she did return fire, she usually scored a direct hit. Professionally, she more than held her own and despite their bickering, they respected each other's abilities and worked as one, performing miracles as a team.

Morgan's cell phone pulsed. He activated it. "Jackson."

"I'm in the parking lot," Hodge's voice sounded thin and strained. Poor kid, probably had no sleep. "Everyone there?"

"Here, or on the way."

"I'm meeting the attorney in Dad's office. Be right with you."

"Okay." As Morgan disconnected, Lorenzo Vargas slid into the chair beside him. "Hi, doc."

Morgan had liked Lorenzo from the first day Edgar hired him away from Disney Animation and put him in charge of Dream Development. Born and raised in Chicago, Lorenzo possessed an artistic talent that had earned him a full scholarship to UCLA film school. After a brief apprenticeship, Disney hired him straight out of school. The younger man seemed to have everything going for him. Women adored his classic Spanish-Italian good looks, black hair, and piercing, dark eyes.

Perfect white teeth gleamed when Lorenzo smiled, but since his divorce, his smiles were scarce. In three years of marriage, his cup of love had overflowed with happiness, then cracked with misery. The young man's courtship, wedding, and honeymoon had been followed by his wife's infidelity before the relationship fell apart, ending in an ugly divorce.

Now Lorenzo lived alone, south of Rosarita Beach, sharing his computer laden mobile home with a family of inbreeding six-toed black cats. Most nights, the trailer housed only the cats, since he frequently worked around the clock, napping on his office sofa. For the life of him, Morgan couldn't fathom such a handsome, charming young man living a dull life, anchored by his job, wasting his finest years in a romantic vacuum.

Rita and Lorenzo were both lost souls. Rita had suffered a great personal loss in the long, slow death of her mother. She still grieved. Last week, he had arranged for her to join them for a dinner celebration in honor of Lorenzo's birthday.

A close friend of both, he knew they'd enjoy each other's company and who knows what might come of it. If nothing else, they'd have a break from work. Morgan arranged to leave the dinner table early, giving them an opportunity to be alone. Later, neither one said a word about the way the evening ended. Their silence was about to drive him mad.

"Nice job with the Tom Harley dream," Morgan said, patting Lorenzo on the back. "Everyone's raving about the background track. Especially the merry-go-round."

"Thanks. I had no use for that bastard, but I had one hell of a feel for his dream. Harley wanted to share time with the kid, wanted to go fishing. We created a simple setting. You know, trees, water, birds and stuff. Jazzed up the background color a little and gave an extra sparkle to the water. I even researched the shit out of dragonflies. Never realized how many different shapes and colors they come in."

"Same as people."

"I heard Harley never made it to the merry-go-round," Jack said.

Morgan nodded. "He only lasted nineteen seconds."

Lorenzo glanced at the doorway. "Rita and Denise are outside. Saw them at Saint Matthew's this morning. I stopped by to fire up a candle for old Edgar." He peered around the room. "Where's Hodge?"

"On his way," Jack said.

"He okay?"

"He's anxious to take charge," Morgan said. "Guess he did his grieving when Edgar took sick and I told him the old man wouldn't make it."

"Guess we all did." Lorenzo smiled. "Somehow, it didn't seem like the old guy was dying. It felt more like he was taking a trip. He said goodbye, everybody hugged him and he went to sleep."

"Not a bad way to go." Morgan looked past Lorenzo and waved as Rita and Denise entered, followed by Lorenzo's assistant; skinny, blond, curly-haired Eddie Driscoll, wearing a loose-fitting San Diego Chargers jersey and a Padres baseball cap pulled down low. Eddie shuffled into the room, hands in pockets, shoulders slouched, eyes locked on the backsides of the two women.

The telltale scent of Royal Secret filled the air as Denise and Rita approached the table, deep in discussion.

"Mexico has given PermaDream free rein," Rita said, making a point. "We should stay here."

"Baloney!" Jack growled, jumping into the conversation. "The first thing we should do is declare a Declaration of Independence from Mexico and go the fuck home."

Cheryl scowled at Jack. "I don't believe that's an option. And your language, as always, is repulsive."

Jack tipped his soup plate and drained it, then wiped his mouth with his handkerchief.

Denise sat beside Lorenzo and squeezed his arm, whispering, "Hi, Renz." Then she turned to Jack. "Cheryl's right. Your vulgarity only waters down your ideas. Makes even the good ones sound foolish."

Jack stood. "That's the kind of hard-on I am. When you get me, you take the whole package. Take it or leave it." He rinsed his soup plate and put it on the shelf. "Everybody knows how I feel. We don't belong here in Mexico. Uncle Sam should fund PermaDream. Give it to the people."

"Get real, Jack!" Lorenzo waved him off. "That's the same tired horseshit you've been peddling for the last five years."

Morgan couldn't agree more. Jack had been peddling it for a lot longer than that.

Jack returned to the table and slumped into his chair. "Every idea has its time. Old Edgar wouldn't buy it, but I bet young Hodge will. Cross the border, apply for some big-time grants, make PermaDream available to all. Tie it to Social Security or Medicare." He snapped his fingers. "Bing-bang-boom, everybody wins."

Denise nudged Lorenzo and whispered. "Jack's right. It's the only way to include everyone."

"If that jerk had his way," Lorenzo said under his breath, "there'd be PermaDream lines at the welfare office." He glared at Jack, raising his voice. "No reason why we shouldn't make a few bucks. Things are fine right here."

Morgan smiled to himself. Rita and Lorenzo agreed on where PermaDream should be located. A positive sign.

Eddie Driscoll stood and leaned toward Jack, tugging at the bill of his Padre cap. After clearing his throat, he said, "Here's the way I see it."

Morgan watched in silence. Here we go. The juvenile delinquent rises to offer his two cents.

"Lorenzo and I don't want to answer to some anal government committee every time we morph a butterfly." Eddie eyed his boss for confirmation. "Right, Lorenzo?"

Morgan almost told him to shut up and sit down. The last thing they needed was to set Jack off again.

Disregarding Eddie, Lorenzo continued scowling at Jack.

"Damn right," Eddie mumbled, sitting again. "Damn right."

Cheryl closed her paperback, leaned forward and spoke with a cool, steady voice. "PermaDream research must continue without any meddling. We should stay put for now and permit the law of supply and demand to govern our growth and bring the cost down. Meanwhile, those who have the money should support our work and pay for our services."

"You said it, Cheryl," Eddie added. "Let the rich slobs buy their own dreams."

Jack slammed a fist onto the table. "What about the *poor* slobs?" His face reddened. "Who pays for *their* dreams?"

Morgan tensed. That's it, he's been sprung.

Jack glared at everyone around the long table. "This probably comes as a big surprise to you people, but not everyone is a fucking millionaire."

Morgan looked toward the door as it opened. Thank God. "Here comes Hodge, just in time to referee."

"Give him a break, Jack," Rita cautioned in a low voice. "His father just passed away." Jack grunted.

The gathering fell silent as Hodge entered, accompanied by a tall dark haired man about Morgan's age, wearing a black mohair suit, gray silk tie, and the first pair of wing-tips Morgan had seen since his high school graduation.

Lorenzo elbowed Morgan and whispered, "Who's that?"

"Attorney."

"Hodge looks like he needs a drink."

Morgan nodded, feeling a pang of uneasiness as Hodge glanced at him, then looked away. The Hodge Michaels he had been with yesterday brimmed with enthusiasm. Now, he appeared ambivalent, wetting his lips, wiping perspiration from his forehead with trembling fingers. Could Edgar's ocean burial have shaken him so much?

Hodge mumbled an introduction to the attorney, who nodded to each staff member before seating himself at the head of the table. Hodge stood beside him, unsmiling. After an uncomfortable pause, the words came. "I want to thank you all for your commitment to the PermaDream project over the past four years," he said in a shaky voice. "No matter what the future holds, I want you to know I love every one of you. You're my family." When his eyes met Morgan's, his face reddened. "I – I look forward to us being together for a long time." Hodge lowered his gaze. "Forgive me, I've just received staggering news."

Morgan stiffened. Here it comes!

"What the hell's going on, Hodge?" Jack asked.

"My dad left us a videodisk. I just viewed it in my office. Now it's your turn."

Morgan frowned. A videodisk. He held his breath as the attorney flipped open his attaché case and handed Hodge a gleaming silver disk the size of a poker chip.

As Hodge inserted it into a slot on the monitor, the attorney addressed the staff in a rich baritone. "I would like to thank you for attending this meeting and bid you welcome in the name of the President of the PermaDream corporation, Mister Oliver Daggett."

CHAPTER FIVE

Rita's heart jumped at the attorney's greeting. Dear God, the rumors about Edgar selling out to Daggett had been true. She glanced at Morgan, hoping for reassurance, but he appeared as shocked as the others, his gaze riveted to the blank video screen.

Before anyone could speak, the grim countenance of Edgar Michaels appeared on-screen, gaunt-faced, his eyes buried in dark hollow sockets. An ill-fitting lab coat buttoned to the neck hung from his small shoulders. Snowy hair stuck up in feathery wisps from his balding head. From his ghastly appearance, Rita knew he had made the video shortly before checking into PermaDream to die.

The elder Michaels sat stiffly at his desk, speaking in tortured spurts, pausing often to wheeze for breath. "Forgive the brevity of this good-bye. My speech is painful, not only for me, but also, I'm sure, for you. Still, I have to give this to you straight from the shoulder and tell you why I no longer own PermaDream." He lapsed into a coughing spasm.

Fighting her own disappointment, Rita looked to Lorenzo, who averted his eyes from the emaciated on screen figure to stare down at his clenched fists. The others had similar expressions as Edgar verbalized again, in a hoarse, cracking voice.

"Early-on, the government endowed us with several modest grants, but they fell far short of what we needed. When they refused more funding, I backed it with everything I owned."

Edgar closed his eyes and took a deep breath, cleared his throat and began again. "I have always marveled at your unwavering dedication. I vowed we'd never fail, but the time came when I couldn't make payroll and I couldn't cover our bills. Lab supplies, computers, and development costs sapped everything. Collectors hounded me. Accountants and lawyers laughed at our vision and derided the concept of computer generated dreaming. The bank was prepared to shut us down until Ollie Daggett stepped in and saved the project."

"Jesus!" Jack muttered, putting his head in his hand and massaging his temples. "We're fucked!" No one else spoke.

Edgar's breathing came slow and raspy as he persevered. "Everyone knows I never made a snap decision in my life. Before committing to clinical trials, I weighed Mister Daggett's offer to fund our future needs in exchange for full ownership. After much soul searching, I accepted, with the stipulation that I maintain administrative control. He paid the bills. I called the shots."

Each word fell on Rita's sinking heart like another rock piled on top of her hopelessness.

"Ollie assured me that he'll honor his commitment to keep the team intact," Edgar continued. "It wouldn't have served any purpose to tell anyone about this until now, but the facts are clear. Without Ollie Daggett, there would be no PermaDream."

He sighed and his eyes took on a faraway look. "I hate to leave you, but I truly relish the thought of embarking on my final dream. I long for the sweet smell of Indiana and the loving arms of my wife." Edgar's voice shook. He scrunched his eyes shut, fighting back tears. One trickled down his cheek. "Dear friends," he said quietly. "The world must reap the benefits of our wonder. Under the leadership of my son, Hodge, PermaDream will succeed. God bless you."

Rita felt as if a giant part of her had been torn out, leaving only emptiness as Hodge switched off the television and stared at the blank screen.

After a short silence the attorney spoke. "Effective immediately, the Morpheus Project is on hold."

Rita caught her breath. Cold twisted in the pit of her stomach. Dear God, all their hard work. Their plans. Their vision.

"PermaDream will live," Hodge snapped. "Make no mistake. This is temporary." He cleared his throat. "I'm meeting with Mister Daggett tomorrow at his Cancun residence."

"Cancun," Jack said with a short, bitter laugh. "Hiding from the taxman. Daggett better stay there too! If he sticks a toenail across the border, the murdering son-of-a-bitch'll go to jail, where he belongs."

"Hold on, Jack!" Hodge pushed himself from the chair. "None of the allegations regarding Mr. Daggett have been substantiated. No one ever proved he had anything to do with the death of that Congressman and his family."

Denise let out an exasperated gasp.

"Tomorrow morning, I fly to Cancun," Hodge said, ignoring her. "I'll fill Mr. Daggett in on my restructuring plans. I'll let him know what funding we'll need to continue. I'll do it for us. Everybody with me?"

"We're with you, Hodge," Morgan said. The others murmured among themselves.

Rita found it difficult to think, much less respond.

Hodge rounded the desk and approached her with a weak smile frozen on his pasty face. "Ollie Daggett wants to meet you," he said. "Wants you to come with me to Cancun." He touched her elbow. "Says you're a key player in the future of the Morpheus project."

Rita backed away. "Oh no, not me."

Hodge pleaded with puppy dog eyes "But Ollie Daggett is insisting that you come. His plane'll pick us up at TJ Airport tomorrow morning."

Rita's sense of well-being rebelled against a trip to the lair of a man accused of being a murdering drug dealer. "Get me out of this, Hodge. I don't want to meet him."

"Come on, Rita," Hodge coaxed. "This is my first meeting too. Give the guy a break. He wants to say hello. He's being friendly and he obviously thinks you're important enough to be part of the negotiations." He pressed on, talking fast. "I'll be with you all the way. Follow my lead. Set his mind at ease and tell him whatever he wants to hear. I'll assure him I can run the company, set a few ground rules, fill him in on my plans, and we'll be home for an early dinner. Hey, you saw Dad's tape. Daggett's the man who saved PermaDream. I'm anxious to meet him."

Rita never realized that Ollie Daggett had been aware of her existence. Now, all of a sudden, he called her a key player? Why?

Hodge pleaded. "The others are counting on us, Rita." The look in his eyes carried less conviction than his voice, but she permitted him to persuade her.

"Okay, I'll go." Edgar would want her to stand by his son.

Rita pressed her burning forehead to the cool Plexiglas of the plane's tiny oval window, peering down at the rugged cliffs of Baja and surging blue Pacific, several thousand feet below. Her beloved Mexico. Her home. So much of it barren, unsettled and untamed. Locating PermaDream down here would mean so much to her people and her country's troubled economy. They deserved a chance. Morgan agreed. So did Lorenzo, who never missed an opportunity to say so.

One night last week, the three of them drank icy Cervezas and ate grilled lobster tail at Eduardo's, a Puerto Nuevo restaurant, tucked in among the dozens of crowded, open-stalled souvenir shops along the main street of the tiny seaside town.

Morgan had insisted she join them to celebrate Lorenzo's birthday. Rita embraced the opportunity for a break from the brutal severity of the final round of testing. Everything seemed to happen at once. Doug's return from Stamford, coupled with Edgar's rapidly failing health and the pressure of wrapping up the final test phase before time ran out and he dreamed his final dream.

It was dark by the time they met Lorenzo at Eduardo's, waiting at a candlelit corner table, nursing a beer, making circular patterns on the dark wood tabletop with his wet glass-bottom.

"Happy Birthday, Lorenzo," Morg said. "Waiting long?"

Lorenzo looked up and shrugged. "Drank a few beers. Thought a few thoughts. Truth is, I'm half-loaded." He grinned at Rita. "*Salud, amiga.* Come to celebrate with me?"

Rita kissed his cheek and took a seat beside him. "*Compleados Años,* Lorenzo."

"*Gracias.*"

Morgan slapped Lorenzo on the back. "Be right back. Have to say hello to Eduardo." He headed for the kitchen and embraced the owner, a long time friend. They launched into an animated conversation about the latest San Diego Charger quarterback.

Lorenzo turned to face Rita. "Nice surprise, seeing you." He graced her with a wide smile.

Her heartbeat quickened.

"I mean that, Rita. I don't socialize enough with the nice guys in my life."

"Wouldn't miss it." She returned his smile, secretly pleased to be considered one of the nice guys by the dark-eyed Lorenzo, who looked quite handsome by candlelight.

He lowered his voice. "I suffer from, "terminal-jerk-syndrome.""

"Huh?"

"Overexposure to Eddie Driscoll."

Rita laughed. "I was beginning to wonder about you two. You spend a lot of time together in the lab."

"Too much time. Eddie's bright, but a weird kid. Normal people collect stamps. Eddie collects computer viruses."

"At least they're not real viruses."

Lorenzo shook his head. "I wouldn't put it past him."

Morgan returned with two wooden bowls of salsa, followed by Eduardo, who toted chips and beer. "Let's get this party going," he said, dropping into a seat. "I ordered a platter of lobster."

Halfway through dinner, Morgan's cell phone rang. It was Hodge. "Needs to talk", he explained, removing his bib and rising with a sigh. "Needs somebody to hold his hand. You two can find your way back. Enjoy. Everything's paid for." He hurried out before Rita or Lorenzo could say a word.

After dinner, Lorenzo suggested a moonlight walk around the tiny coastal town. As they strolled a bustling street, filled with tourists and Southern California regulars who came to enjoy the famous Puerto Nuevo lobster dinners, he said, "Guess you noticed, Morgan figures you and I should be friends."

"I thought we *were* friends."

"I mean, *friendlier* friends. Morgan's been trying to play matchmaker. If it was up to him, you and I would be out shopping for furniture."

"I don't think either one of us is ready for that," Rita blurted. Scarcely were the words past her lips, when, she regretted speaking them. She felt his steady gaze, but avoided his eyes. "I mean, with all the work, pressure, commitment, it's difficult to have a personal life."

Lorenzo nodded. "We're either martyrs, heroes or damned fools."

In one of the souvenir shops, Rita spied several shelves of votive candles; tall, opaque, wax-filled-glasses with pictures of Jesus or the Virgin Mary imprinted on them. "Wait, I want one of those." She took hold of his arm and steered him inside. "The anniversary of my mother's death is tomorrow. I plan to light one for her every year."

"Go ahead," Lorenzo said. "I'll poke around the shop."

While Lorenzo browsed, Rita took her time selecting the candle, choosing one with an image of Christ praying in the garden of Gethsemane.

Outside again, they strolled to the end of a cobblestone street where the crowd thinned and rickety wood steps led to the beach. They stopped under the pale glow of a solitary mist-shrouded street lamp, peering into the darkness where unseen gulls cried and waves pounded the sand.

"Walk on the beach?" Lorenzo asked.

Rita started to say, "Yes", when a rat scurried across the steps in front of them. A sudden chill gripped her.

"No." She hugged herself to stop the shivers. "Can't stand rats."

Lorenzo took off his jacket and draped it over her shoulders. "Me neither. I collect cats." He reached into his pocket. "Bought you something." He dangled a delicate silver chain, with a tiny charm in the shape of a winged angel in front of her.

"How sweet." Rita smiled. "Some celebration this turned out to be. It's your birthday and I get the gift." She held it out.

Lorenzo placed the wisp of silver chain around her neck, leaning close, his forearms brushing her shoulders as he fastened it. "This has been a wonderful evening, Rita," he whispered. "Thanks for being a part of it." He kissed her, barely brushing her lips. Rita closed her eyes.

"Ollie Daggett's going to love my plans for PermaDream," Hodge shouted from the seat behind, wrenching Rita out of her reverie.

"I hope so," she muttered, trying to tune Hodge out, holding on to the sweet memory of Lorenzo. If he were here with her on the plane instead of Hodge, she would feel a lot safer.

"I'll do most of the talking." Hodge's voice cracked as he yelled to be heard over the throaty roar of the motor. His high-pitched voice grated in her ear. "You back me up. We'll be home in no time."

Rita nodded. She reached up and touched the silver-winged angel she hadn't removed since that night in Puerto Nuevo. What would she have done if Lorenzo had really kissed her? Perhaps, sometime. Perhaps soon. *Que serra'.*

The small plane turned and headed inland over miles of green jungle until she saw a white-walled enclosure of several dozen acres, about twenty miles inland from the non-stop casino action of Cancun, gambling Mecca of the young century. Isolated by lush vegetation, the compound contained several outbuildings, a large Quonset hut, a guest dwelling, and in the center, an imposing Mediterranean villa surrounded by expansive lawns and color-splashed tropical gardens.

They banked low over the mansion's terra-cotta roof, rippling the shimmering surface of a crystal pool. "Seat belts!" the pilot called over his shoulder.

Rita tightened her safety belt.

The engines roared and the plane shuddered as the pilot reversed the props. Rita's stomach dropped as they nosed toward a limp windsock dangling from a pole at the end of a narrow pitted mud strip. Ribbed like a washboard and pocked with puddles, the dirt runway scarred the rain forest a short distance from the walled compound. Her heartbeat throbbed as she rechecked her seatbelt.

"Jesus Christ, the runway looks like it's been bombed," Hodge shouted from behind her. "Hang on!"

Rita clenched her teeth and jammed her feet against the bulkhead. The tiny plane rocketed over the treetops and wobbled toward the runway. She crossed herself, then grasped the arm rests and squeezed her eyes shut.

The plane touched down smoothly, then slammed into a mud hole with a window-rattling jolt. A forward utility door clanged open. Rita heard breaking glass and smelled whiskey.

The pilot braked hard, throwing her forward. The seat belt, pressing against her stomach, felt as if it would tear her in two. The wings creaked, the tail skidded left, right, then straightened. She opened her eyes as they jounced to a stop at the end of the runway. A moment later, the pilot unlatched the door. "*Vamos,*" he said, then leaped out.

Heat and humidity smothered them. Rita stood, weak-kneed and trembling, desperate to be outside in the fresh air.

"I'm getting the hell out of this sweatbox." Hodge shouldered by and stood in the exit. "Jesus, it's even hotter out here," he said, hopping down.

As Rita climbed out of the plane, a dirt splattered jeep sped toward them, bouncing along the edge of the runway.

"Who's this?" Hodge asked.

The jeep skidded to a stop alongside the plane, spraying mud. A lanky, blonde thirty-something-woman wearing a straw Stetson, cowboy boots, khaki shorts and a poplin top, tapped the passenger seat beside her. "Right here, *señorita*. He's waiting." Raising her sunglasses, she squinted at Hodge. "Back seat. Let's go!"

Hodge climbed into the back. Rita sat in front, grabbed the dash and held tight as the blonde wheeled the jeep onto an overgrown jungle path. Gear jamming, double clutching, and avoiding contact with the brakes, she steered deftly around tree trunks, boulders and potholes.

Soon, they roared into a hard packed clearing and raced toward a gate in the towering compound wall. Guards, armed with Chinese FongKar laser rifles, waved from searchlight studded parapets as steel doors slid open and the jeep entered the enclosure, slowing to turn onto a cobbled road through the steamy jungle surrounding the villa.

Parking in front, the blonde led them up some steps and across the wide veranda where she opened the ornately carved door and ushered them inside. A swarthy man armed with a laser rifle stood inside the door. A second man sat in a shadowed corner cradling a sawed-off-shotgun. Open, barred windows in the cavernous vestibule granted no relief from the smothering heat.

"*Señor* Daggett's in his private quarters," the blonde said to Rita. "Head of the stairs."

As they followed the blonde up a wide staircase, Rita glanced over her shoulder at Hodge. Ashen-faced, tight-lipped, face greasy with sweat, he climbed as if in a stupor, staring at the closed door at the top of the stairs with the wide-eyed gaze of a child watching a horror movie.

Where are you Lorenzo, she thought.

CHAPTER SIX

The blonde unlocked the door and led them into a room with unadorned walls and a polished hardwood floor.

A droplet of perspiration tickled the small of Rita's back as she stood beside Hodge in the sweltering reception room. A soft hum followed by a whirring sound told her that the pair of corner mounted, motion sensored cameras had locked onto them like twin gun barrels. She pictured Ollie Daggett, sitting in his air-conditioned quarters, studying their faces for signs of weakness.

Rita vowed to show him nothing. Keeping a straight face, she stood absolutely still, staring straight ahead. If she could will herself to stop perspiring, she would. She was here for Edgar, his vision of PermaDream, and the memory of her mama, not for Hodge and certainly not for this cabron, Ollie Daggett.

"Shoes!" the blonde said, removing her boots. "Take them off, *señorita*. It's a rule. Leave them here." She stepped aside, waiting by the door.

Stepping out of her heels and smoothing her skirt, Rita felt a surge of compassion for poor sweat-soaked Hodge, who leaned against the wall breathing hard, pulling off his shoes without undoing the laces. Circles of perspiration stained the armpits and darkened the back of his buttoned brown suit coat.

A barely audible series of clicks punctuated the stillness and the inner door opened. A blast of frigid air hit Rita like a splash of ice water. Her feet sank into the plush white carpet of Ollie Daggett's inner sanctum when she followed Hodge through the doorway. The blonde took up the rear, closing the door behind them.

"Feels like twenty below," Rita whispered, rubbing her goose bump prickled arms.

A clammy, crawling sensation fingered her spine as she and Hodge approached the mahogany bulwark of Ollie Daggett's desk. The burly man's grim scowl, abetted by a black widow's-peak-hairline and bottle brush eyebrows gave him the look of a mindless brute, yet he had the pale smooth skin and shiny pink cheeks of an elderly female. The grotesque combination reminded Rita of the Frankenstein monster, created with exhumed male body parts and a woman's severed hand.

In spite of his unsettling features, Daggett looked elegant in a white suit and matching brocade vest, burgundy silk cravat, and silver cufflinks. His pinkie ring, though smaller than his horseshoe shaped diamond studded tie tack, more than held its own in the glitter department. Though she couldn't see his feet, she suspected that, despite his rules for visitors, Ollie Daggett wore shoes. She pictured the blonde on her knees, tying white laces.

His glassy eyes singled out Hodge. "You're Edgar's kid."

Hodge nodded. "It's a pleasure to finally meet you, sir." He wiped his trembling hand on his thigh and offered it to Daggett. "I want to assure you that we're ready to roll up our sleeves and devote every waking hour to the success of PermaDream. I'm proud and honored to be..."

"Remember the shoe rule, Hodge," Ollie growled, ignoring the proffered hand. "You don't want to fuck up my white rug."

Hodge paled. "No, no, of course not," he mumbled, putting his hand in his pocket and shuffling his feet.

Ollie turned to Rita, looked her up and down, cocked an eyebrow and spoke in crude Spanish. "*Me llamo Oliver Daggett. Como se llama, señorita?*"

Damn this patronizing son-of-a-bitch! Rita's rising temper overwhelmed any prior feeling of awe. "My name is Rita Cariño," she enunciated in a crisp, clear voice, then glared over her shoulder at the blonde. Might as well set her straight too. "I'm an SDSU graduate." she said. "Magna Cum Laude. I speak English, if you don't mind."

The blonde said, "Hell, I don't mind, honey."

"Of course we don't mind." Ollie leaned forward, unsmiling. Rita's stomach churned. Had she gone too far? His empty-eyed stare turned to icy menace and the warning in his voice sliced like a machete. "We don't meet many big-shot college girls here in the jungle. Do we call you, Mizz, or, Ma'am, or Queen Shit or what?"

"Rita."

Daggett studied her in silence.

Beside her, Hodge cleared his throat.

After a moment, Daggett's nostrils flared and his liver lips parted, revealing tiny pointed teeth. The cold unrelenting look in his eyes remained. "Rita it is," he said. "So, you picked up a degree from SDSU. Ain't many chiquitas ever pulled that one off. You must be hot tamales upstairs."

He tapped his temple, then slid the soggy stump of a cigar from between his lips. "Tell you the truth, Rita, I admire educated women. Always have." He plopped the cigar butt into a wastebasket, then dabbed at his chin with the back of his hand. Brown spittle darkened the corner of his mouth. "Only thing is, sometimes they get snotnose. I can't stand snotnose women, no matter how fucking brilliant they are."

Daggett looked past Rita to the blonde. "Where's Chazzy?"

"Over the Atlantic, first class to Paris. Limo to Denmark. Presidential suite at the Copenhagen International."

"Did you get him everything he wanted?"

"Hot women and chilled Dom Perignon."

"Good." A genuine smile flickered across Ollie's face, briefly touching his eyes. He turned to Rita and Hodge. "My son's on a whorehouse tour of Denmark," he said in a matter-of-fact tone. "Left this morning."

"Excuse me," Hodge said. "We're on a tight schedule here. I'd like to run a few ideas by you."

"Shut up!" Ollie snapped. The anger in his voice stabbed like a knife. Rage boiled in his eyes. "Nothing is more important than my son," he snarled. "Nothing!"

Hodge stiffened.

Daggett gestured to the blonde. "Take Hodge to the guest house. Fix him a drink. Unload that fucking suit and get him into some comfortable clothes. Calm him down." Ollie pointed to Rita. "You stay. I want to talk to you."

Rita swallowed hard, puzzled by Daggett's attitude toward Hodge. Why did he want her to stay? This was not her arena. Her job was caring for people and keeping them as healthy and comfortable as possible.

"C'mon, Hodge," the blonde said.

Hodge didn't move. "Hey, hold on here." He held out his hands and shrugged. "What about PermaDream? My plans?"

"I have my own plans." Ollie returned his attention to Rita. "Hodge'll be staying with me about six months."

"Six months?" Hodge stepped forward, red-faced. "I can't stay here six months," he whined. "I'm needed at PermaDream."

"I told you I have plans," Ollie snapped, dismissing Hodge with the wave of a huge hand. "Unless you want someone else running PermaDream."

Hodge glanced at Rita, then back to Ollie, pleading with his eyes, but remaining silent.

Ollie's words hung in the air for an uncomfortable moment, then he nodded, softening his tone. "Go on, relax. Everything'll be okay. We'll talk later."

"C'mon, sugar." The blonde brushed past Rita and reached for Hodge. "I'll fix you that cold drink. I'll bet you're one of those hot blooded, Southern California, Margarita boys."

Hodge didn't resist as she grabbed his elbow and pulled him to her. Slipping her arm around his waist, she led him away.

"She'll loosen his tie," Ollie said when they were alone. The big man shook his head and frowned. "Hodge sure didn't inherit his father's *cajones*. Old Edgar would've told me to kiss his ass."

Stunned by the abrupt turn of events and shocked by Hodge's sniveling capitulation, Rita fumbled for a response. "Hodge is in mourning. He's not himself. You'll see, he'll do fine, just fine."

"Maybe he won't." Daggett leaned back and clasped his hands behind his head. "Maybe somebody else'll run the show. Somebody with a bigger pair of balls."

Rita caught her breath. Did Daggett intend to run PermaDream? Did he have the gall to think she would abandon Hodge? She folded her arms and returned his stare while her stomach flip-flopped. If Daggett took over, she would quit on the spot.

Ollie slid open his top drawer and pulled out a mirror etched with lines of white powder. "Toot?"

Rita's anger flared, but she managed a civil tone. "No thank you," she said evenly. "What's this all about?"

He closed the drawer and gestured for her to take a seat on a straight back cane chair.

"I don't belong here," she said. "I should be at PermaDream and so should Hodge."

"I told you I'd deal with Hodge," Ollie said. "Don't worry about him. He's a young guy. Six months is nothing." His tone softened. "Be sweet, sugar, I need your help."

"My help? You need my help?"

"Yeah."

Rita held her breath. So far, nothing about this situation made sense. After being treated like the court jester, Hodge permitted himself to be led away like a donkey. Now Daggett topped everything by asking for help.

"It's my son," he said, adding an unnatural, fuzzy tone to his voice that sounded surprisingly warm and human. "I want to talk about Chazz."

In spite of the frigid air, Rita felt a flush at the mention of Daggett's repulsive, lizard-eyed son. Her hand went to the silver angel at her throat. Had she come all this way to discuss Chazz Daggett?

"You know Chazz?" Ollie raised his eyebrows expectantly. "My boy?" He grinned. "Aaaaah, sure, you know Chazzy. All the girls do. Tall, handsome guy. Looks like me. Except for his shaved head." He covered his hairline with his palm. "See?"

"I've seen him."

"Bet you didn't know you're Chazzy's type."

"And what type is that?"

"Smart and sexy."

Rita's cheeks burned. She was Chazzy's type all right. Female and breathing. "We've never met."

"Y'know, poor Chazzy never had a mommy. Bitch took off a few weeks after he was born." Daggett's pinkie ring flashed as he tapped his chest. "I've been mother and father to him. It ain't easy raising a boy without a woman. Especially for a man with big huevos, like me. I jacked Chazz up real good in the macho department, but the poor kid came up short-changed in the, "sweet and gentle" section. Got a few rough edges." Ollie lowered his voice. "Truth is, my young lion could stand to go to some kind of charm school."

"If you're asking for advice, I seriously doubt that charm school would benefit Chazz."

Ollie brushed aside Rita's sarcasm with another cheesy smile. "In six months, my boy turns twenty. A year later, on his twenty-first birthday, I'm considering naming him President of the PermaDream Corporation."

Ollie's statement hit Rita like a shotgun blast. Chazz? President? "But, but, Hodge..."

"If Hodge insists on leaving with you, I'll accept his resignation, but if he shows some smarts and stays with me for six months, I'll teach him a few moves and bring him in on my game plan. He'll have a year to show me what he's got between his legs. I hope he makes it, but if he falls on his ass, you can bet your skirt, Chazz'll be ready to take over. Some birthday surprise, huh? It'd top everything I ever did for him."

"Pardon me, but that doesn't make sense." Rita crossed her arms. "It's obvious that Chazz never had a decent education. Hodge is a college graduate. It takes someone with schooling to run an operation as complex as PermaDream."

Ollie glared across the desk. "I never made it past ninth grade and I own PermaDream." He held out his hands and looked around the sumptuous quarters. "Not too shabby for an ignorant gringo, huh?" His expression softened. "Look, honey, education's not the issue here. The issue is following orders. Chazz will do exactly what I tell him. That's all that matters. We'll see who's who in the zoo when he's twenty one. I want my boy to be ready, that's all."

Rita opened her mouth to speak, but thought better of it when she saw the glazed, faraway look in Ollie's eyes.

"Y'know, I get misty-eyed thinking about all the birthday parties I gave him over the years," he said. "We never miss having his favorite chocolate cake, covered with that white shit and sugar flowers." He sighed. "Chazzy always eats the whole thing by himself. He blows out the candles, then sits there and sucks the fucker up. It's a family tradition."

Rita forced a weak smile. "How cute."

Ollie kept talking, each memory stirring more. "Of course, 'Daddy Ollie' always comes up with a big surprise. On his third birthday, I named a racehorse after him. When he turned fourteen, he became a man. I flew him to Vegas and tossed him into a suite at Caesar's with four of the fanciest hookers in town. Show me a boy who wouldn't die for that. Chazzy came home feeling like King Kong."

Rita had grown tired of this asinine, one-sided conversation. She wished Daggett would get to the point so she could go home and pull her thoughts together.

"I never once let him down. Never will either. It ain't easy coming up with a gift every year for a kid who gets whatever the hell he wants, whenever he wants it. That's why you're here, Rita. I'm giving you the chance to earn a big fat raise."

"A raise?" Rita's anger began to boil. "What are you getting at, Mr. Daggett?"

"Near the end, old Edgar talked about you more than his son. Told me how his 'little angel,' took care of him, how you were sweet and good and nice. My Chazzy needs an angel too. Someone to mother him. Teach him some manners. Love him." Ollie's pig-eyes locked on her. "Someone like you."

"Me?" Rita stood. "Me?" A torrent of revulsion overwhelmed her.

Ollie waved his hands. "Okay, okay, you don't have to love him. Just take care of him. Teach him. Mother him. He held up four fingers. "I'll pay you four times what you're making." He added a thumb. "Five times."

Rita's anger carried her. "This is ridiculous! I'm not interested in mothering your son at any price."

Ollie's face reddened, but he didn't speak, only stared wide-eyed as her anger erupted like hot lava, burning brighter with each word. "You have a hell of a nerve. Offering me drugs. Trying to buy me, like some crooked PLC politician. You ignorant-foul-mouthed..."

"Hey, hey, show me some respect here, *señorita*! Cool it, with the names. Skip it, for Christ's sake. I'll get somebody else." Ollie raised his hands in mock surrender. "*La siento, señorita, la siento.*"

"And knock off that *señorita* crap! Listen, Mr. Daggett. Don't get the idea that I'm the house Mexican, here to serve the new gringo boss. It was my decision to accept Edgar's offer to work at PermaDream and it was my decision to come to Cancun to meet you. Now it's my decision to leave here and go back to work, so call your blonde flunky and get me back to the plane."

"Ease up, Rita, you made your point. Now, forget it."

"I will," she lied, knowing she would never forget this oddball day. "What about Hodge?"

"Joe College needs to calm his jittery ass down and learn a few things. Don't sweat it, honey. Soon he'll get the picture that I only want

47

to show him the ropes so he'll know how to get things done, Ollie Daggett's way. In six months, Hodge'll be in charge of the whole enchilada. I told Edgar that I'd take care of him and I will. He'll have his chance. Ollie Daggett's word is a royal flush in spades. If Hodge blows it, still no sweat. He can be Chazz's assistant." Daggett's voice iced over. "Don't discuss our conversation with anybody, Rita." His prison yard stare drilled home the warning. "Got it?"

"Yes." She replied as emphatically as possible, knowing full well she would discuss the day's weird events with Lorenzo and Morgan, first chance she got. More than ever, Rita needed to confide in someone and Morgan and Lorenzo were *familia segundo*.

Without another word, Ollie nodded toward the door. It opened again with its distinctive whispering clicks.

The faint odor of whiskey lingered in the cabin of the northbound plane; a chilling reminder of the morning's jungle landing. Rita loosened her safety belt, kicked off her shoes and lowered her seatback as the private plane achieved altitude and followed the twinkling lights of the Mexican coast. She wanted to say goodbye to Hodge, but as they sped toward the waiting plane, the blonde smiled and told her he had fallen asleep in the air-conditioned guest house.

By now, Rita's anger had cooled. She fingered Lorenzo's silver angel, replaying the day's events in her mind, cringing at the recollection of telling Ollie off and happily surprised to have gotten away with it. She lingered on the unreal, unexpected, ludicrous conversation about Chazz and tried to calm her stomach-churning-anxiety over Hodge's well-being. Wait until Lorenzo and Morgan heard this one. Imagine, big, bad, murdering Ollie Daggett, saddled with such a glaring weakness. A blind, inflexible, unconditional love for his disgusting son.

How pathetic.

CHAPTER SEVEN

Morgan Jackson sipped his coffee and stepped onto the elevator, studying the front page of The San Diego Union Tribune with mixed emotions. After pressing the button to Z level, he started to read, page one, lower right.

DIGITAL DREAMS
By Mark Clements (UPI)

The second stage of the controversial PermaDream Euthanasia Center is near completion. Following several months of dormancy, the frenzy of construction that began in August on a huge circular building remains shrouded in secrecy at the center of a heavily guarded area south of the California/Mexico border. Several hundred yards from the soon to be expanded Otay Mesa Crossing, stands a new facility, housing powerful hardware and high-speed memory modules that give Morpheus, the dream computer, what Denise Moore of PermaDream calls, "the magic that makes the miracle".

Since the death of PermaDream founder Edgar Michaels last May, his son Hodge is reported to have been the guest of international businessman and suspected drug kingpin, Oliver Daggett, at his Cancun,

Mexico compound. Daggett is sought by U.S. authorities for questioning in the Christmas Eve plane crash deaths of Texas Congressman, Roberto Manzur and his family, three years ago.

At the time of his death, Manzur headed a joint task force with an investigative branch of the United States Food and Drug Administration and had initiated extradition proceedings against Daggett with the Mexican government. Warrants have been filed for Daggett's arrest on several tax-evasion charges in both state and federal courts. To date, the controlling PLC Party in Mexico has rejected any such overtures from the United States. Sources claim that Daggett, a resident of Mexico, is in fact the true owner of PermaDream. Unconfirmed reports state that Hodge Michaels accompanied Daggett to France and the Philippines in an attempt to expand PermaDream.

According to Denise Moore, Project Administrator of the PermaDream research labs in Las Puerta, "Dream technology has grown at a phenomenal pace thanks to a recent breakthrough in synaptic modulation by a team of experts, headed by renowned neuroscientist Cheryl Martin and Jack Scanlon, a leading microprocessor engineer."

When questioned about the future of PermaDream, Moore remained close-mouthed, saying only that, "Hodge Michaels will hold a press conference soon, to announce new plans." While rumors about the further growth of PermaDream and its effect on the burgeoning border employment picture continue to run rampant in Mexico, Moore acknowledged that the PermaDream hospital facility, headed by the eminent American physician, Morgan Jackson, has recently undergone significant expansion. Jackson is reportedly supervising a series of tests on extended dreams for terminal patients.

(See Digital page A-4)

The door whooshed open. Morgan folded the newspaper, tucked it under his arm and stepped out of the elevator. The air conditioning in the new Z-level PermaDream patient care facility blew cold, dry, and steady. Since coming on-line, Morpheus had done a faultless job controlling the environment, but giving a machine responsibility over so many tasks left Morgan uneasy. He still preferred a hands on approach. What he wouldn't do for a good, old fashioned thermostat right about now. Fastening the top button of his new red flannel shirt, he braced himself against the chill and entered Pre-Dream.

Oblivious to his presence, Rita Cariño huddled over a console, dark eyes intent, her small hands moving quickly, making notations on an IPad. Not wanting to startle her, Morgan cleared his throat.

She looked up with an expectant smile, then jumped, sending the IPad clattering to the floor.

"Rita!" Morgan dropped the newspaper, rushed to her and took her by the shoulders. "Are you all right?"

Her frightened look turned to one of relief, but her hands trembled as she retrieved the IPad. "I'm okay."

"Sorry. I tried to warn you I was here."

"It wasn't you." She touched his sleeve, then drew back as if burned. "It – it's that shirt. My grandfather had one just like it. Same color, same pattern. When I saw you standing there I thought..." She breathed in deep, shaking her head. "He was wearing it the last time I saw him."

Her agitation made Morgan uncomfortable. This wasn't the Rita he knew. He tilted her chin and spoke in his father-to-daughter manner. "Something you want to talk about?"

"I haven't thought about it for a long time," she said, speaking more to herself than to Morgan. She gazed past him, then looked him in the eye. Her expression changed as if she had come to some inner decision. "I was five," she said, her voice soft and childlike. "Grandpapa's little girl. Nothing made me happier then waking up before the sun on Saturdays to go fishing with my *Abuelito*. I'd sit on his shoulder and point the way as we followed the trail to the ocean."

The far away look returned to her eyes. "It was my job to help push the panga into the surf, then he rowed for a long time. The sun rising over the mountains behind us sent a golden path across the water that seemed to reach all the way to the end of the world. Grandpapa said it pointed to the place where the biggest fish waited. Our secret spot. He never took anyone else there but me."

Morgan swallowed hard. He treasured the few scattered memories he had of his own grandpa. Talked about him all the time. Why had Rita never mentioned hers until now? Why the sudden, haunted look? He hoped she was okay. Right now things were critical, especially with what he was about to tell her.

"He disappeared," she said. "It concerned me when I didn't see him all week, but I knew he wouldn't forget about me on our fishing day. I got up Saturday, same as always and followed the path to the ocean. I knew he'd be waiting..." Her voice trailed off, then picked up again. "I was so happy when I saw his red shirt." She nodded toward Morgan. "Exactly like yours. He sat against a rock down near the water's edge with his back to me. I ran to him calling his name. He seemed to be doing something with his hands, in his lap. Unraveling fishing line or something."

"What was he doing?"

"It wasn't his hands," she said softly.

Morgan steeled himself. "Then what?"

"*Raton!*" She said as if spitting something rotten. Then she repeated the word in English. "Rats!"

Morgan's stomach lurched. "Oh Jesus!"

"Apparently, he had a heart attack. The rats had eaten into his stomach. His face was all purple and bloated. Lips. Eyelids. Gone." A tear rolled down her cheek. She took a deep breath. "I ran home. Later, they found him. I never told anyone. I couldn't." She hugged herself and shuddered. "You're the first person I ever told. To this day, even the thought of a rat..." She sobbed.

Morgan pulled her to him. "Poor Rita." He hugged her as a father would a child, saddened by the warm tears on his shoulder. "It must've been awful."

She straightened and brushed her sleeves.

"Rita." Morgan looked her in the eye and took hold of her hands. "I know it's been hard for you, but I have to give this to you straight. And it won't wait."

Her big eyes widened. "What's wrong?"

"You and I are setting up Ollie Daggett's son for a two hour recreational dream."

"Recreational dream?" Rita pulled away, dark eyes flashing with anger, her face turning grim. "Chazz Daggett?"

"He's in my office."

"Good Lord, Morgan, dying people are waiting and that creep's taking a recreational dream. Who the hell authorized this?"

"Hodge."

"Dammit! It's not fair," Rita said. "After six months of rumors, Hodge pops up and tries to force this crap down our throats."

"Looks like Daggett kept his word about schooling Hodge."

"Come on, Morgan, call him. Tell him to talk to Daggett again. Convince him he's wrong."

Morgan shook his head, knowing she'd be angry. "Hodge is on the plane headed home. Ollie won't see him any more. You told me yourself, how crazy the old man is about Chazz. The dream is a gift. Who's going to tell Ollie he can't give the kid what he wants?"

Rita's stomach burned. She crossed her arms. "So that arrogant bastard Ollie Daggett gets me to play nursemaid to his Neanderthal son after all."

"I wouldn't let him do that to you." Morgan offered a reassuring smile. "Just help me hook Chazz up to Morpheus. As soon as he closes his eyes, you're finished. I promised Hodge we'd help. He needs us."

She sighed. "I'll be there for him, but I won't sleep much tonight thinking about it. The others'll be mad as hell. Hodge has a lot of explaining to do."

"He's scheduled a noon meeting," Morgan said. "I guess he'll deal with it then. Whatever you do, don't miss it. Hodge said he had big news. I'll stay with Chazz until he wakes up."

"Aren't you going to be there to hear his big news?"

"He's emailing it to me as we speak. I'll read it while I watch Chazz."

Rita wrinkled her nose. "Ollie Daggett is a vile, ignorant man. God knows what's in that email! "

"Chazz is waiting in my office. We'll meet you in Pre-Dream as soon as he signs some papers." He picked up the newspaper. "Brought you this. Another story about us in it." Morgan avoided her gaze, rubbing his palms together, trying to warm his suddenly cold hands. He hated doing this to her, but there was no other way. "Sorry to stick you with this. We won't have any problems, will we?"

She shook her head and sighed. "No problems."

He handed her the folded newspaper. "Story's on page one. Seems they know more about what's going on than we do."

CHAPTER EIGHT

After a solitary flight and a quick taxi from the airport, Hodge rushed through the recently built Hall of Dreams, a long curving corridor lined with hundreds of framed color portraits of men and women of all ages. He recognized many of the faces smiling down from the walls. The person behind each glowing countenance had been granted PermaDream happiness.

He followed the corridor around the structure's inner circumference and entered the Gallery of Angels; photos of children who dreamed away their final moments playing with friends, picnicking with parents, and riding glittering carousels in fanciful settings, designed by Lorenzo Vargas.

Further along in another section of corridor, a one way floor-to-ceiling mirror served as the inner wall. Behind it, banks of consoles, blinking panels and illuminated work stations faced the glass for non-invasive scrutiny of the electronic heart of Morpheus. Behind a roped - off area, in front of a blue velvet curtain, a red lettered sign cautioned:

NO ADMITTANCE

Behind that, in a specially cooled clean room, Morpheus maintained vigil through a fiber optic network that kept tabs on such diversified tasks as patient monitoring, intravenous drug and nourishment delivery, facility temperature control, front lobby traffic, and Eddie Driscoll's clandestine, after hour games of Toxic Mutant.

A satellite link downloaded and updated video and text files from the Internet directly to the research department where Lorenzo, Eddie, and their staff previewed, manipulated and recorded the stream of data for use in the production of increasingly sophisticated dream sequences. For the past three months they had labored in secret behind closed doors. Soon the world would realize the full impact of their efforts. First, Hodge wanted to share the secret with Denise, who waited in his office.

He hurried past Z lab, marked by a darkened section of mirrored inner wall. Behind it slept nineteen Phase II PermaDream volunteers, spending extended time in a computer-controlled life support environment, enjoying their waning hours in times and places of their choice.

His stomach boiled at the thought of Ollie Daggett's healthy son occupying one of twenty prized dream beds, fulfilling obscene fantasies for two full hours while terminally ill volunteers clung to what little remained of their lives, praying for a happy PermaDream finale. No sense even thinking about it. Hodge knew he had no choice. He wanted to get it over with as quickly as possible. Quickening his pace, he left the corridor, climbed to the fifth floor annex and ducked into his office.

Denise stood at the bar, clinking ice cubes into two glasses. She added several fingers of Chivas Regal to each, smiled and drifted toward him with the drinks, looking gorgeous and leggy in a short teal skirt and low cut white blouse. A sexy treat for the senses, but for Hodge, as untouchable as a hot wire.

In Cancun, thoughts of Denise were the only thing that kept him from losing it during the half-year of humiliation he suffered at the hands of Ollie Daggett. Ollie had even controlled Hodge's sex life, sending him off with the blonde for extended sex breaks several times a week. "Listen to me, Joe College, take advantage of that woman," Ollie told him. "Learn. You'll never luck into another piece of ass like her." During their lengthy sexual interludes, Hodge often closed his eyes and fantasized about Denise, longing to be with her instead.

Denise set the drinks down, kicked off her shoes and eased closer. Pressing her body to his, she whispered, "Did you miss me?" She slipped her arms around his waist and squeezed, making him burn inside.

He smiled. Had she reconsidered?

Her cheek felt soft and warm against him. If only this moment would last forever. He smiled, inhaling the essence of her perfume, wishing he didn't have to tell her about the Daggett kid. "Denise, there's something you have to know," he blurted, anxious to get it behind them.

"What is it?" she asked in a soft sensuous tone.

"We have to give Chazz a two hour dream for his birthday."

She stiffened and backed away, frowning. Her voice came harsh. "Why, in the name of God, would you allow that?"

Hodge's bliss popped like a camera flash. "Ollie demanded it."

"I knew it! That lowlife pig! Raping our miracle!"

"Our miracle belongs to Ollie. Like it or not, we're working for him. If I learned anything over the last six months, I learned that. When he approached me about the dream, I stood my ground as long as I could, but he wouldn't back down. I'm sure everyone will understand."

"Don't count on it. Don't count on me understanding, either."

Her words hit like cold punches. "For Christ's sake, Denise, we're talking about one lousy bed. Two hours, that's all."

Her face reddened. "Is that really all? What'll we talk about when half our beds are tied up for recreational dreaming by the Daggetts?" She put her hands on her hips. "Talk about pearls before swine. Daggett's depraved son enjoys a two hour recreational dream, while a volunteer patient suffers, maybe dies in agony. Some birthday present!"

Turning her back, she huffed to the window and pressed her forehead to the pane, peering at the whirlwind of construction kicking up dust in the area beyond the parking lot, five stories below. "I'll bet Rita told you to go straight to hell when you asked her to baby-sit that gutter trash. I would have."

Hodge drew a long deep breath and downed his scotch. His stomach tightened. So much for the easy part. Now for the shocker.

CHAPTER NINE

"Chazz! C. H. A. Z. Z. Chazz Daggett! Got it?"

Morgan nodded, gazing across his desk at Ollie Daggett's only offspring; a tall muscular pink-cheeked young man with a shaved head, wearing a dark tee-shirt, black leather jacket and hobnailed boots.

"I'm Doctor Jackson."

Chazz fingered a walnut-sized, ruby eyed, silver skull ring, then looked up, pale blue eyes glaring under lowered brows. "The idea of you gawking at me while I'm lying there out of my skull gives me the creeps. My father might believe you're the best doctor in the world, but the thought of you touching me makes my skin crawl."

"Your father's the boss, Chazz. He insisted that I supervise your well being while you dream."

Chazz made a long face. "I told him I wanted a white man."

"Come on, son, we're in the twenty first century and you're still hung up on the color of a man's skin. I've seen enough blood and torn flesh to know we're all the same inside. Don't sweat it, Chazz, you'll get the same care as our terminal patients. I'm only here as a precaution. Morpheus will be in control and computers are color blind."

Chazz grinned. "Well now, ain't you hot shit! Talking all that philosophical jive. Just like Uncle Remus."

Morgan eyed young Daggett with a steady gaze. "Don't waste your racial slurs on me, Chazz. That kind of garbage stopped annoying me long ago. Another time and place, I'd laugh at your shaved head, your funny leather outfit, and your big mouth. Push your snotty attitude too far and I'd work you over with a can of Whip-ass, but those days are long gone. I've been a doctor for too many years."

Chazz waved his hands in mock terror and spoke in a child's voice. "Oooh, the big black boogie man scared me. I tink I'm gonna cwy." He giggled. "My old man ever heard you talking to me like that, he'd cut your widdle wee-wee off."

"Let's get this over with." Morgan shuffled several forms. "About your dream." He looked up. "I believe you'll be uncomfortable with your destination."

"Who gives a shit what you believe?" Chazz picked up a framed photograph of a silver haired, dark skinned woman and smirked. "This one of your ancestors?"

Morgan took his late mother's picture from Chazz and gently placed it in a desk drawer. Focusing his anger on the computer screen, he attacked the keyboard with his index fingers, spitting out words, "You volunteered several times during our final phase of testing. Alabama, 1952, Germany, '43, Atlanta, '54, Johannesburg, South Africa, 1980. Last time you dreamed, you went to..."

"Washington, D.C., 1924," Chazz shouted. He balled his fists and squared his shoulders. "Marched my pink ass straight down Pennsylvania Avenue. Right down the middle of the street. Me and 40,000 Klan Brothers." He slammed a fist against his chest. "God bless America!"

Morgan leaned forward, lowering his voice. "We didn't develop dream travel to cater to the likes of you."

Chazz showed his palms. "Shit happens." Leaning an elbow on his chair back, he lowered his voice and drawled, "It's happening to you right now, ain't it?"

Morgan shook his head. "Why in God's name would anyone in their right mind want to spend time in Hartville, Mississippi in 1860?"

"There are more blacks in Mississippi than anywhere in the USA. I stuck a hatpin in a Mississippi map." Chazz shrugged. "Hartville won."

"And the hundred thousand in Confederate money?"

Chazz smiled, exposing a mouthful of tiny yellow teeth, like two rows of dried, shoe-peg corn. "Slaves." He studied his fingernails, then looked up smiling. "Got a problem with that?"

"It's not my problem, it's yours. Take my advice, Hartville isn't..."

"That's enough advice!" Chazz growled. "Where do I sign?"

Morgan slid pen and paper across the table. "Bottom line."

"That's better." Chazz scribbled his name, then stared at the ceiling whistling, "We Shall Overcome", while Morgan tapped the keyboard and rattled off information.

"You'll experience pleasure and pain, exactly as if you were awake. The day you've chosen will continue for the length of the dream. We'll wake you in two hours. Remember, to dream-travelers, seconds can seem like days or weeks. Two hours can feel like a lifetime. Questions?"

"Nope." Chazz stood and spread his arms. "Beam me aboard, Mister Spook!"

With his Klan robe draped over his shoulders like a royal cloak, Chazz strutted beside the doctor through a doorway marked, PRE-DREAM and down a dimly lit corridor to a darkened room where a myriad of miniature lights embedded in a coal black ceiling twinkled like stars.

Against the opposite wall, dark eyed, diminutive Rita Cariño, wearing a powder blue jumpsuit and silver hooped dream-catcher earrings sat at a terminal behind an illuminated desk. She glanced up as the men drew near.

Chazz bent down beside her to study her nametag, his lips barely moving as he mumbled her name phonetically. "Ree–tah Car–een–yoh." He straightened, speaking it aloud. "Rita Cariño!" He raised his eyebrows. "Hey, what do you know, *Rita-the-Señorita*? I heard all about you. C'mon, honey, stand up and shake your enchiladas." Grabbing his crotch, he swiveled his hips and made a loud kissing sound.

Rita touched a finger to her lips, ignoring his gyrations.

Chazz's expression darkened. "You telling me to shut up?"

"People are sleeping."

He lowered his voice to a hoarse whisper. "Listen sweet cheeks, you're talking to Ollie Daggett's son."

"I know who you are!" she snapped.

"Then you should learn my rules," he snarled. "Nobody in this third rate country tells Chazz Daggett what to do. If Chazz wants to shit on your desk and wipe his ass on the carpet, he'll drop down and do it." He leaned in close, inches from Rita's face. "Got that, Rita the *Señorita*?"

Before she could reply, Morgan tossed a folder onto the desk between them. "Chazz is in a hurry, Rita. Want me to wait?"

"No."

He turned to leave. "See you in Pre-dream."

"Yowsah, boss!" Chazz muttered. He dropped into a chair and straightened his legs, balancing his right heel on his left toe.

Rita glanced at the robe draped across his lap. "Want to hang that thing up?"

Chazz scowled. "That thing stays right here with me."

She pointed to his boots. "You sure you'll be comfortable wearing those?"

"Steel plated ass-kickers. Why not? Been wearing them for years."

She keyed the computer. "And the leather jacket?"

"What about it?"

"We've duplicated the exact ambiance of your chosen time and place."

He scratched his head. "What the hell does that have to do with my leather?"

"No official Mississippi weather data is available for August ninth, eighteen-sixty. Our research department has estimated it, based on readings over the past half-century. Temperatures in the upper nineties. Humidity in the 80 percent range. I'd suggest lighter clothing."

Chazz raised his arm and sniffed. "Sweat makes me smell like a man." He leaped to his feet. "I'm wearing my jacket now, and I'm wearing it in my dream. Leather's part of the Daggett image. Same as these tattoos." He slammed his palms onto the desktop. A steely-eyed bald eagle, clutching a Nazi banner in its talons glared defiance from the back of each hand.

Rita stood and pressed a button on her desk. Behind her, a door slid open. "This way."

Chazz swaggered through the doorway, eyeing her backside. He pursed his lips to whistle, then stopped. "Hey! This is an elevator. Thought I was going to bed."

"You are." She fingered a button and the doors closed. "We're placing you downstairs in the PermaDream facility with the terminally ill."

"Terminally ill? You mean, I'll be hanging there like one of them dying turnips? If I catch some Goddamn disease, my daddy'll shit all over you people."

The elevator lurched, then descended.

Chazz leaned against the wall, ankles crossed, picking at his fingernails. "I know you assholes don't appreciate what I'm doing, but I don't give a shiny shit what you like." He sucked his teeth. "Just don't play games. The old man'll freak out if anything happens to me. Know what I mean? You better take extra special care of Chazzy."

"Doctor Jackson is the best. Your father knows that."

"My father and I don't think alike when it comes to niggers." Chazz smirked. "If there's an emergency, that old jungle-bunny's liable to pound a drum and shake a spear over my head."

Rita stared at the floor, showing no emotion.

"Know something, Rita-the-*Señorita*?" Chazz licked his lips and wiggled his tongue. "Your ass is as pretty as your eyes. Chazzy'll kiss it on the fifty yard line, during the next Charger game."

Rita looked him in the eye. "And Rita-the-*Señorita* will kick Chazzy so hard, he'll need an eye, ear, nose, and throat specialist to put his little balls back down between his legs."

Chazz's eyes widened and his mouth dropped. "Smart-ass little bitch!" He moved toward her and the elevator stopped. The doors whooshed open onto a bustling hallway. He stopped, balling his fists.

Rita's voice tinkled like diminutive celestial chimes. "Kindly step to the left upon exiting, Mister Daggett."

Chazz tightened his grip on the robe, wishing it was the little jumping bean's throat. His dream came first. He'd deal with the bitch later. Clicking his heels, he snapped to attention, stepped smartly off the elevator and paraded down the hallway, heart thundering like a kettle drum, blood sizzling in his veins. Soon, he'd be in Hartville owning slaves. He smiled. They would call him Massa Chazz.

Rita-the-*Señorita* guided him to a hospital bed where he stretched out, clutching his robe to his chest.

"Lie still, we're connecting your life support to the monitors," she said.

Chazz grunted and watched the tight-assed little chile-pepper attach sticky pads containing several thin multi-colored wires to his wrists. He smiled to himself. Dark hair, dark eyes, tight butt. Snotty little Rita Cariño would make one hell of a birthday present. Just the two of them, all alone on an island or a boat where nobody could hear her scream and he could take his time with her.

A humming sound made his body tingle.

"We're hooking you up to PermaDream control," Rita said. "When the system kicks in, you'll feel a rush of blood to your brain. Don't fight it. Let yourself slip away."

"Yeah, yeah, I know all about it." Chazz squinted. "Too damn bright in here."

The jigaboo doctor dabbed at his forehead with petroleum jelly. "After we secure the electrodes, Nurse Cariño will place moist cotton pads on your eyelids. It's quite soothing. You'll be dreaming before you know it."

"About time." Chazz closed his eyes and exhaled, letting his heart slow. The mattress felt firm against his back. His pillow floated like a cloud beneath his head. A gentle crawling sensation began in his extremities and spread throughout his body before shimmering across his mind like soft, warm fog.

Sweat dripped from his armpits and trickled down his rib cage. His lips felt thick and dry. He called out, "Hey, what happened to the air conditioner?"

A fly landed on his nose. Chazz shooed it away, but it kept buzzing around his head. "Hey, there's a fly in here. How the hell am I supposed to fall asleep with..."

He opened his eyes and saw that he lay on his back in the center of a rocky dirt road. Overhead, golden sunshine blistered a pale-blue sky. Leaning on an elbow, he looked around at endless fields of ripe cotton.

He stumbled to his feet, heart pounding. "I made it!" Howling with glee, Chazz danced in the narrow road, stopping when he noticed three black men standing in the shade of a big green-leaved oak. Bingo! Three buck niggers, right off the bat. Might as well get started. Chuckling, he stepped behind a wild berry thicket at the side of the road and slipped into his Klan robe.

Unseen, he worked his way through the roadside brush until he stood close enough to hear their voices. Being careful not to soil or crease the pointed hood, he raised it over his head. Sucking in a deep breath, he bounded to the middle of the road and headed for them, laughing and yahooing, stirring up clouds of powdery dust with his steel-plated ass-kicker boots.

The men stared as Chazz swooped from one shoulder of the road to the other, arms outstretched, fanning the satin robe like angel wings, shouting, "Gonna buy a bullwhip, then I'm gonna buy you." A strong acrid odor stopped him.

He lowered his arms and sniffed. No mistaking it. He looked

around, squinting through the eyeholes. A stream of black smoke, rose from a nearby maple grove. "All right!" he shouted, feeling exhilarated. "Smell that? Hot tar! Which one of you raisin heads wants to show Chazz Daggett some disrespect?" Squaring his shoulders, he stiffened his knees and goose-stepped toward them, chanting, "Eeny-meeny-miny-mo..."

Rita removed the cotton pads from Chazz's eyes and dropped them in a waste basket. "Sound asleep. Morpheus is in control."

Morgan smiled down at him. "Hartville, Mississippi, August ninth, eighteen-sixty."

"Why Mississippi?"

"Chazz gets his kicks terrorizing people. This time he wanted to own slaves."

"I never heard of Hartville."

"Chazz stuck a hatpin into his great-great-great-great-grand-daddy's hand-drawn, post Civil War map of Mississippi. The old man's map placed it somewhere between Port Gibson and Liberty. The only information Lorenzo's department could garner had been passed down verbally from descendants of former residents. From there, Morpheus took over the Hartville recreation."

"What happened to the real town?"

"Hartville was never more than a collection of shacks that served as a hideout for an outlaw gang led by Freedom Hart, a former plantation slave. One Christmas Eve, he beheaded his owner's family and chopped off the man's hands, leaving him alive. Hart and his band of runaways terrorized rural Mississippi, riding by night with the mummified hands of his former master lashed to his saddlehorn."

"Whew." Rita shivered. "Some story."

Morgan washed his hands as he spoke. "Hart drowned during the spring floods of 1862 and the group disbanded. No trace of the settlement has ever been found." He turned to leave. "I'll pick up Hodge's fax and watch over young Mister Daggett. See you after the meeting."

Rita stared at the monitor, observing the high, rapid pulsing of Chazz's heartbeat. "Must be having some dream."

Morgan paused in the doorway. "I tried to warn him, but he wouldn't listen. The Hart gang kept a barrel of boiling tar on the fire in case any foolish white men dared to enter their camp."

Before turning off the lights, Rita blotted a bead of perspiration from Chazz Daggett's upper lip.

CHAPTER TEN

Hodge moved to where Denise stood by the window and inhaled the sweet fragrance of her perfume. Time to reveal the future of PermaDream, first to her, then to the staff. Chazz should be dreaming by now and Morgan would spend the next several hours reviewing the email. Later, they would talk.

For now, he needed Denise beside him at the meeting, showing support for Ollie Daggett's plan. He choked out the words, "I have something to tell you."

She tensed, still peering at the construction hubbub below. "I won't listen to any more bullshit about Daggett's disgusting offspring, or his vile two hour dream. You knuckled under to that drug dealing, murdering scumbag!"

"I did the right thing," Hodge said. "The only thing." He touched her elbow. "Forget Chazz's dream. Big things are happening. Wonderful things." He wanted to spin her away from the window, take her in his arms and hear her say she trusted him to make the right decisions. Instead, he stood behind her feeling far away, dreading the pain he would see in her eyes when he told her the news. "Give me a chance. Please. Look at me, Denise."

She faced him, holding out her drink, a look of sullen indifference on her face. "Here." She wrinkled her nose. "I only wanted a sip."

He took the glass and set it on his desk. His heart thumped. "I came here straight from the airport because I wanted you to hear the news first." He reached out for her, but she brushed past him like a cold breeze and sat on the sofa.

"More news?" She raised the pitch of her voice and fanned her face with her hand. "Heavens, how much of this Goddamned euphoria can a girl stand?"

Her sarcasm sparked a slow burn in Hodge. He felt his face flush and his throat tighten. "C'mon, Denise, give me a break! I just spent six months with Ollie Daggett." Without you, he thought.

"It was probably like being alone on Easter Island."

"I was hardly alone." Hodge couldn't bring himself to mention the blonde, who rarely left him during his time with Ollie. He leaned against the edge of his desk facing Denise, recalling the long hours in Daggett's refrigerated office looking at photos of Chazz, listening to Ollie's incessant rants about past birthdays and his plans for number twenty-one, should Hodge fail to make their operation profitable. "In June, I accompanied Ollie to the Philippines," Hodge said. "Negotiating for a second PermaDream site outside Manila. What a disaster! Name-calling, racial slurs, and physical threats. In Paris, Ollie and the members of the French Diplomatic Corps couldn't even agree on which cheek to kiss. The meeting disintegrated into a shouting match, then fell flat on its face." Hodge finished his drink and picked up hers. "Ollie called the Minister of Protocol a cocksucker. Poor guy, nearly dropped dead from shock. The French put away the champagne and we were out of there." He paused, watching for a reaction. None. "We had to come up with another way to make money."

He studied her, hoping for a hint of empathy or a gesture of compassion, but her severe expression only deepened the way his grade school teacher's did when he offered his school skipping alibi.

"What has Daggett done to you?" Denise frowned, shaking her head. "Jesus, all this money crap."

"What the hell's wrong with earning money? Money is..."

"There's that word again! You're really caught up in it, aren't you?" She spit out the words. "You sicken me!"

In spite of his feelings for her, his hostility flashed. "Sicken you?"

Her narrow-eyed arrogance diminished her beauty, making it easy for him to speak the words, "Here's something else to sicken you." He paused, took a breath, and delivered the news like a slap.

"PermaDream is being replaced by a commercially oriented recreation and educational facility for the general public. It's to be called DreamLand." He tossed off his drink.

"DreamLand?" Denise paled. "An amusement park?"

"More than that. Much more."

She lifted her gaze to meet his. Her voice went flat. "You sold us out."

Hodge looked away, unable to bear the disappointment in her eyes.

"Sold us out for an amusement park."

"I didn't sell you out. Without Ollie Daggett, we would've folded long ago. In the beginning, when other investors laughed, he backed Dad. Time after time, he came up with the money for clinical trials. Now he figures a return on his investment is past due." Hodge shrugged. "Hey, I can't disagree. We're talking millions here. Now we can pay Ollie back and get rich in the bargain. We're all due something. I talked Ollie into waiting until the end of Phase II, before shutting PermaDream down."

"Shutting it down? I don't believe it. Everything we worked for, the good things we accomplished. The end of pain and suffering."

"I felt disappointed at first too, but with Ollie's encouragement, I worked out the guilt. I'll help you. Same as he helped me."

She rolled her eyes. "Oh, please, spare me!"

"Believe me, Denise, there's something much more exciting than PermaDream in our future." Hodge forced a smile. "Much more." He brightened his voice. "There'll be a demonstration of DreamLand at today's meeting. A sample dream, created by Lorenzo and Eddie Driscoll. You'll be amazed."

Denise stared at the floor, biting at her fingernail. "Lorenzo too?" She lowered her voice. "Jack will quit for sure."

"With his attitude, Jack'd be lucky to find work repairing video games. I suspect he knows that." Hodge paced back and forth, talking fast, pitching hard. "Look, I'm not enthusiastic over the prospect of repairing video games either. I've had lots of time to think this over and I'm riding it out. If we don't stay, outsiders will take over. I won't stand for that. I assumed you'd feel the same way. Why cast aside a life's work because of a simple change in direction?"

"A simple change in direction?" She put her hands on her hips and glared. "Come on, Hodge, PermaDream is..."

"Dead." Hodge's tone had the effect of slamming a door. "Ollie has appointed me CEO of DreamLand Enterprises."

Denise caught her breath. "CEO?"

"He's giving me my chance."

She tensed. "You accepted? Just like that?"

"I can run this place, Denise. Make decisions. Make us all rich. You'll see."

"You didn't even discuss it with me?"

"You would have talked me out of it. We'd all be out on the street." He reached for her hand. "Come on, it's time for the meeting." He helped her to her feet. "You've been with me all along. Stand beside me now. I need you when I break the news." He stood close and searched her smoke gray eyes for a hint of forgiveness.

She pulled away and frowned, empty-eyed, ashen-faced, hands clenched at her sides. "I don't want any part of your meeting, or your sample dream," she said in a flat, impersonal voice. "Go tell the others about Ollie Daggett's amusement park."

KEN REETH & MATTHEW J. PALLAMARY

CHAPTER ELEVEN

S oon after Rita settled into an aisle seat beside Cheryl, the presentation room lights dimmed and a wall-sized screen behind Hodge flickered and faded to black. After a moment of silence, shimmering stardust sparkled across the ebony background and a torrent of music filled the air. A green fluorescent dot pulsed in the center of the screen, accompanied by the sizzle of musical stingers and the booming thunder of timpanis. The fanfare soared to a crescendo and the dot quivered while rocketing forward from the void, expanding into a multicolored geometric configuration that shifted and changed dimension, growing to man-sized proportions.

Cymbals crashed and children's voices filled the room, singing an upbeat version of the old tune, "Mister Sandman." The pattern morphed into a tall, thin computer generated figure with shoulder length white hair, feathered cap, and a hooded cloak of midnight blue. Gold neon eyes sparkled from behind a black mask that concealed the upper portion of his lined face. "Welcome to DreamLand," he said in a soft purr. After a low, sweeping bow, he added, "I am your host, the Sandman."

Smiling, the Sandman beckoned with long slender fingers. "Follow me, to the land of dreams." With the flourish of a master magician, he produced a red satin sack from the folds of his cloak. Reaching in, he removed a handful of shimmering light and tossed it overhead.

Colored sparks rained down, blurring his image and a computer drafted circular building with mirrored windows came into focus, surrounded by trees, flowering shrubs and fountains spouting pastel water. The Sandman reappeared, romping across an expanse of plush green lawn. He leaped onto a wide path and pranced toward the building, stopping at the entrance.

"Step up and see the wonders inside.

Your eyes won't believe our incredible ride."

Spreading his arms and billowing his mantle, the Sandman vanished in a cloud of luminescent green smoke. The building loomed closer, as if the viewer were being drawn into it and the mirrored facade dissolved, leaving only a rotating skeletal framework that stepped through a series of cad renderings and three-dimensional drawings showing a maze of corridors, rooms, and entranceways arraying outward from a central control center.

Another puff of emerald smoke and the Sandman appeared beside a series of holographic archways. He pointed to one containing figures of elves, wizards, and witches. "Storybook Kingdom," he said.

"Have some fun and have a scare.

The dream machine will put you there."

Above a second arch, a baseball player swung a bat, a football player made a diving catch and a basketball player slam-dunked a ball. "Sports Land." The Sandman waved an arm, in a sweeping gesture.

"Pitch to Babe Ruth.

Make a slam-dunk.

Sink a hoop.

Score a goal and win the game.

Feel the glory, live the fame."

Leaping high, he performed a triple back flip, landing by a third arch, on which toothy dinosaurs prowled. George Washington crossed the Delaware and a World War Two Navy fighter ace stood beside his Grumman Hellcat, chest swelled with pride.

"In HistoryLand the past is now.

The dream machine will show you how."

A spectrum of colors flashed, punctuated by sharp stabs of music from the brass section. As the archways blurred and faded, a deep off screen voice said, "The Sandman is waiting to put *you* in that special dream. More great dreams are on the way, including the exciting new SpaceWorld where you'll pilot a rocket to the moon, journey to Mars, or be lost in an uncharted universe. Don't miss it."

The Sandman reappeared on the path in front of the mirrored

DreamLand building. Smiling, he turned and with a dramatic flourish of his cape, vanished. The building shimmered and expanded outward, atomizing into stardust.

Silence, as the darkened room slowly brightened to full illumination.

Hodge spoke. "Now you know everything. I've explained DreamLand to you and you've seen a sample DreamLand commercial. When we're ready to go, it'll be downloaded onto the Internet and played over cable and satellite TV systems, cell phone apps – the works. Plans have been ready to roll for some time. Even as we speak, interior design specialists are presenting final proposals to the creative department. Construction plans were approved months ago."

More silence greeted Hodge's words as if he had announced the death of a loved one; a far cry from the excitement Rita knew he sought. Like a gathering storm, scattered whispers and angry grumbles zig-zagged through the group, punctuated by Jack's angry voice, booming above the others. "What is this, a gag?"

Hodge glanced at Jack slumped in his front row seat, eyeglasses pushed up on his forehead, staring at the floor shaking his head, arms folded, legs crossed.

From beside Rita, Cheryl's voice rose, bristling with anger. "I don't like this, Hodge."

Rita watched Hodge tense, grasping the edge of the dais. No doubt he had planned on Cheryl being in his corner. He always referred to her as pure intelligence wrapped in plain paper; a walking Nobel prize waiting to happen. "DreamLand's research budget will give you the opportunity to dig deeper than ever into the workings of the mind," he said.

"You should have consulted us before making this commitment," she shot back.

Jack snorted. "Consult us? Ask the experts? Hell, no!" An angry look darkened his face. "No need to ask the experts for an opinion, is there, Hodge? You got that clown dancing around up there to do your thinking."

Hodge flinched and his cheeks flushed. "He's not a clown, he's..."

"A Goddamned puppet, same as you! A rhyming puppet!" Jack launched himself from his chair, wide-eyed, ears red. He hunched his shoulders and spoke in a mincing voice.

"You sold your soul, you got no class.

You and Daggett can kiss my ass."

Rita barely breathed.

Tension held the room in silence.

Hodge looked like a wide receiver who had just fumbled the winning pass. Obviously forcing his voice to remain calm and steady, he said, "Don't jump to conclusions, Jack. First experience a dream that Lorenzo and Eddie have been working on. We're set up in the next room. Come on up, Lorenzo."

Rita stared at Lorenzo as he took his place beside Hodge. So he knew all along. Never said a word, not even to Morgan. Even Eddie Driscoll knew.

Hodge seemed remarkably composed, considering the chilly reception. Jack's performance had come as no surprise, but Cheryl's objection obviously hit hard. Rita watched in silence as he continued to hold things together.

"We have a well laid out plan." His voice cracked. He took a sip of water before continuing. "When we activated Morpheus, we never anticipated the vast scope of dream technology. We simply zeroed in on the distant horizon." He took a breath, letting his words sink in. "Of course that was before the concept of neural based microprocessors, brain wave modulation, and neurotransmitter stimulation hurtled us into an astounding new dimension." He raised his hand and closed it into a fist. "We now hold the potential to aim the sights of Morpheus at the future. We have lowered the horizon."

Jack snorted. "Our horizon's been lowered, all right." He sighed. "I should be on the freeway, hauling my ass back to Sausalito."

Hodge ignored him. "With the new hardware on-line, Lorenzo and Eddie have already developed the initial sequences." He faced Lorenzo. "Everything ready?"

Lorenzo nodded.

"Okay, take it from here. It's your baby."

Lorenzo stepped forward. "Be prepared for an intensely personal taste of the DreamLand experience. It'll only last a few moments in real time, but you'll remember it for the rest of your lives. Guaranteed."

"Scuse me." Eddie Driscoll elbowed Hodge aside and stood beside Lorenzo.

Touching his chest and sucking in his breath, Lorenzo shook his head and let out a nervous chuckle. "This must be how Columbus felt the first time he lost sight of land. Nothing you've ever imagined can hint at the sheer magic of the DreamLand experience. Believe me, this'll knock your socks off."

He nodded to Eddie who pointed a hand held remote. The projection screen slid away revealing a portal into another room where colored lights flashed and twinkled, and pastel shadows skittered back and forth. A familiar cloaked figure emerged from the flickering shadows.

"Ladies and gentlemen," Lorenzo announced. "Your DreamLand host, live and in person."

The Sandman paused to offer a smile, then spoke in the deep rich voice of a trained classical actor. "Welcome, dream travelers, to the land of nod." Scattering handfuls of shiny confetti, he stepped aside. "Enter and be amazed." He bowed, making a sweeping gesture of invitation with his cape.

Hodge went first, stopping inside the doorway to greet the others as they joined him in the purpled shadows. Rita followed Jack Scanlon, stopping when he shouldered past Eddie and looked in the doorway frowning, his neck and ears still red. "This is it, eh, Hodge? From now on we work in a Goddamn carnival." He glared at the Sandman. "With this clown!" He balled his fists.

The Sandman backed away. Hodge grabbed Jack's arm and softened his tone. "Easy, Jack. Give us a chance."

Jack pulled away, raising his voice. "You mean give Ollie Daggett a chance. Now our technology belongs to that pig."

"We never owned it, Jack. It always belonged to him. We have to trust him to do right by us."

"The only one I trust is Uncle Sam. We should have turned this whole thing over to the U.S. Government months ago. Shit, they've been trying to nail that drug-selling, tax-evading, murderer who lives off..."

"Get out the hip boots," Eddie Driscoll said. "Here comes another pile of bullshit."

Jack glared at Eddie and thrust his head forward like an angry rooster. "Shut your mouth, punk! Nobody wants to hear from you. We devote years of our lives to a project so the citizens of the world can share in a miracle. All of a sudden, Hodge takes our hardware and turns himself into fucking Walt Disney."

He stomped off to join the others in front of a row of human-sized, egg-shaped shells, reminiscent of space capsules. Each shell tilted back at an angle. Multicolored L.E.D.'s flashed down both sides in succession, like winking runway lights. "All right," he said, his voice bristling with contempt. "Show us this money making miracle."

Rita watched in silence as Hodge backed into the console shadows and eased out the side door.

The Sandman pointed a remote toward the row of gleaming pods. The front of each egg slid open with a soft whoosh, revealing a contoured, padded recliner. "Please be seated in the nearest dream chamber, folks," he said. "Lean back. Make yourself comfy. When you arrive in Storybook Kingdom, you'll find yourself in a clearing in the Enchanted Forest. Trails lead in every direction. Only two have been completed. Pied Piper or Hansel and Gretel. Choose one and follow it. Pleasant dreams."

Rita held her breath as the cloaked figure approached, reaching out for her.

CHAPTER TWELVE

The Sandman led Rita to the row of blinking dream pods where she stood in front of one, staring at the flickering lights, trying to fathom how she had become caught up in all the craziness. Her heart felt heavy. PermaDream. Gone. After her meeting with that *cabron* Daggett, she should have known.

Hodge had slipped away. He would be looking for Denise to comfort him. So much like a little boy. Ollie Daggett had pounced on his vulnerability the way a lion took down prey.

Rita had accepted Edgar's invitation to join the staff during the second year of the Morpheus Project, vowing to battle debilitating pain and the stigma of death; something she had wished to free her mother from.

Now PermaDream had been cast aside. For what?

"Pleasant dreams," the Sandman said, pointing to the empty pod.

Rita's throat grew tight and her pain simmered into anger over this new turn of events, but she decided to reserve judgment until after the presentation. Curiosity alone dictated that she keep an open mind. Hodge had referred to the program as, "Lorenzo's baby". She would close her eyes and visit Lorenzo's dream world, hoping to learn something more about this intriguingly distant man with so many personal shadows.

Following the Sandman's instructions, Rita squeezed into the pod. As she settled into the dream cradle and the soft, satiny gel-foam molded to her form, she felt a sense of security. She breathed easily, but her heart pounded in anticipation of sharing Lorenzo's fantasy.

A young man and woman costumed as elves stepped from the shadows and moved along the line of cocoons, leaning into each one. As they approached, she read the young man's name tag.

WILL GREENWAY

Svelte and handsome, he could pass for a boy's underwear model in a clothing store ad. The girl elf, about seventeen, had pretty silken blonde hair, full red lips and sparkling blue eyes. Her name tag read.

EMILY FULBRIGHT

She looked like she belonged in a fairy tale. Whoever had hired these two knew what they were doing.

After the "elves" saw to her comfort, Rita watched Lorenzo pace back and forth issuing instructions to the dreamers. "When the Sandman's helpers secure you to the dream pod, they'll direct you on the use of the escape device embedded in the capsule wall."

She loved the sound of his voice. So soft, so strong. Cute butt too, and great shoulders. The male elf peered into her face, obviously speaking from a memorized script. "Your dream will only last a few moments, but it'll seem longer. If you feel you've dreamed enough and want to call it off, the escape words are mama, or mommy. Speak either one and you'll pop awake feeling rested and refreshed."

"Why, Mama and Mommy?" someone asked.

Lorenzo answered. "Research tells us, mama is the most recognizable word in both English and Spanish. This is especially true among children who will make up eighty-five percent of the Storybook Land dreamers. We added mommy in deference to North American kids."

Eddie Driscoll cleared his throat, adding, "Except for some French Canadians and an Eskimo or two, the English-Spanish combo pretty near covers the eastern hemisphere, right, Lorenzo?"

"Worldwide, mama tested at the top of the list in almost every tongue. It could be the world's most familiar word." Lorenzo smiled. "Hell, we probably wouldn't even have to tell the escape word to most kids. Who's the first person they call for when they're in trouble?"

Rita snuggled deeper into the cocoon. What a bullshit artist!

Emily the elf leaned into her capsule. "You'll love the Enchanted Forest," she gushed sweetly. "Follow the path marked Hansel and Gretel. It's the best one." She grinned, showing perfect teeth. "I was a test volunteer. Been there twice. The escape word is Mama, but it's so much fun, you won't want to leave." She moved to the last cocoon. The one occupied by Jack Scanlon.

As the elf saw to Jack's comfort, Rita heard him grousing. She almost laughed out loud at the thought of him crying out for mama. Jack would be more comfortable with an escape word like "asshole".

Emily the elf rejoined her partner and the Sandman in front of the bank of pods. "Pleasant dreams!" they shouted in unison. Holding hands, the trio skipped through the same door Hodge had used for an exit. The panels of Rita's cocoon whooshed shut.

Disoriented by the sudden darkness, she blinked, looking for a glimmer of light along the door seams. None leaked through. Perspiration dampened her skin. In the velvet blackness, clammy tendrils of claustrophobia reached out to smother her. Her heart pounded, but a calming puff of warm air touched her face and she heard the distant, ethereal tinkle of bells. She took a deep breath, assuring herself that everything would be okay. If little, sparkle-eyed Emily could do it, so could Rita.

A humming sound filled her ears and the cocoon seemed to spin. Faster. Faster. Secure in her cradle, Rita fancied it tumbling through the air. She caught her breath and laughed aloud as she felt it whirling and falling like Dorothy's house in the Wizard of Oz. She closed her eyes...

...opening them to find herself on her side in sweet smelling grass, listening to the warbling of birds and the drone of insects in a small clearing surrounded by dense greenery. Sunshine warmed her shoulders. Lifting her head, she squinted, momentarily blinded by a sudden spray of sunbeams twinkling like gold dust on flower petals and glinting off the wings of rainbow spangled butterflies.

The Enchanted Forest.

Deciding to stand, she seemed to float to her feet without using her hands. The sensation made her stomach quiver. Signs marked two separate paths into the woods, THE PIED PIPER and HANSEL AND GRETEL. Emily had recommended Hansel and Gretel. Rita would have chosen that one over the Pied Piper anyway. She wanted no part of rats, even in Lorenzo's harmless dream fantasy.

She stepped onto the path.

From far away she heard a children's chorus singing a song she remembered from an animated Hansel and Gretel video she'd watched hundreds of times as a little girl.

"The witch is coming for you,
The witch is coming for you,
She'll nibble your fingers and snack on your toes,
And fatten you up for stew."

Rita smiled. Silly little song, yet it filled her with the same tingling excitement she delighted in as a child, when every new morning glistened like a dewdrop and nights brushed by steeped in soft woolly shadows. And every story had a happy ending.

She looked over her shoulder. Ponderous trees. Velvety bushes. Dark boulders. The clearing had vanished. Rita tingled from head to toe as she followed the path into the forest, marveling at its verdant beauty. She sniffed the balmy air. Intoxicating. With a growing sense of well being, she strolled deeper into the cool hush of the Enchanted Forest where sunlight threaded the leafy ceiling and sparkled like diamond dust on the grass beneath her feet.

"Hello." A blonde girl, about twelve, with blue eyes, rosy cheeks and a pink organdy dress stepped out of the woods to block the path.

Rita stopped. Jesus, Emily the elf had a little sister. "Don't tell me, your name is Gretel."

The girl nodded, grasping Rita's hand. "I'm so happy you came. I need your help."

"What's wrong?"

Gretel's eyes filled with tears. "The ugly witch has stolen my brother, Hansel." She sobbed. "Keeps him locked in a cage, fattening him up for Halloween dinner." She squeezed Rita's hand. "Please say you'll help."

Rita grinned. Very good, Lorenzo. Right on script so far. "Of course I'll help. What can I do?"

"Come with me. The witch's house isn't far." Gretel pulled her off the path, deeper into the forest. "Every day she puts boys into the oven and bakes them into gingerbread." Gretel picked up the pace. "Hurry. She'll check her oven any time now. Our only chance is to slip up from behind and push her in."

Rita had to run to keep up. "What if she catches us? Do we go into the oven to make gingerbread girls?"

"Only the boys. We'll be turned into wiggly worms and fed to the birds."

"Yuck." How about that? Lorenzo's wife cheats, so the girls are turned into worms. Running to keep up with the little girl, Rita raced into the shadowy gloom of the Enchanted Forest, drawn straight into the action.

Gretel slowed. "We're close now," she whispered.

Rita sniffed and smelled wood smoke. "Smell that?"

"The witch is heating up the oven."

"Where?"

Gretel stopped and parted the bushes. "There."

Rita gasped, taken aback by the quaint beauty of a tiny gingerbread cottage with a fudge brownie roof, milk chocolate shutters trimmed in pink frosting and spun sugar window panes. A gingerbread-boy-fence bordered the tiny clearing. Smoke puffed from the chimney. Through an open window, she heard singing in a high-pitched, off key cackle.

"I am coming for you,

I am coming for you,

I'll nibble your fingers and snack on your toes,

And fatten you up for stew."

"Follow me," Gretel whispered.

They tiptoed down the path, stopping outside the kitchen door where Gretel pressed her mouth to Rita's ear. "We'll wait outside until she bends over the stove. Then we'll sneak in."

Peeking over Gretel's shoulder, Rita caught her breath at the shaggy profile of an enormous black form. "She's much bigger than I imagined."

Gretel nodded. "It'll take both of us to push her into the oven."

"I hope she fits." Rita swallowed hard, pressing her shoulders tight against the gingerbread wall.

"All right, Hansel," the witch croaked from inside the house. "Time to fetch the other little boys from the pantry. Mmmmmmmm, they'll make a scrumptious dessert. First I'll check the oven. Should be nice and hot for gingerbread."

Rita and Gretel exchanged glances. Rita wet her lips and tried to still her trembling knees. She heard a squeaking metallic sound.

The oven door!

Gretel eased forward. Rita followed, drying her palms on her skirt as the two slipped through the doorway. Across the room, the witch bent over, peering into the oven, her broad backside waving in the air. Hansel squatted in a wire cage beside the stove. Gretel pressed her fingers to her lips and shook her head, cautioning him to be still while she and Rita tiptoed across the floor, arms outstretched, ready to shove the witch into the oven.

Suddenly, the witch straightened. "Who's here?"

A boom of thunder rattled the sugar windows. Rita's legs went wobbly.

"Who dares to enter my house?" The black robed hag snarled and spun around, towering over the trespassers. Her voice screeched like fingernails on a blackboard. "Girls!" Bloodshot eyes bugged out, her warty nose wrinkled, and her hairy lip curled. "Girls!"

Gnarled fingers, with long green nails clawed the air in front of her chalk-white face. "C'mere, you two! I'll turn you into fat slimy worms."

"Bullshit, sister, not this girl!" Rita scrambled for the door.

"Come back here!" the witch shrieked.

"Run, Rita, run," Gretel shouted. "She's after you!"

"Christ!" Rita leaped outside and skittered off the path, darting through knee high weeds. She heard footsteps behind her. Fetid breath burned her neck.

"I'll get you before you reach the woods, honey!" The witch cackled.

Zig-zagging like a jackrabbit, Rita crossed the open field, running as fast as she could. She stopped at the edge of the woods, gasping, mouth dry, lungs afire. Surely she'd left the witch far behind.

A hand grabbed her shoulder and lifted her off the ground.

A red light flashed at the far end of the room, a soft beep pulsed, and a pod slid open. Lorenzo checked the digital timer. "Someone only lasted twenty seconds." He peered down the row of cocoons. "Who the hell's in the second module?"

Eddie glanced at his IPad. "I'll be damned, it's Rita."

"Rita?" Lorenzo frowned. "Who would've figured on Rita using the escape valve?"

"I had her pegged for the whole ride."

Lorenzo hurried to the open cocoon, smiling. "Made our record book, Rita. DreamLand's first escapee."

"Screw you sick bastards!" Rita squirmed in the encompassing cradle, red-faced and perspiring. "Get me the hell out of here, right now!"

"Rita, what's wrong?" A look of concern crossed Lorenzo's face. He took her hand and helped her from the cocoon. "What happened?"

She gasped, "I don't believe you're going to send kids into that nightmare. You're insane. It's too scary for little people. You'll traumatize them."

Lorenzo tightened his grip. "Hey, Rita, calm down." He moved closer, lowered his voice to a near whisper. "It was only a dream, you were perfectly safe."

Rita pulled away. "Safe?" She stamped her feet, straightened her dress and fluffed her dark hair. "Your goddamned witch threatened to turn me into a worm. Chased me across a field. Lifted me off the ground."

Eddie interjected. "That's when you shouted for Mama?"

"You bet your ass I shouted for Mama!" Rita snapped. "I won't suffer the indignity of being turned into a worm, even in your nasty dream."

"You acted too fast," Eddie said. Another second and you'd have met Hansel and Gretel's papa, the woodsman. It was Papa who picked you up, not the witch. He would've rescued you."

Lorenzo laughed. "You left too soon. Missed the happy ending. The old man chases off the witch, Gretel frees Hansel, and the gingerbread figures on the fence turn into happy little boys. The worms in the garden revert to beautiful little girls."

"Worms." Rita sighed. "You'll terrify children."

"The dream world you experienced was meant for teenagers and adults. Younger children frolic with friendly witches. I didn't think you'd enjoy doing that. A parental advisory board will give approval to every kid's dream."

"Suppose the Mama signal didn't work?" Rita asked. "Suppose she turned me into a worm?"

"Impossible."

"Suppose I hurt myself?"

"In DreamLand?" Lorenzo smiled. "Nonsense. Nobody gets hurt here." He shrugged. "It was only a dream. You missed the good part. A wonderful celebration. Music, dancing, food. Dream food tastes unbelievably delicious. All senses are heightened."

Another beep and the end module whooshed open.

CHAPTER THIRTEEN

"Enough of this gingerbread boy bullshit!" Jack Scanlon's voice bellowed from the end cocoon.

In spite of her anger, Rita turned aside to hide her smile. Jack had called for Mama after all.

Eddie Driscoll blew on his coffee. "Scared of the witch, Jack?"

Jack squinted at the younger man. "How would you like your legs chopped off at the ass, Junior?"

Eddie raised his middle finger and thrust it toward Jack.

"One of these days I'm going to bust your little hummingbird balls Eddie," Jack said.

Rita wanted to tell them both to go someplace else to shoot off their mouths, but reconsidered. "Easy guys," she said, seeking to calm herself as much as them. The last thing they needed at a time like this was to be fighting with each other. "With all the changes going on around here, we need to stick together."

"Stick together?" Jack leaned forward, poking his head out of the capsule. "Wise up, Rita, this punk is one of them! Eddie and Lorenzo created that Goddamned Hansel and Gretel nightmare." Eddie's face flushed.

Jack pulled himself from the capsule, mumbling as he adjusted his clothing. "Programmer geeks're all full of shit."

Rita felt shamed at the way Jack embarrassed people with his foul language and waving arms. His anger seemed far out of proportion to his grievance. Granted, Eddie's sense of timing stunk, but he had only been teasing.

Lorenzo handed Jack and Rita questionnaires. "Fill these out and get them back to me in the next day or so."

Rita glanced at her paper. Several questions, room for comments and personal impressions of the experience. "Okay." She slipped it into her coat pocket.

Lorenzo said, "We need to know how the escape worked and I'd like some feedback on the dream."

Jack skimmed his with an index finger. "I'll give you feedback, Lorenzo. The dream sucked." He crumpled the paper and tossed it in the wastebasket. "Don't bother me with this garbage."

Hey, asshole!" Eddie said. "We worked our tails off on this project."

Jack stiffened. "Asshole?"

"You heard me!" Eddie started toward him.

"Be cool." Lorenzo grabbed Eddie's arm.

Jack hunched over, motioning with both hands. "Let him go." He shuffled forward, fists clenched, piercing blue eyes needling Lorenzo. "Junior needs a spanking."

Hodge hurried through the door, blocking Jack's way. "What the hell's going on here?"

Jack stopped. "I opened my nose and smelled the bullshit, that's all. I'm wise to you." He faced Rita. "Look at your hero now, baby. Fast-buck Hodge is snatching up his chips and cashing them in. Screw the rest of us. To hell with the elderly and the homeless. From now on, little kids'll pay this bastard for having the shit scared out of them."

Realizing the pressure Hodge had to be under after six months with Daggett, Rita stifled the urge to side with Jack. Her stomach felt queasy. She wanted to scream at everyone to stop bickering. Hodge was doing his level best with an impossible situation. He desperately needed their support. At least for now.

Hodge sighed. "Can't you understand what's at stake here? Ollie Daggett bet a long shot on PermaDream. We pulled off the miracle and he won big. He owns everything; patents, programs, equipment, the works. We can win too, but if we quit now, our positions will be filled before we can empty our desks. We won't take as much as a stamp out of here. Stay and we'll be treated like royalty. Jesus Christ, am I the only one who understands?"

"Sure, Hodge, everybody's wrong but you." Jack's narrow shoulders slumped and he shook his head. "The only thing worse than someone who sells out their friends is someone who sells out and tries to justify it." He closed his eyes and shook his head. "All our hard work," he muttered, spreading his arms. "For this Humpty-Dumpty shit!"

"Hodge is doing all this to fight for PermaDream," Rita said. "Don't you see that?"

Jack snorted. "So that arrogant bastard kid of Daggett's can feed his sickness. Hell, he's doing it right now."

"You're wrong, Jack," Lorenzo said. "Before you know it, PermaDream'll be back and available to everyone. Some day we'll..."

"Attaboy, Lorenzo!" Jack cut in. "Pucker up and kiss Hodgie's ass, same as always."

Rita saw Lorenzo stiffen. Fire flashed in his eyes. Fearing he'd harm Jack, she grabbed his arm. "No more arguing! Can't you see we need each other?" She looked him square in the eye. "Need each other, uh...we...I mean, uh, all of us," she blurted, flustered by his smoldering passion, while being weakened by the tingle in the pit of her stomach. She willed herself to turn away.

Jack's wild-eyed-glare flashed from Hodge to Lorenzo. "None of you give a shit if some poor sick person suffers and dies a lonely agonizing death staring at the walls of a hospital room."

Rita flinched, recalling the painful sorrow of her mother's final days.

"You knifed us in the back." Jack shook his fist, eyes glistening as he choked back tears. "We stuck with you every step and you sold us out!" His mouth kept moving, but no more words came. He stormed out, knuckling his eyes.

Hodge put his face in his hands.

"That bastard can't walk through a doorway without doing a five minute exit scene," Eddie said.

Rita looked away. Everyone had witnessed Jack's wild outbursts during PermaDream discussions, but seeing this sad tormented side of him unnerved her. She felt a shiver of pity for him. Despite his rotten attitude, he was right. Deserving people would be cut off.

Jack Scanlon, the crude loud-mouthed jokester cared more than any of them. Though he teased Cheryl mercilessly and directed baleful wrath toward Ollie Daggett, Jack Scanlon had never uttered a harsh word to Rita. Perhaps he sensed that she understood his hurt as he understood hers. Her hopes had been dashed as much as his by the day's events. She wanted to be alone. When the blinking console lights blurred, misted by burning tears, she excused herself and slipped away.

Hodge felt a lump rising in his throat when he watched Rita leave without looking back. If only his father had lived. PermaDream would be a reality and he would still be a good guy in everyone's eyes.

"Jack is an asshole," Eddie said. "We busted our asses so the jerk can keep his job and this is the way he thanks us. Screw it." Jamming his hands into his pockets, he shuffled out.

Hodge exchanged a sober glance with Lorenzo. "Our team is shrinking."

"Hey, what'd you expect? The boat's being rocked." Lorenzo patted Hodge's shoulder. "They're disillusioned. So were we at first. Don't sweat it, nobody's leaving. Wait'll they get a whiff of the big money." He headed for the door. "I'll go give Eddie an attitude adjustment."

"I'll look after things here," Hodge said. "The others will be waking up."

"And they'll be sold on it. You'll see. The worst is over." Lorenzo whistled as he followed Eddie into the conference room.

Now that he was alone, the faint clicks, soft whirs, and muted tones from the DreamLand hardware provided an eclectic soundtrack for Hodge's spinning thoughts. The explosive face-off with Jack left him hurt and angry. Would the staff cheer and dance him around on their shoulders if he told them to go sign up for unemployment? Would Jack have led the celebration if Ollie Daggett hired another person to take over his job at twice the pay? Rita had obviously been shaken too. She had probably gone to Morgan for consolation. Thank God for Morgan. He would set things straight.

Behind him, the door whispered open and he turned to see a perfumed shadow step through the doorway, haloed in golden light from the outer room. The scent of Royal Secret came to him and his heart leaped. Denise! He swallowed hard, choking back tears. With her at his side, nothing would stop him. "Baby," he whispered, reaching for her hand.

"Don't!"

His heart sank as she pulled away.

"I can't support you in this, Hodge. That's not why I'm here."

"Then – then why?" He stopped when he saw something wrong in her eyes. "What is it?"

"I just left Morgan."

The telephone rang, shattering the tension. Hodge triggered the speaker. "Yes."

"Get down here right away," Morgan said, his voice tight with urgency.

"What's going on?"

"Chazz Daggett."

Denise stiffened.

"What the hell is Chazz up to now?"

"He isn't up to anything. We can't wake him."

CHAPTER FOURTEEN

DreamLand's longest lines formed outside Storybook Kingdom. Giggling children with sparkling eyes queued behind red velvet ropes at the base of four soaring archways. Holographic images of The Three Bears, Sleeping Beauty, Rumpelstiltskin, and Hansel and Gretel smiled down from above each pastel-lit portal.

At the fifth portal, black velvet curtains hung beneath the darkened hologram of a feather capped musician, parading in front of a long line of grinning rats. The Pied Piper dream had been shut down until further notice.

The Sandman, with shoulder length white hair and a hooded cloak of indigo satin, sang, juggled, and performed sleight of hand magic, keeping the folks entertained while waiting in line.

A chubby, red-haired boy at the end of the Hansel and Gretel line tugged at the Sandman's cape. "Why is the Pied Piper closed?"

The Sandman offered the little boy a toothy smile. "Piper's on vacation, son." Moving closer, he touched the boy's shoulder. "What's your name?"

"Albert."

"Visiting the Enchanted Forest, eh?"

"Yep." The boy nodded. "Hansel and Gretel."

"How old are you, son?"

"Nine."

"Big boy for nine." The Sandman bent closer, knitting his brow and lowering his voice to a near whisper, so only Albert could hear. "Not scared of the ugly witch, are you?"

"Nah." Albert shook his head. "Ain't scared of no witch. Anyway, she's a funny witch. Besides, it's only a dream."

"Attaboy!" The Sandman beamed. "Nothing to be afraid of in DreamLand. Sleep tight." He pulled a yellow sunflower out of Albert's ear, turned it into a balloon, popped it, and with a flourish, transformed the broken balloon into a handful of silver confetti which he tossed over his head. Albert smiled as the Sandman romped off through the twinkling cloud to entertain the kids in the Rumpelstiltskin Dream line.

"Welcome to DreamLand. Please remain in line." A recorded woman's voice, soft and smooth as butter fudge filled the air. "If you wish to awaken from your dream at any time, speak the word Mama or Mommy."

A pause, then, "Hi, folks, I'm your host, Hodge Michaels, reminding you that HistoryLand opens on Labor Day with twelve different events to choose from and dozens more to come. Make reservations now to dream travel to that special time and place in American history. Be in the front row when Lincoln delivers the Gettysburg Address. Visit New York in 1789 to cheer Washington's inauguration. Slap leather in the gunfight at the OK Corral. See the attack on Pearl Harbor from Diamondhead. Don't be disappointed. Plan ahead and enjoy your stay at DreamLand."

Another pause, then the woman's voice, restated the initial message, this time, in Spanish. "Welcome to DreamLand. Please remain in line. If you wish to awaken from your dream at any time, speak the word, Mama or Mommy."

At the reservation desk, under the glare of TV lights, a pretty, blue eyed young blonde smiled as she answered a reporter's questions. "Beginning midnight, New Year's Eve, DreamLand will be open 24 hours a day, instead of closing at eleven." She added, "HistoryLand will be on-line in two weeks."

"Tell us about the upcoming dream-trip to the moon," a reporter said.

The blonde nodded, her blue eyes sparkling with excitement. "Space Adventure opens Thanksgiving week, but it's been sold out through mid-February. We're really proud of it."

Five stories above the crowded atrium lobby, behind his glass office wall in a private section of the complex known as North tower, Hodge watched a massive traffic jam on a large HD screen.

A stark headline crawled across the bottom.

DREAMLAND TRAFFIC A BORDER NIGHTMARE

"They're here from all over the world," a reporter said from his vantage point on a freeway overpass. "Members of virtually every race on the planet are swarming to the U.S. Mexican border, southeast of San Diego, hoping to literally fulfill their dreams and fantasies. The magnet drawing them all is the newly opened one-of-a-kind fantasy world, where dreams do indeed come true. For a price."

The camera panned back revealing a massive, circular complex looming several hundred yards beyond the international border. "DreamLand literally dominates the horizon here at the border crossing, southeast of San Diego," the reporter said. "In the eyes of some critics, thumbing its nose at the United States Government, rendered virtually powerless by the leaders of the controlling PLC Party in Baja, California, Mexico.

"While Mexican and U.S. officials bicker over how many new lanes are needed for an enlarged border crossing, the wait at Otay Mesa currently averages three hours. Throngs of vendors on both sides of the border do a brisk business, selling souvenir sleep masks, T-shirts, fish tacos, Churros and cold drinks to a captive throng of would-be dreamers."

The photograph of a fiftyish looking Edgar Michaels appeared on screen.

"In the year and a half since the death of PermaDream founder Edgar Michaels, father of computer generated dreaming, rapid and unprecedented changes have come about in the use of the brain-wave modulation techniques he pioneered at the end of the century. According to his son, Hodge, CEO of DreamLand Enterprises, they are all being utilized at DreamLand."

A tight shot of Hodge's face replaced his father's photograph. "If we had stayed on the U.S. side of the border, none of this could have happened," Hodge said, in a take from a press conference held on opening day, a month earlier. "Government agencies and paperwork would have hamstrung us at every step. Here in Mexico, the PLC has the foresight to allow us unfettered research and expansion as long as we continue to make safety our primary concern. Since our very first series of tests, our medical facilities have exceeded AMA standards and will continue to do so. Everyone is welcome to travel through the wonderful worlds created by Morpheus, our dream computer. The DreamLand experience is both exhilarating and completely safe."

Over a stock helicopter shot of the huge facility, the reporter said, "Rumored to be the brainchild of alleged drug lord Oliver Daggett, who has never been photographed, DreamLand opened its doors last month to record numbers and the lines have been growing longer every day. When questioned on his association with the reclusive Daggett, Hodge Michaels consistently offers the same statement.

"Mister Daggett was a close friend and adviser to my father," Hodge announced, in another clip from the press conference. "I welcome his continued input as a consultant. Without Mr. Daggett's unique vision, DreamLand would never have come into existence."

The reporter added, "Daggett, who lives in Mexico is wanted on tax evasion charges in the United States and is also sought for questioning in the deaths of Congressman Roberto Manzur and his family in a Christmas Eve plane crash four years ago. Prior to the crash, the ruling PLC Party in Baja California, Mexico, had refused to consider Manzur's extradition request. Unnamed sources have accused Daggett of masterminding the sabotage of the private plane in retaliation. He remains unavailable for comment. Meanwhile, at the Mexican border, construction maintains a breakneck pace and the money continues to pour across."

Hodge switched off the TV and peered down into the crowded atrium lobby. He smiled. The spike in DreamLand's revenues since the grand opening a month earlier had come as no surprise. Ollie Daggett had assured him it would be spectacular. The need for swift expansion had been made clear during his half year at the compound in Cancun. Already, the skeleton of a twin structure stood beside the main facility. Lorenzo's team had Genesis, the opening attraction, on the BibleLand drawing board a full year ahead of schedule.

At a corner desk, Denise switched off her monitor and joined him near the window.

"I break out in a rash over the potential earning power of this place," she half-whispered in her husky voice. "Don't you think twenty dollars a minute is overkill?"

Hodge shook his head. "I could raise the price to fifty and they'd keep coming. Don't forget, not everyone pays full price either. There's student tickets, seniors, and group rates. Soon, we'll have a family plan. Just wait'll BibleLand opens and the churches start asking for discounts. They'll get them too."

"Even with group rates," she countered, "when we're open twenty-four hours, each dream cocoon will generate between twenty and twenty-five thousand a day running full tilt. That's scandalous."

"Nothing scandalous about hard earned money, Denise. It's given us this." Hodge swept the elegantly furnished office with his arm. "Ollie kept his word too. I'm running the business with no interference." He smiled, lowering his voice. "He's here, you know."

"He is?" A stunned expression flitted across her face. She peered across the atrium at Daggett's curtained private quarters opposite Hodge's office. "I suppose we'll have his toadys in our faces until he leaves."

"Ollie's too smart for that. He's alone. Slipped in last night. No crowd, no armed guards, no hooplah. Nothing to alert anyone. Tomorrow, he'll slip out the same way."

She smirked. "Slick son-of-a-bitch!"

"Smart too. Why let Uncle Sam's boys know he's available for kidnapping? A hundred bodyguards wouldn't stop them from taking him." Denise's pretty face pinched into a frown and her voice went flat. "Daggett may get away with his drug deals, but he'll pay with his life for murdering Congressman Manzur and his family. Those poor kids, going home for Christmas. The bastard!"

Hodge sighed. "Let's not start that again."

"I can't believe we're finally going to see him." She paused, then added, "And he'll get to see his precious Chazz." She smiled. "I can't wait."

Hodge swallowed hard. News of Ollie's visit had shocked him. Fearful for his safety, Ollie rarely ventured beyond the walls of his compound and had never visited Chazz since the ill-fated dream trip a year ago. Hodge should have known Ollie would rather die than miss his son's birthday. With a shudder, he realized that the moment would soon arrive for Ollie to see the appalling state of his son's condition.

Terrified of what would happen to him if he told the truth about Chazz, and certain that given time, Morgan could solve the problem, Hodge had lied, assuring Ollie that his son's condition was stable, even going as far as sending monthly video-disks of a healthy, slumbering Chazz recorded in the early days of his coma. So far, Morgan had failed. Now that Ollie waited in his quarters, Hodge regretted not telling him the truth from the beginning.

How would he react when he discovered that Hodge lied and his beloved son had become little more than an emaciated vegetable? Hodge had played out countless gut-wrenching mental scenarios over the past year, but nothing he envisioned offered solace.

Ollie Daggett could be violently explosive, or menacingly quiet, depending on his mood. The blonde who had been Hodge's companion in Cancun told him she preferred the explosion. At least then, she knew his thoughts.

After a long silence, Denise turned from the view across the atrium to face Hodge, her smoke gray eyes searching his. "Does Daggett know about the Pied Piper?"

"No sense telling him. He'll be gone tomorrow."

"Anything new down there?"

"Nothing."

"You haven't done anything other than shut it down?"

"Can't until I meet with Emily Fulbright."

"The girl who sent that ridiculous memo?"

"She's due any moment. Stick around?"

Denise shook her head. "I promised Lorenzo I'd lend a hand with the investigation. He's swamped."

"Should've seen the look on his face when I pulled him away from Genesis to investigate Pied Piper."

"Bet he was thrilled."

"These things happen. Lorenzo understands." Hodge put his hands in his pockets and rocked back and forth. "You're right, Denise. The Fulbright girl's probably a whacko, but you never know. Hell, she could be a scam artist. I'm following through with my own personal investigation just in case."

"Good idea."

Hodge sat at his desk, watching and wanting Denise, wondering if he impressed her with his new-found, "take charge" attitude. Things had never been the same between them since he'd returned from Cancun, but, she *had* stayed. He didn't want to think about why – only that he still had a chance to love and be loved. With the corner of a silk handkerchief, he buffed the emerald eyes of the bronze Sandman statuette, an opening day gift from the staff.

A woman's voice from a hidden speaker filled the air. "Emily

Fulbright is waiting, Mr. Michaels."

Hodge turned to Denise. "She's here. Let's have a look." Taking a remote control from his top drawer, he pointed it at a paneled wall and touched a button. The wall whispered open revealing an array of eight nineteen inch color monitors surrounding a seventy two inch screen. The image on each monitor sequenced through different areas of DreamLand, panning ticket booths, waiting areas, hallways, the research and development section and the near empty PermaDream facility. With the touch of a button, Hodge could peer into any area. Ollie's idea. Hodge swallowed hard. Ollie hated surprises.

He aimed the remote at the top left monitor and activated the outside camera above his huge oak office door. A long hallway appeared on the large central screen, ending at the reception desk beside the North Tower elevator where a frail form slumped on a black leather couch. A woman with her face buried in her hands. "There's our trouble maker," Hodge said. "Emily Fulbright."

"Zoom in. See if I recognize her." Stepping behind Hodge, Denise took hold of his shoulders and kneaded his muscles. "You're really tense."

His heart soared at her touch. "Yeah." He clicked the zoom button and the camera telescoped into a tight shot. Withered hands and long dirty fingernails filled the screen.

"Jesus!" Denise gasped. "She's a DreamLand greeter?"

"So she says."

"With those hands?"

"I know."

"Greeters are supposed to be young girls. Emily Fulbright has liver spots. C'mon, Emily," she muttered, "lower those claws, give us a peek at your face."

The bony hands didn't move.

"Who hired her, anyway?" she asked.

Hodge shrugged. "She slipped through the cracks. I'll sure as hell find out, though." He rolled his shoulders, moving his back muscles beneath her probing fingers. "Damn, that feels good. Why don't I turn off the Emily Fulbright show and take off my jacket?"

"Sorry." Denise patted his shoulder and backed away. "Enjoy your investigation. I'm joining Lorenzo and Morpheus. See you." She entered Hodge's private elevator. As the doors closed, she blew him a kiss.

The winking elevator lights showed her arrival at Z level, the heart of Morpheus. He sighed, feeling rejected. Should have kept his mouth shut and she'd still be rubbing his back. Lately, she'd been more at ease with their arm's length relationship. Hodge tried many times to get through to her and ended up under many a cold-shower for his efforts. Denise had never come close to letting him in.

Hodge surprised himself at how quickly he had grown accustomed to his new status as CEO. He no longer yearned for the daily hands-on experience of working with Morpheus. True, he still supervised every DreamLand project and even designed several dream features, but mostly from the comfort and security of his office. Lately, he viewed the creative end of the operation more as a hobby than an obsession. Like Ollie Daggett said, 'Empire building can also be a satisfying pursuit.'

Still feeling the warmth of Denise's fingers on his shoulders, he clicked the remote again. As the wall slid back into place, he tapped the intercom button and told his secretary, "I'm ready for Emily Fulbright."

CHAPTER FIFTEEN

As Cheryl passed Hodge's private elevator, the Z-level doors slid open and Denise stepped from the illuminated cubicle flashing a brilliant smile, looking like an eye stopper on the cover of a fashion catalogue.

"Hi, Cheryl."

Cheryl nodded, quelling a surge of envy. As always, Denise exuded professionalism, despite her form-fitting skirt, curve-revealing blouse and beauty counter makeup.

Denise held open the elevator doors. "Going up?"

"No." Cheryl's lips barely moved when she spoke. "I'm off to do some homework." She held up her notebook computer. "Too many interruptions around here."

"I'll walk to the parking lot exit with you," Denise said, falling into step beside her. "I'm on my way to help Lorenzo dig into Pied Piper."

Cheryl turned away, concealing a smile. Pied Piper, indeed! She had seen Denise's eyes searing Lorenzo's backside often enough to recognize her desires. "I'm sure he'll appreciate your help," she said, keeping her expression even. Watching the two work together during the opening days of DreamLand had made one thing crystal clear. Hodge and Rita be damned, Denise Moore longed to be the one to help Lorenzo forget his ex-wife. She turned men's heads wherever she went, but the handsome Lorenzo, God bless his soul, never responded to her advances.

"Poor guy's been working so hard," Denise said, batting her eyelashes. "Sometimes he doesn't go home for days."

And I bet you'd like to be there waiting for him, Cheryl thought. "Some people are dedicated to their work."

Denise frowned as if hearing that line for the first time.

Cheryl couldn't fathom how Hodge failed to discern her interest in Lorenzo. Could he be so intoxicated by Denise's allure that he never noticed the "come-get-it" gleam in her eyes when she smiled at the fire-eyed Adonis?

Hodge was young and handsome, with sandy hair and clear brown eyes, but not a strong man like Lorenzo. Denise kept Hodge in a constant state of sexual bewilderment, playing him like a Stradivarius.

Cheryl rooted for Hodge to have his way with the tall, chestnut haired beauty, but she knew his hunger would remain unfulfilled.

Cheryl fumbled for her key card when they reached the exit. "Hodge must be steamed having to shut down a top attraction."

Denise nodded. "Pied Piper's his favorite. He designed the Hamelin rats."

"I know."

"Disney's mouse, Hodge's rats." Denise laughed, showing perfect teeth.

"What's the problem with Pied Piper?" Cheryl asked.

"One of the StoryWorld greeters supposedly had a strange experience during a dream. She's with Hodge now."

Cheryl jabbed at the bridge of her glasses, pushing them higher on her nose. "I'll ask him about it." She found her key card and opened the door leading to the rain swept tarmac of the staff parking lot. "Tell Lorenzo I'll come by later to lend a hand."

"Okay." Denise waved. "See you."

Tilting her head, Cheryl listened to the clicking of Denise's heels on the tile floor fading in the direction of the Commissary, then like a slender shadow, she slipped out the door into the cold rain.

When she arrived home, Cheryl went straight to her bedroom where she set her IPad on the nightstand and flipped up the screen. She kicked off her shoes, removed her hose, unzipped her dress and pulled it over her head. After draping it over a chair, she unhooked her bra and laid her undergarments on top of the dress.

Naked, she drew a deep breath. Humming softly, she swayed from side to side, stroking her body with her fingertips, making her skin prickle. Free at last! She flicked a wisp of moon-colored silk from the closet. Her heart fluttered in her throat as she slipped into the shimmering garment, thrilling to the tingle of cool silk on burning skin.

She stepped up to the mirror and batted her lashes, trying to make her eyes sparkle the way Denise's did when she smiled at Lorenzo. Cheryl's mirrored smile fell far short of the desired effect. Her thick lensed glasses didn't help. Pulling them off, she wet her lips and attempted a broader smile.

Another dud, even with blurred vision. Perhaps she had waited too many years to learn to sparkle. At fifty she barely knew how to smile. Cheryl sighed. Seemed as though she had grown old without ever having been young.

She turned away from her reflection and reached into her bag, removing, with care, the prototype light-weight silk hood that she and Jack had developed. Holding it up, she studied the array of miniature high-output, low power magnetoresonators stitched across its surface.

Nothing they had thus far designed matched the field strength of this configuration. Easing it over her head, she adjusted the Velcro straps until it felt comfortable, then plugged its shielded cable into the computer's USB port and keyed in the access code. Stretching out on her bed, Cheryl closed her eyes.

Too late for sparkling eyes.

But not too late to dream...

CHAPTER SIXTEEN

Hodge opened his office door and eyed a pallid, flat chested woman with beanpole legs, wearing a green skirt that stopped short of her bony knees. She wore scraggly dishwater colored hair in a pony-tail tied with a stained pink satin ribbon. No lipstick brightened her hairline shadow of a mouth and her skin looked pale and dry as parchment.

Stunned by Emily Fulbright's appearance, Hodge stood aside and motioned for her to enter. Clutching her sweater at the neck, she slipped past him, her shiny gaze darting into every corner of his office.

"Hi, Emily, I'm Hodge Michaels," he said, trying to set her at ease with a broad smile. He took her hand, flinching inwardly at its cold roughness. "Please, sit down." He gestured toward the plush leather covered chair in front of his desk, beneath a concealed video camera. "Can I get you something? Coffee? Glass of water?"

"No." Staring at the floor, she shuffled across the white carpet and perched on the edge of the chair.

Hodge sat behind his desk, wiped his sweaty hand on his pants and studied her. He had instructed Human Resources to cast bright-eyed, apple-cheeked young girls as DreamLand Greeters. This bandy-legged, middle-aged frump had a face like a cantaloupe and looked utterly ridiculous in her short skirt. Sucking in a deep breath, he exhaled slowly, hoping to calm his anger. "What seems to be the problem, Miss Fulbright?"

Emily squinted. "Light bothers me, Mister Michaels," she piped. "Hurts my eyes."

"Sorry." Hodge pressed a button and the drapes swished shut.

"Still too bright," she squeaked.

A second button subdued the lights, leaving the room in shadows. "How's that?"

"Better."

"Good." Hodge waited for her to speak.

Emily rubbed her eyes and dabbed at the inner corners with her fingertips. Her tiny pink tongue flicked at cracked lips.

Hodge opened her file on his desktop flat screen and eyed her over the top of it. Who the hell could have hired her? He guessed her to be at least fifty, closer to sixty.

He turned the screen toward her and pointed at the displayed color photo of a familiar looking young woman with sparkling blue eyes, full red lips and shiny teeth. "Who's this girl?"

"Me."

Hodge raised an eyebrow. "Pardon?"

"It's me, Mr. Michaels," she whined. "I swear."

"When was it taken?"

"Six weeks ago." Her voice cracked on the final word.

Hodge squirmed in his seat. "How old are you, Emily?"

"Nineteen."

Nineteen? Hodge's gaze flashed from Emily to the youthful face in the photograph and back again. Where had he seen her before? He had heard of pictures flattering people, but this one confounded the imagination. He checked to make sure the video-disk recorder had been activated, before continuing. Later he'd review the video with Morgan and Cheryl. "So, you claim to be nineteen."

Emily lowered her gaze and heaved a long quivering sigh. When she looked up, tears glistened in her pink-rimmed eyes. "I am nineteen."

Hodge turned the monitor back to face him. "I, uh, hadn't seen your file before. Give me a second to bring myself up to speed."

As he studied her file, he became aware of Emily's incessant movement; smoothing hair, adjusting sweater cuffs, scratching, crossing and uncrossing her ankles. Every time he looked up she seemed to be in the middle of a complicated repertoire of blinking, squinting and lip-licking. When he tried to concentrate on reading, she distracted him, clearing her throat, sniffing and making sucking sounds with her teeth.

Folding his arms, he pressed his elbows to the desk and reached for another smile. "So you originally came to us as a test subject."

She nodded. "Two years ago, when you were developing PermaDream, I volunteered. I mainly tested teenage dreams. Later, I was the girl elf at your first demonstration."

"You?" He looked at the picture in the file again and remembered, then glanced up. His stomach lurched at the sight of the withered crone in front of him. "That was you?" She nodded.

"Sorry, I don't recall you being there." Hodge avoided looking at her face, first studying his Sandman statuette, then surveying the office. He would certainly remember this old fart if she showed up at his demonstration wearing an elf outfit.

Emily stiffened. Her chin trembled. "I'm scared sir." Her lips puckered and her nose wrinkled. "Real scared. I'm scared to sleep anymore." She hugged herself, sobbing as she rocked back and forth.

Hodge raised a hand to calm her. "Easy, Emily. Settle down." Jesus, he didn't want her losing it in here. He should have met with her someplace else, maybe Morgan's office. "Just take it easy," he said.

"I'll – I'll try." She wiped her eyes, leaned forward, raised off the seat and scratched her behind.

Hodge winced at the thought of her standing in the DreamLand lobby picking her bony ass while welcoming twenty dollar a minute family dreamers to Storybook Kingdom. What could she be up to? Lawsuit? Blackmail? Most likely a nut case. "Exactly what do you think happened, Emily?"

"I don't think anything. It happened."

"Tell me about it."

"Last week, I dream-traveled to Pied Piper Village. DreamLand Greeters are supposed to regularly visit the different dream worlds."

"My idea. Go ahead."

"In my dream, the Hamelin town square was empty, except for the Pied Piper dressed in green, wearing a little hat with a feather. When he saw me, he started to play his flute and march around the square. It was a wonderful tune." Hodge beamed. "I helped compose it."

"I wanted to follow him to hear more. Before I knew it, I was skipping along behind him."

"Yeah, it's infectious, all right."

Emily's eyes grew wide and her voice tightened as if someone had squeezed her windpipe. "All of a sudden, the square filled with rats. They came from everywhere. A huge one with beady eyes and long brown teeth crawled out of a sewer and bit me."

Hodge swallowed hard. Having read and re-read her memo, he anticipated the rat story, but to actually hear her utter it… Struggling to control his anger, he spoke in a steady, even tone. "I personally supervised the development of the Hamelin rats, Emily." After a short pause, he added, "My rats are lovable."

"Lovable?" She stuck out her hand and raised her sweater cuff, revealing a mass of tiny scabs. "Lovable?"

A cold, crawling sensation writhed through Hodge's midsection. Good Lord, the marks on her skinny wrist did resemble bites. Could she have made them herself? Despite the churning in his belly he measured his words, speaking softly. "Be reasonable, Emily. It was a computerized sequence. You were dreaming."

She held up her arm, little more than skin stretched tight over bone with a series of scabbed puncture marks. "Rat bites."

Hodge made a note to have an exterminator come by after hours to give the building a once over as a buffer against the possibility that the DreamLand complex might have rodents. You never know in Mexico. As he wrote, Emily's voice scratched at his concentration.

"Rats followed me home."

Hodge set down his pen. "Followed you home?"

She raised trembling hands, holding them about two feet apart. "Big ones."

He skimmed the memo. Not a word about the damned things following her home. Jesus, she's making it up as she goes.

Emily's gaze narrowed. "They come at night and wake me. I hear them squeaking in the dark." She tilted her head as if to listen and whispered. "Then their claws. Tap tap tap on the kitchen linoleum, scampering down the hallway, scratching at the bedroom door."

"Better discuss that with your landlord." Hodge scrutinized the wounds on her wrist. Could a rat have somehow been trapped in her dream capsule? No. She had to have been bitten in her apartment.

Emily's eyes glittered as she leaned forward and whispered, "Sometimes they crawl into bed with me. They wriggle and squirm around my bare feet and legs, all warm and hairy. Except for their tails. When I throw back the covers they skitter away. The other night I was lying in bed watching TV when something flashed and I found myself in a dark tunnel, waist-deep in cold, smelly water." She shuddered. "Couldn't see. I ran my fingers over the wall. All slimy." Her voice trembled. "I picked big water bugs off my arms, then from far away I heard the Pied Piper, playing that same song on the flute. The song I marched to in my dream."

"My song," Hodge muttered.

Emily shivered, then continued. "The water lapped at my armpits, my neck and my chin. My heart beat so hard I could feel it in my throat. I couldn't breathe. I stood on my tiptoes and squeezed my mouth shut tight as I could," she whispered. "Soft, jelly things touched my lips. Garbage, feces, decomposing food. Rotting hairy lumps – and all the time that pretty song on the flute. Drawing me..." Her voice faded.

Hodge poured himself some water. Emily grabbed the glass, drained it and returned it to the tray without apology. "The light flashed again," she said in a strained voice. "I found myself standing in my bedroom, soaking wet. The stink was awful. I ran to take a shower." She dabbed at her eyes with a crumpled piece of tissue. "I know it'll happen again."

Hodge couldn't believe his ears. He uncradled the telephone. "I'd like you to speak with our psychologist."

Emily's face reddened. She rose to her feet. "You don't believe me!" She screeched. "I shouldn't have sent the memo! Shouldn't have said anything!"

"Okay, okay." He hung up. "Only trying to help." He pressed the button, opening the drapes, signaling the end of the meeting. He wanted Emily Fulbright's ugly face and pathetic whining out of his office, out of his life. "Take the next few weeks off with pay." He came from around his desk, grasped her bony elbow and led her to the door. "The Pied Piper dream's been shut down. I'm personally supervising the investigation. Stay home. Wait for my call." She left without another word.

Hodge returned to his desk, eyeing the monitor, smiling as he watched the poor wretch shuffle down the long hallway to the elevator. Christ, he'd almost told her to have a nice day. He wanted the others to see the tape. Switching on the speakerphone, he tapped out Cheryl Martin's extension. If he knew Cheryl, she'd have a cerebral orgasm confronting the weird psychosis of Emily Fulbright.

CHAPTER SEVENTEEN

Cheryl Martin adjusted the stereo, fine tuning the music until the shimmering strings of Mantovani felt like another layer of skin and the bass line throbbed to the beat of her heart. Soft voices massaged her mind.

"Who can I turn to,

When nobody needs me."

Drawing aside the drape, she peered out the sliding door. Rain drummed on the glass and splattered in puddles on the balcony. Far below, wild surf raged against dark rocks.

"I only know I gotta go,

Where destiny leads me."

She ran her hands down her sides, reveling in the cool feel of silk against her naked body. The floor length negligee clung to her hips and rubbed against her bare nipples when she moved, making them tingle and grow hard. A man's tongue probably felt smooth and silky like this, she thought. Several of her all-time favorite authors used those specific adjectives to describe the sensation.

Danielle Steele, Jackie Collins, Jaqueline Susann, and many writers since them utilized every adjective imaginable to describe intimate sensations. Cheryl had read them all again and again.

Someone tapped on the door. Her breath caught and her hand darted to her throat.

Three quick knocks. A pause. Two more.

A warm glow surged from deep inside of her and her heart raced.

Breathing hard, she pulled the filigreed comb from her hair and shook loose long amber tresses. The perfumed negligee clung to her thighs as she glided across the room and opened the door.

Lorenzo Vargas stood on the porch in a trench coat, hair blowing every which way, smiling in the teeth of the howling wind and driving rain. She stepped aside. "Come in, quickly. You'll catch your death."

"Death?" He laughed. "A small price to pay for a night with you." Lorenzo stepped through the door, his wet face glistening golden in the firelight.

"You're such a tease." Trembling, she helped him off with his coat and tossed it into a corner. "You're soaked to the skin. Come sit by the fire before you catch a chill. Slip out of those clothes. I'll bring a towel and a drink."

"Sounds wonderful." Lorenzo kicked off his shoes and undid his shirt. "Make it Amaretto, darling," he said in a gentle tone. "The sweet liqueur of love."

She tossed him a towel and a cotton robe, then busied herself at the bar filling two aperitif glasses with Amaretto. When she faced him again he stood in the glow of the fireplace, legs spread, nothing but a towel wrapped around his hips. The robe lay at his feet.

Her legs went tingly.

Lorenzo smiled. "Come. It's warm by the fire." He beckoned. "Please Cheryl. Don't be frightened."

Roberta Flack's voice floated from the speakers.

"The first time ever I saw your face,

I thought the sun rose in your eyes."

She sighed, drinking in the splendor of the moment. The thought of the tall, handsome younger man being her lover made her heart pound so hard she could barely utter the words, "Lorenzo, please understand, you're – you're naked."

"I'm not naked." He raised his arms. "I'm wearing a towel."

"You have nothing on under it."

"And you have nothing under your negligee. Soon we'll be skin to skin. Soul to soul. Our hearts will beat as one. Don't stand in the gloomy dark, Cheryl. Come over here where it's cozy and warm. Slip out of that negligee and press your burning flesh to mine. I want to hold you, kiss you all over, smother myself in your essence."

She trembled at his words, spilling Amaretto on her hands. She set the glasses on an end table. His muscles rippled as he took her wrists and drew her to him. "Don't torture me, Cheryl. I kneel at your throne. The promise of you is the reason for my being."

She didn't dare breathe for fear of breaking the spell.

"*Mi preciosa.*" Lorenzo's voice smoldered with desire. Firelight blazed in his dark eyes as he brought her fingers to his lips. His hot tongue flicked at each sweet, sticky drop. "I'm going to lay you down, drizzle the liqueur between your thighs and kiss it away."

The thought of Lorenzo's silky tongue caressing her nearly drove Cheryl out of her mind. She lusted for the feel of his burning lips on her mouth, her breasts, her stomach.

Lorenzo pulled her close. She slid her arms around him and gazed into his fiery eyes. His back muscles hardened and flexed beneath her fingertips when he bent to brush her lips with his. "Cheryl," he whispered. "Darling Cheryl."

"Sweet Lorenzo." She touched the back of his neck. "Your hair's dripping. I'll bring a towel."

"Wait." Holding her with his gaze, Lorenzo placed her hand on the knot at his waist. "Use my towel."

Her heart fluttered as she kneeled to undo the knot.

"And the moon and the stars were the gifts you gave,

To a dark and endless sky, my love – to a dark and endless sky."

The towel fell to the floor.

Cheryl gasped as Lorenzo vanished in a puff of smoke!

Earsplitting rock music blasted from the TV, accompanied by brilliant flashing lights. The music rose to a crescendo, then crashed to a stop, leaving her in stunned silence.

Dear God, what's happening? Harsh laughter followed and the wide-eyed, disjointed face of Eddie Driscoll came into focus on the screen.

"Eddie," she sobbed, folding her arms across her breasts.

"Hi, Cheryl, baby. Look, I'm a TV star!" Eddie grinned, turning his head from side to side. "Couldn't resist putting myself into this horny little dream of yours." He laughed. "I figured you were up to something when you encrypted your files. That hurt my feelings, Cheryl. Lorenzo and I never hide anything. We share all our data. Naturally I had an obligation to investigate. When I saw what you were hiding I was shocked to find out what a nasty little girl you are. Who would've figured on our resident genius having hot pants? Hell, you never know."

Eddie smirked. "Time for a commercial break, Cheryl. Pay close attention." His eyes glittered green as he spoke in an announcer's voice. "Need screwing? See Eddie Driscoll! Eddie has the right equipment and knows how to use it. He can give it to you anyway you like it, long, strong and all night long. So don't dream your life away, let big Eddie give you the real thing." His tone hardened. "You better come see me when you wake up or I'll share your little dream with everybody."

Eddie's face faded until nothing but a Cheshire Cat smile remained. "And now, a surprise guest, just for you, Cheryl baby. You're gonna love this one!"

The TV screen went blank.

CHAPTER EIGHTEEN

Morgan awoke with a start, finding himself in a darkened room, feeling as if someone had just spoken to him. He listened, hearing only the steady beep of life support. Blinking at the gloom, he saw only flickering displays and the winking lights of the shadow world ruled by the life sustaining super-computer, Morpheus.

He sipped his coffee, then spit it back into the Styrofoam cup. Lord, how he hated cold coffee. When he settled into his chair earlier, the darn stuff had been too hot to drink and while waiting for it to cool, he dozed. Pushing his long thin frame from the easy chair, he listened to the muted beeps and scanned the pulsing lights of PermaDream.

Tapping a waveform on a touch screen, he watched young Daggett's body temp flash across the top of the monitor. Steady at 102.

He checked the twenty four hour readout. Often, it jumped four or five degrees in a heartbeat and stayed that way for an unsettling moment before lowering and stabilizing at 102. No fluctuation for the past twelve hours. Good. No problems today. Please.

Instinctively cross-checking the computer's efficiency, he touched his digital thermometer to the young man's ear. 102. Body weight as of yesterday, ninety-four pounds. He flashed a wry grin at the console. Right again, Morpheus.

Morgan felt it important that everyone under his care had human contact. Despite the steady stream of feedback from Morpheus, he made it a point to periodically rest his hand on his patient's forehead, lift an eyelid and check beneath it with his penlight. Even when held open, the ostensibly sightless eye maintained rapid movement. For 365 days there had been no change.

Permitting the eyelid to close, he peered down at Chazz's comatose form. His head, with its purple temporal vein throbbing, appeared too massive for his spindly neck. Stringy, chalk-white hair curled like wisps of dry spittle from the once shiny pate. The hair, a deep shade of brown when it first grew back, had turned white several months later. Patches of gray beard covered waxen cheeks and a quivering chin. "Happy birthday, Chazz," Morgan muttered.

Beneath his beetled brow, under closed lids nearly buried in dark hollow sockets, Chazz Daggett's eyes darted back and forth like frightened rodents.

The rapid eye movement had been a constant from the outset of the boy's year long coma. The overall symptoms seemed consistent with high level viral infections, but Morgan had checked and tested his blood scores of times. Hundreds of labs had analyzed it worldwide. Every one came up empty. Strangest thing. Every sign of a virus and none of the etiology. His file on Chazz continued to expand. Plenty of theories. Every one a gut-wrenching dead end.

Soon, Ollie Daggett would arrive. Since he rarely left the safety of his compound, this would be his first visit. According to Hodge, he refused to approach Tijuana or any border town, wary of being kidnapped and brought back to the United States for trial. He trusted no one, but this was his son's twenty-first birthday. There would be a celebration. Ollie Daggett would attend. Nothing on earth could prevent that.

He issued orders that Chazz be dressed in his favorite outfit. The leather jacket, T-shirt and jeans hung over a chair. Shiny black boots stood beneath the bed. Morgan lifted Chazz's bony right foot and pushed it, bending the younger man's knee until it cracked. Setting the foot down, he picked up the other and repeated the motions. "Rita's coming by to get you dressed, so you'll look extra nice for your daddy. Haven't seen him for a long time. Between you and me," he said, lowering his voice, "I'm not looking forward to his visit."

"Don't expect an answer from him," Rita said from the doorway.

"Can't ever give up hope." Morgan lifted the other eyelid and clicked on his penlight. "Textbook REM."

Rita went to the console. Her silver hoop earrings sparkled in the reflection from the display and her dark eyes glistened with intensity as she scanned the readouts. "If only Morpheus could speak."

"He's speaking to us. Only we don't understand his language." Morgan tilted his head, listening to the soft beeps. "Yeah, he's talking, all right." She looked up, frowning.

"Don't sell Morpheus short, Rita. We've spent a lot of time together this past year. I've had the luxury of watching over Chazz, trying to figure out what's going on. Before long those beeps and clicks start to sound like a language, like Morpheus is trying to tell me something. Listen."

Rita did a slow scan of the room. "You're making me nervous. This place is creepy enough with him lying there like that."

Morgan continued, "You and I go home at night and sleep, absorbed in our own dreams, escaping reality, but our benevolent friend Morpheus never slumbers. Even though Chazz's dream sequence was terminated a year ago, all indicators tell me that he remains trapped in his nightmare." Morgan shook his head. "Poor Chazz. Wanted to own slaves."

"We should've pulled the plug on him long ago, in spite of Ollie's instructions."

"They weren't instructions. They were orders. Ollie is the patient's father. We have no choice. Besides, no hospital can give Chazz the care and attention that we can."

"Should've done it anyway." Rita brushed a fly from Chazz's forehead. "This is insane. He'll look absolutely ludicrous wearing that stupid leather outfit. More of Ollie's asinine orders. How ironic. This sorry excuse for a human being hooks up to PermaDream for his own sick pleasure and winds up in a coma."

Morgan fingered the panel. "I blame myself. I knew about Freedom Hart and his renegade slaves. Should have told Chazz, whether or not he wanted to hear it. I kept my mouth shut. Figured on teaching him a lesson. Treated it as a damn joke."

Rita touched his hand. "Morg, it's only a dream. It's not real. Besides, how can you be certain that – that..."

"That the boy's still locked in that nightmare? Of course he is. I watched the background track. Correlated it in real time to his physiological reactions. It's still following the same sequence of changes. I can set the clock by Chazz's reactions. Haven't you seen enough twitching and sweating? Look at his eyes. Constant movement.

I'm aware of the God awful misery he must be enduring because I didn't warn him. I pray for the boy to die and end his suffering, but Morpheus keeps him alive, and somehow, even though he's disconnected from the dream machine, Chazz continues to hallucinate."

Rita said, "If my mother was alive, she'd swear he was possessed."

Morgan grinned. "My mom would be inclined to agree. Hell, I'm about ready to buy into it. Why not? Nothing else fits. How often has he repeated the same agonizing nightmare? It's been a year for us. How many lifetimes for Chazz? How much pain?"

The twinkling lights dancing before Morgan's eyes seemed to blink out a cryptic message. "That damned computer knows everything. Every bit of research and testing we've done is stored in it. All my theories. My hunches. Morpheus has all the pieces to the puzzle. I can't help thinking that if I knew how to listen better, he'd give me the solution." He shrugged. "I keep trying." Morgan touched a finger to his lips. "Listen again, Rita," he whispered. "And look." He pointed to the monitor.

Rita cocked her head, her diminutive features set in an attitude of concentration. After a few moments her dark brown eyes searched Morgan's. "Sorry. Nothing but lights, beeps, and air conditioning." Once again, she waved her hand over Chazz. "And this damned fly." She raised an eyebrow. "I think you've been working too hard on this, Morg."

Morgan spoke over his shoulder while checking the IV. "I'm not crazy. Not yet. It's just a fantasy I've had, that's all. Wishful thinking."

"You've been spending too much time down here in PermaDream, blaming yourself for this. You need a break."

Morgan turned with a smile. "Good idea. I'll take the rest of the week off. Do some fishing. Give my best to Ollie Daggett."

"Hey, wait!" Rita wagged her finger at him. "Not until after the birthday party. You're not leaving me alone with Chazz and Ollie."

Morgan chuckled. "Only teasing. I wouldn't do that to you."

The console phone rang. She picked it up. "PermaDream. Hi, Hodge. Yeah, he's right here."

Morgan set his IPad down and took the phone. "Jackson."

"Just met with the Fulbright girl," Hodge said.

"And?"

"I need your take on her."

"I'll bring my medical bag."

"Don't bother, I sent her home. Got her on videodisk though. I'm not certain if this is a hoax, blackmail, or God knows what, but something's wrong. A hoax, I can deal with, but if it's anything else..."

"Sounds serious."

"It's damned strange, Morg. I'd like to clear it up fast. We're laying out the ad campaign for BibleLand. The last thing we need hanging over us is a lawsuit."

"That bad?"

"You tell me once you've seen the disk."

"Be right there. When's the Daggett birthday thing?"

"Nine."

Morgan glanced at his watch. "Ollie won't be down for five hours. Plenty of time."

"Hurry. If you see Cheryl, bring her along. I haven't been able to locate her."

"Okay." Morgan cradled the receiver and looked up to see Rita studying him, the concern in her eyes clouding her expression.

"Problem?" she asked.

"Hodge wants me to take a look at something important. Can you prepare our patient for his daddy's visit?"

"Chazz is in my loving hands."

"Ollie's due at nine. I'll be back by then." Morgan hurried out of PermaDream, leaving Chazz to the tender care of Rita Cariño and the ever watchful Morpheus.

CHAPTER NINETEEN

Cheryl adjusted the stereo, fine tuning the music until the shimmering strings of Mantovani felt like a second layer of skin and the bass line throbbed to the beat of her heart. Soft voices massaged her mind.

"Who can I turn to,
When nobody needs me."

Drawing aside the drape, she peered out the sliding door. Rain drummed on the glass and splattered in puddles on the balcony. Far below, wild surf raged against dark rocks.

"I only know I gotta go,
Where destiny leads me."

She ran her hands down her sides, reveling in the cool feel of silk against her naked body. The floor length negligee clung to her hips and rubbed against her bare nipples, making them tingle.

Someone knocked on the door. Three quick taps. A pause. Then two more.

Lorenzo! A warm glow surged from deep inside of her and her heart raced. Sweet Lorenzo. Breathing hard, she pulled the filigreed comb from her hair and shook loose long amber tresses. The perfumed negligee clung to her thighs as she glided across the room and opened the door...

Jack Scanlon stood on the porch, wearing nothing but a trench coat, grinning like a jackass in the teeth of howling wind and driving rain, hairy legs sticking out from beneath his wet coat. He twitched his hips and stepped into the room.

Trembling, she followed him to the fireplace. "Sorry, Jack, I'm expecting someone."

Jack stared at the fire. "Dance card's all filled up, is it?"

"Please leave."

He turned to face her, wet face gleaming golden in the firelight, green chips of light glittering in his eyes. "God, but I hate rejection." From a trench coat pocket, he pulled out a cat-o-nine tails and slapped it across his palm. "I really do."

"Stop this, right now!"

Jack spoke softly. "I know who you're waiting for, Cheryl." He moved closer. "Shame on you, spreading your legs like a Goddamn chimpanzee for Lorenzo Vargas. Where's your self respect?" He grinned. "Don't get me wrong, a lack of self-respect isn't necessarily bad." Jack held out his arms. The cat-o-nine tails dangled from one hand. "Hell, more often than not it gets in the way of a good piece of ass." He swung and the barbs whistled through the air, inches from her face. "Know what I mean?"

Cheryl backed away. "Jack, please." She sobbed. "We're friends. Colleagues. This is offensive."

"Think so?" He placed the whip between his teeth. "Wait'll you see this!" Slowly, he opened his trench coat, exposing his pale naked body, narrow pimply shoulders, knobby knees and pot belly.

Cheryl struggled to catch her breath, backing away as Jack stripped off his coat. He rolled his bony hips, causing his horse-sized, purple-knobbed appendage to wave back and forth. "You're staring at my magic-wand, baby. That isn't polite." Green flashed in his eyes.

Tossing his coat aside, he removed the cat-o-nine-tails from his mouth and faced her, hands on hips. "Ever beg for food, Cheryl? Ever wear a leash? Ever been ridden like a donkey?"

"Please, Jack," she sobbed. "Please, don't hurt me."

"Sorry, Cheryl, can't promise that." Jack stepped closer, tapping her cheek with the whip as he spoke. "Jack Scanlon never made a promise he couldn't keep." Grabbing her chin, he jammed his mouth hard against hers.

His tongue slid between her lips. Cheryl choked as he eased it deeper into her mouth. She struggled to escape, but he overpowered her, jamming a knee into her crotch and pinning her to the wall. She slumped against him, limp and helpless.

He pulled his mouth away and whispered, "You'll kneel at my feet every night, Cheryl, begging to be my footstool." He stepped back and snapped her nightgown strap. "Take it off," he said. "Let's have a look at that ass."

"No."

"Then I will!" He ripped off the gown and tossed it aside. The cat-o-nine-tail's barbed stingers whistled past her ear. "Oh, baby, am I gonna smoke those hams!"

"Stay away!" Cheryl's fluttering heart made her whole body tremble. Her teeth chattered as she backed through the open door into the cold rain.

"Get back here!" he shouted.

She turned and ran into the arms of Eddie Driscoll, who laughed. "Not yet, Cheryl, Jack isn't finished."

"Come here, donkey!" Jack grabbed her hair and pulled her back across the threshold. "I'll teach you some manners." He kicked the door shut. From the other side, Cheryl heard Eddie's coarse laughter. "Mama!" she shrieked, at the top of her lungs. "Mama!" Everything went blurry.

Cheryl plucked off the dream hood and sat straight up, gasping for breath, bewildered by the flickering reality of her bedroom.

With Jack Scanlon's harsh profanities echoing through her mind, she stumbled down the hall on trembling legs to the bathroom, where she hovered over the toilet bowl. Head throbbing, eyes glazed, knees sore from the unyielding tile, she kneeled, shaking her head, trying to calm her frenzied mind. How ridiculous, she thought. Cheryl Martin, the world's leading researcher in brain wave modulation, kneeling on the bathroom floor, skin crawling from thoughts that seemed to bubble up from the bowels of hell.

With shaking fingers, she tore off a section of toilet tissue and dabbed at sweat on her lip. Tears blurred her vision and her stomach burned from the humility of Jack's cruelty. Sobbing like a frightened child, she closed her eyes and relived the degradation she suffered in the dream.

Behind her, the bathroom door opened. A shadow fell across the floor.

Jack!

"No more," she gasped. "No more. I won't let you do this. I want to wake up, I want to wake up. Mama!"

Jack's voice croaked at her ear. "What makes you think you're asleep, donkey?"

A hot burst of fear exploded inside her. She couldn't be awake. "Mama!" she screamed again, but nothing happened. She sobbed, "Dear God, I am awake, I'm wide awake!"

Jack's laughter echoed in the tiled room. She tensed. Any second now, her bare behind would quiver beneath the sting of the cat-o-nine-tails. She closed her eyes and held her breath, anticipating the first scorching blow.

A small eternity passed before Cheryl opened her eyes and looked over her shoulder at an empty bathroom. Taking a long, shuddering breath, she went to the sink and threw cold water on her face. A chill shook her. Hurrying back to the living room, she checked the locks and turned on every light. No dark corners for her tonight. She slipped into a soft cotton robe to cover her nakedness and sat on the edge of the bed to ponder her situation. This called for a cool rational interpretation of facts. Back to basics. For every effect, a natural cause.

She hadn't anticipated any side-effects from the increased field strength of the portable unit. Perhaps it had provoked such a powerful synaptic response that they still fired in some sort of aftershock. Yes, that was it. The residual synaptic buildup was still firing, resulting in a ghosting effect.

Her hand fell to her lap, brushing her thigh. Pain lanced her, sending needles of fire up and down her spine. She raised the robe and peered between her legs. A mass of purple welts mottled the alabaster skin of her inner thigh.

Her mouth went dry and her heart hammered. Bruised thighs? She stared at them, recalling Jack's nightmare assault and that old cliché about pinching yourself to see if you're dreaming. Rationality shattered like a pane of glass and icy terror rushed in to occupy the empty space. Dream pinches do not leave real bruises!

She took up her pen and held it over a clean sheet of paper, finding herself doodling a stick figured rat with crooked whiskers and a long tail that spelled, "Eddie", in an elegant cursive. Her romantic dream had been invaded and devastated by Eddie Driscoll. He had broken her encryption and modified the sequence, even inserting himself into her dream. Then Jack. The oversized penis gag no doubt tickled his low power intellect. Adolescent Eddie with his frat-house-wit would think of Jack and his "magic wand" as being terribly funny. The little bastard.

Glowering, Cheryl reached for the telephone.

CHAPTER TWENTY

"Bitch!" Eddie slammed down the phone and flopped into a chair at the animation lab work station beside Lorenzo. "Ugly-ass humorless-bitch!" He shook his head.

Lorenzo looked up from the slow motion Pied Piper sequence unfolding on the screen in front of him. "What's your problem?"

Eddie fiddled with the touchpad, a further sign that something irritated him. "Somebody should slip that uptight old bitch a big stiff cob."

"Who the hell are you talking about?"

Eddie nodded toward the phone. "Cheryl. She's nuts." He tapped his temple with an index finger. "Nasty bitch. No humanity, no compassion, no sense of humor. She just threatened to get me shit-canned."

Lorenzo's dark brow furrowed. "Jesus, Eddie, what kind of garbage did you stir up now?"

"All I did was play a little trick on her."

"Stay the hell out of her way with your damned tricks," Lorenzo snapped. "I told you not to screw with Cheryl. You know how focused she is when she's working on something."

"Yeah, she's focused all right. If Morpheus had a dick..."

Lorenzo's eyes narrowed. "You will get yourself canned with an attitude like that, only I'll be the one to do it. I take a lot of crap from Hodge about giving you too much freedom. Why can't you be cool and stop drawing attention to yourself? How many times do I have to tell you to keep a low profile?"

Eddie stared at the floor.

"Keep acting up," Lorenzo said, jabbing his finger at Eddie. "Cheryl's going to start investigating you. If she finds out about that damned virus collection you've been keeping, Hodge'll have both of our asses."

"That's my personal business. None of hers."

"Then where do you get off mucking around in hers?" Lorenzo shot back.

Eddie opened his mouth, then stopped. "You're right." He shrugged. "To hell with her. She ain't worth my attention." He nodded toward Lorenzo's display. "What's up with the Piper?"

Lorenzo bit his lower lip. "One of the girl Greeters said she was bitten by a dream rat."

"Bitten?" Eddie raised his eyebrows and whistled. "No shit?"

"Hodge is a nervous wreck. Kid swears it was an ugly vicious rat."

"She's nuts!"

"Hodge pulled me off Genesis to investigate. I was creating Eve." He smiled. "Gave her Rita's eyes."

"Never mind Rita's eyes, give her Denise's ass." Eddie grinned. His fingers danced across the keyboard and tapped the touchpad, stepping it through a series of screens until the Pied Piper sequence on Lorenzo's monitor appeared on his own. "You looked at this frame by frame?"

"Frame by frame, stop motion, slo-mo, reverse video. Four times so far."

"Nothing out of whack? No drooling rats with big sharp teeth?" Eddie's keyboard clicked and the video froze. Zooming in on a rat's fuzzy little head, he enlarged it until it filled the screen. With a flurry of motion, the rat's big, soft brown eyes shrank, turning red, feral and beaded. Its tiny nostrils widened, and its pink mouth blurred into a gaping black maw, studded with jagged fangs, slimy and wet with shimmering strings of saliva.

Lorenzo let out an exasperated sigh. "Get serious, Eddie."

"I am. How about it, y'gonna give Eve Denise's ass?" He grinned. "Oh, baby, what a work of art! I swear, Denise has the finest ass in the..."

Behind them, the door opened. With two taps of the touchpad,

Eddie returned his rat to its fuzzy cuteness. Turning, he flashed a toothy smile when he saw Denise. "Hello there." He looked her over as she approached. "Looking lovely, as always."

Denise smiled and turned to Lorenzo. "How're things going?"

"Plodding along."

"Nothing new?"

"Afraid not. Seen Hodge?"

"He's interviewing Emily Fulbright."

Lorenzo leaned back in his chair and crossed his arms. "The bane of my existence. Hodge is overreacting to her craziness. She's obviously a nut."

"Oughta give that dopey kid an ink blot test." Eddie muttered.

Denise touched Lorenzo's arm. "You don't think it's serious?"

"How can it be?" He held up an IPad with a thick stack of notes on it. "But Hodge wants hard copy. We're maintaining a low profile, trying to keep our problem within the family."

"Good."

"We're hustling, Denise, really hustling." Eddie said. "Everyone but Cheryl."

Lorenzo pinned him with a frosty stare. "Eddie's about to pay a visit to Hansel and Gretel."

"I am?"

"You sure are. Move."

"C'mon, Lorenzo, I can't stand all those happy people. Why can't I go to Rumplestiltskin? I love that nasty little shit."

Lorenzo jerked his thumb over his shoulder. "Hansel and Gretel." Eddie scowled and shuffled out the door.

Several wisps of Denise's chestnut hair brushed Lorenzo's stubbled cheek when she leaned over for a closer look at the flickering image of the Pied Piper village on his screen. He stiffened and moved his head until her hair no longer touched.

"Your settings are so mystical. So charming." She moved closer. Her breast brushed his shoulder. "The village square background is absolutely enchanting."

"Thank you." Lorenzo shifted away from her and stood. "Coffee?" He smiled. "Fresh brewed."

"Why not?" She followed him to the coffee maker.

Lorenzo poured. "How about you, want to do some dreaming?"

She shook her head. "I'd rather help out here in the lab. I'm not much of a dreamer." She touched his hand. "I'm into reality."

Lorenzo looked toward the door. "Just for the record, Denise, this is a waste. Nobody's buying the Fulbright kid's story."

"Of course not." She laughed. "Only Hodge."

"True. The way I figure it, by tomorrow morning Hodge can drop a net over Emily Fulbright, reopen Pied Piper and forget this lousy farce. We can't devote our lives to this nut. I have Genesis to create. The Garden of Eden. Adam and Eve. The serpent."

"Amen, Lorenzo." Denise smiled, squeezing his arm.

CHAPTER TWENTY ONE

Steely clouds from an unexpected afternoon storm cast a somber gloom over the San Diego waterfront. The steady gentle sea breeze gave way to a gusty, palm rustling north wind that kicked up dust and sent trash scudding along the curb. Drivers switched on headlights. Benches emptied and tables cleared in open air restaurants as people hurried to seek shelter.

Wearing dark glasses, Emily Fulbright raced along the Embarcadero running into the wind, head down, legs pumping, as if some unseen abomination snapped at her heels. Gasping, lungs aching, she struggled to breathe. Damn Mister Hodge – hadn't believed one word of her story – figured her to be a liar – thought she was crazy – Damn him! Damn! Damn! Damn Mister Hodge to hell!

The sky grew darker, the air more dense. Her itching raged as if she had erupted into a blistering case of poison oak, head to toe. Emily resisted the urge to tear off her clothes and dive into the cold white-capped waters of San Diego Bay.

Flailing her arms, she hailed a taxicab, then changed her mind and waved the driver on his way. She would run all the way home.

Another block and her throat felt as if she'd swallowed a live coal. Hot tears stung her eyes and her feet felt like raw meat. She'd never make it. Better catch a taxi after all. Darting into traffic, she dodged a bus and flagged another cab.

As the first fat raindrops splattered onto the pavement, the driver reached back and opened the door. Emily climbed in and wheezed out her address. "Please hurry, please."

"Sure thing." The cabby studied her, a look of concern clouding his unshaven face. "You all right?"

"Yes. Just go."

Skin smarting as if her body had been assaulted by a swarm of stinging insects, Emily huddled in a corner of the back seat. Twisting her pinkie finger into her ear, she dug as deep as she could, unable to reach the itch. Writhing, she scratched her armpits and rubbed her sweaty thighs together, vainly trying to relieve her suffering.

Finally reaching home, she rushed past the waiting elevator, raced up five flights to her apartment, slipped inside, locked the deadbolt and fastened the security chain. In the kitchen, she kicked off her shoes and leaned against the wall, raking the soles of her feet with filthy nails. Filling a glass with water, she guzzled it and wiped her mouth on her sleeve.

Something moved behind her.

Trembling, she set the glass down and peered over her shoulder. A long dark tail slid behind the refrigerator. On the counter, beady eyes peered out from an open box of corn flakes. A clatter came from inside the dish cabinet.

Emily backed away. Several fat hairy creatures scurried between her legs, claws clicking on the linoleum.

She stood in the living room doorway wheezing, trying to catch her breath. Thick drapes stretched across windows and nailed to the wall kept out the painful light. Wind rattled the panes and raindrops drummed the roof like tiny hammers, causing her head to pound. She leaned forward, peeking into the room, heart thumping. A bubble of fear rose in her throat. Dozens of tiny eyes glinted green in the shadowed gloom. She knew they'd be there. Waiting.

Dark squeaking forms scrambled from her path as she ran through the living room and dashed down the narrow hallway, scattering her clothing. Naked by the time she reached the bedroom, she snapped on the light and stopped before the full length mirror. The sight of herself made Emily's eyes bulge. Her stomach twisted into a cold knot and a quivering sob wracked her feeble body.

"God, help me!" She staggered backward from her image and stumbled into the bathroom where she grabbed the soap and stood under the steaming shower, lathering herself with a fury, scrubbing with her fingertips, muttering as she tried to scour the gray fuzz from her upper torso, taking great care to avoid touching the six tiny pink nipples.

"The Fulbright girl's on the losing end of a serious bout with depression, Hodge. From what you've told me, I'd bet on it." Morgan spread butter on his hot Apple Danish until it oozed off the sugared cake and dripped onto a paper plate. "Severe depression can be a gauntlet through hell."

"You shouldn't eat so much greasy crap," Hodge said. "You're a doctor, for God's sake."

"I'm also an ectomorph. I burn energy twice as fast as you." Morgan slipped a napkin under his paper plate, unfolded a second and spread it over his knee, then forked off a bite-sized piece of Danish and dragged it through the melted butter. He popped the sweet cake into his mouth and spoke while chewing. "Ectomorphs have to eat."

"You're a junk-o-morph." Hodge tasted his own coffee, then added more sugar. "Ready for the Emily show?"

Morgan swiveled his chair to face the monitors. "Roll 'em."

Hodge pointed his remote. The lights dimmed, monitors flickered, and Emily Fulbright popped onto every screen the way Hodge first saw her, slumped on the black leather couch at the far end of the hallway, face buried in her hands. "There she is, Miss America," he sang. The camera zoomed in until her withered hands and long dirty fingernails filled the huge central screen.

Morgan stopped eating. "Look at those hands. It'd be a stretch, but if she's truly only nineteen and the hands represent her overall condition, we could have a woman with Werner's syndrome or a Progeroid disorder."

Hodge raised an eyebrow. "What the hell are they?"

"Progeroid children are born with an accelerated aging gene or no aging control gene at all. Kids develop and deteriorate at a highly accelerated pace, like when you fast-forward a videotape. Werner's is similar."

Hodge rubbed his arms. "That's disgusting."

"They're fatal genetic disorders."

"Genetic?" Hodge leaned his elbow on the desk, cupped his chin in his hand and tapped on his cheek with his index finger. "Let me get this straight, if it's Progeroid or Werner's, it's genetic and DreamLand is off the hook, right?"

Morgan frowned at Hodge's lack of compassion. "Don't pop open your victory champagne yet. At best, the Progeroid thing is a long shot. Few victims ever make it into their teens. Never heard of a full-blown Progeria syndrome that began in adulthood, or Werner's for that matter, unless this is some new accelerated form. Emily should be examined by a specialist."

"Or interrogated by the cops. She's probably some ugly old hag trying to rip us off."

On the screen, Emily's face popped into focus as she sat at Hodge's desk.

"Jesus," Morgan said. "Something is wrong here. Turn up the volume."

"Light bothers me, Mister Michaels." Emily's squeaky voice piped from the monitors. "Hurts my eyes." The images dimmed, hushing the room in deeper shadows.

Hodge looked away as Emily relayed the details of her nightmare while Morgan watched in silence, sitting forward, neither talking nor eating.

"I personally supervised the development of the Hamelin rats, Emily," Hodge's voice, swollen with pride, bellowed from the screen. "My rats are lovable!"

Morgan watched intently as Emily slid the sweater cuff up her bony arm. "Rat bites."

The punctate abrasions on her arm, in concert with the fear etched in her creaky voice gave him a chill. He raised his hand. "That's enough, Hodge."

"Good." Hodge aimed the remote and Emily's image disappeared, replaced by the usual DreamLand surveillance scans. "I never want to see that face again." When the lighting returned to normal, he held up the Fulbright file. "The old bitch insists that the pretty kid in the Fulbright file photo was her a year ago. Tell me she doesn't look forty years older than the girl in this picture."

Morgan sighed. "At least." He closed his eyes, unable to shake the haunting memory of Emily Fulbright's appearance. "That face, all withered and wrinkled, like one of those dried apple head dolls. And her eyes. Glassy. Beady. Almost inhuman. Strange things happen to people under the stress of depression, but this seemed like some sort of physical aberration. He shook his head. "Beats anything I've ever seen."

"So?" Hodge loosened his tie and unbuttoned his collar. "What now?"

"I'll pay her a visit. Hell, if I looked like that I'd be scared too. And confused."

"Or a Goddamned liar."

"Come on, man, don't be so quick to condemn her. This calls for a measure of compassion. Emily Fulbright needs a friend. Someone to calmly and rationally explain what's happening to her. That's my job."

"What about the marks on her arm?"

"They could be accidental or self-inflicted. I won't know until I see them close up. Where is she?"

"I sent her home." Hodge found Emily's number in his shirt pocket and punched it into his cell phone. "I'll ask her to see you, but she won't. You should've seen her freak when I tried to set up an appointment with Cheryl."

"Permit the doctor to speak with her." Morgan took the phone, listened for a moment, then canceled the call. "No answer. I'll just head for her apartment."

"Did you get rid of the nursing staff?" Hodge asked. "Ollie doesn't want extra people hanging around when he shows up."

"Rita's alone. She's covering for us. I'll be back by nine. She'll kill me if I leave her alone with the Daggetts."

"She'll be safe, I'll be there," Hodge said. "Lorenzo's coming too. And Denise. What a trooper! She's even showing up for a slice of cake."

Morgan frowned. "Cake?"

"Ollie's having one sent over from Chez Cake in La Jolla."

"A birthday cake? For God's sake, Hodge, this is insane! Chazz looks like he's been dead for a week and Ollie's bringing him a birthday cake?"

Hodge shrugged. "What the hell do you care if he brings a cake?"

"Doesn't Daggett realize what kind of shape Chazz is in? He hasn't stopped by once since the boy slipped into the coma."

"Ollie rarely leaves the compound. Never comes near the border. He's afraid he'll be kidnapped, but he's here for the birthday." Hodge pointed to the glass wall behind his desk. "In his private quarters."

Across the atrium, a thin crack of light framed the window around the edge of Ollie Daggett's closed velvet drapes. "Without his entourage," Hodge added.

"No bodyguards?"

Hodge shook his head. "He traveled alone. Wore drab clothing. Flew commercial, Mexico City to Ensenada. Hired a car and drove the rest of the way." He tapped his temple. "Brains, Morg. Ollie Daggett has brains. And commitment."

"And a temper," Morgan added. "And eyes that will soon see Chazz." He grasped the edge of the table as if feeling the initial tremor of an earthquake. "This'll be one hell of a bombshell, Hodge. He should be warned."

"Don't look at me." Hodge raised his hands. "This isn't my fault. I'm no medical man."

"He should be warned," Morgan repeated.

"Then you warn him!" Hodge gave a final wave, then leaned back in his chair and crossed his arms. "The phone's in your hand. Call him. Tell him his son looks like he belongs on a slab."

"Come on, Hodge."

Hodge said, "Tell Ollie we plan to prop Chazz up in a corner and staple a party hat to his scabby head before we sing Happy Birthday. And while you're at it, ask him if he'd prefer us to shove the birthday cake up Chazzy's ass or needle it into his veins."

Morgan raised his hands in surrender. He couldn't believe how much had changed since their first experiment. Hodge still bore a stunning resemblance to a younger Edgar Michaels, but he exhibited a callousness that Edgar could never imagine. He was about to tell Hodge he was behaving like a stupid insensitive fool when the cell phone pulsed.

"That's probably Denise," Hodge said. "She's concerned." He snatched the phone from Morgan. "Hello," he purred, then paled and straightened, throwing back his shoulders, and deepening his voice. "Of course everything's ready, Mister Daggett. We'll all be there at nine sharp." His expression froze. He tilted his head and listened. "Pardon?" His facial muscles seemed to collapse and his voice returned to its normal pitch. "Uh – gee – uh – I'm sorry, sir. I can't make it right now. I'm in an important meeting with Doctor Jackson and – Hello – Hello?" He stared at the phone, then eyed Morgan and spoke in a barely audible voice. "Jesus, he hung up." He set down the phone. "He wants me to come by his quarters, now, Morg. For a little talk." Ashen-faced, Hodge slumped back in his chair, closed his eyes and let out a deep sigh.

Morgan stood. "I'm off to see the Fulbright girl. Be back as soon as I can." He crumpled the napkins and paper plate and stuffed them in the wastebasket. "Stand tall, Hodge. Show Daggett you're a man."

"Yeah sure." Hodge shook his head and ran his fingers through his hair. "This is all Dad's fault. Why couldn't he have gone after a government grant? We wouldn't even know Ollie Daggett. PermaDream would be a reality by now. Denise and I would probably be married and working on a family. Dad really fucked up."

Morgan swallowed the burst of anger he felt at Hodge's change in attitude. A young woman needed his help. He would tell Hodge off later. He headed for the door. "I'm off to see the Fulbright girl. Been years since I made a house call."

Hodge snorted. "Better bring along a strait jacket when you make this one."

CHAPTER TWENTY TWO

Morgan parked under the only street light on a narrow hillside cul-de-sac and tapped out Emily Fulbright's number on his cell phone. After a dozen rings, he disconnected, dropped the phone into his medical bag and turned up his collar against the steady rain.

After hurrying the short distance to the aging apartment house, he climbed the front steps, opened the glass door, and entered a tiled vestibule illuminated by a circular neon ceiling tube set flush against the ceiling. Behind him, the door clicked shut. He tried the barred inner door.

Locked.

Spying a bank of several dozen numbered buttons on the wall, he moved closer, squinting as he tracked the names with an index finger until he found E. Fulbright. Top floor. 5A. He pressed the black button beside the printed name.

An ear-piercing electronic squawk assaulted his ears. "Who is it? Who's down there?" a thin raspy voice demanded.

"Morgan Jackson, Miss Fulbright. Hodge Michaels asked me to stop by. I'm a doctor." He quickly added. "A medical doctor."

"Go away! Nobody can help. Mister Michaels thinks I'm lying."

"I know you're telling the truth, Emily. Let me in so I can ease your discomfort. I'll only stay a moment. That's a promise. Trust me.

Please."

"You alone?" she whispered.

"Yes."

After a breathless moment the buzzer sounded. Morgan pushed open the door and stepped inside. Peering up the shadowed staircase, he pulled his phone from his bag. A moment later Hodge's voice came on the line. "Morg, where are you?"

"Emily Fulbright's downstairs hall," Morgan said in an urgent half whisper. "The girl is home. She'll see me."

"Terrific. Examine those bites closely. We'll need plenty of documentation. There may be a law suit."

"I'll call you later."

"Don't waste too much time on her, Morg. Remember, first things first. Ollie Daggett'll want detailed medical facts about Chazz."

"Relax, I'll be there. Call you later."

Morgan stepped onto the elevator and watched the floor lights change as it rose, trembled, and shuddered to a standstill at the top floor. Holding the door open with his foot, Morgan peered into the darkness beyond the rectangle of illumination. The lone source of light, a bare incandescent ceiling lamp had been shattered in its socket, leaving the hallway dark, save for the dim glow from the elevator.

Glass dangled from the ceiling by a bare wire. Jagged shards from the broken bulb formed an inverted crown. Glass crackled underfoot as he stepped off the elevator. Casting a long slender shadow, he eased down the hall toward apartment 5A. Halfway there his shadow disappeared when the elevator door whooshed shut, plunging the hallway into darkness.

He heard a scratching sound, then silence.

Morgan stopped and stood still, blinking. "Emily?" he whispered. "It's Doctor Jackson. Are you here?"

The razor-edged sibilance of night and the muffled sound of rain answered. He shrugged. No sense standing poker-straight in the gloomy hallway counting heartbeats in his throat. He had a house call to make. Tightening his grip on his medical bag, he reached out and inched along the wall until he felt the door frame beneath his palm. End of the corridor. Apartment 5A.

He tapped on the door and heard shuffling footsteps, followed by the unexpected crunch of broken glass. His breath caught. He backed against the door, hand to his chest, heart thudding against his ribs.

The footsteps came from the darkened hallway.
Behind him.

CHAPTER TWENTY THREE

"Welcome to the Enchanted Forest."

The man's recorded voice, soft and deep, reminded little Albert of his pastor's during Sunday morning services. The boy stood in the center of a moving walkway, gliding through a seemingly endless tunnel. Overhead, soft colored lights diffused by gossamer clouds pulsed to the tune of "Three Blind Mice" coming from behind banks of artificial trees and kaleidoscopic bunches of fake flowers.

A prickling sensation tickled the nape of Albert's neck, as if someone lurked behind him, then the tunnel went dark and a door whooshed open.

"Follow the elves to your dream cocoon," the friendly voice said.

Tiny lights twinkled like Technicolor fireflies as the walkway carried him into a circular room. He looked at the domed ceiling and a comet streaked across a starlit sky, trailing sparks.

Dozens of man-sized opalescent Easter eggs faced the walkway from both sides, with tiny multi-colored lights outlining each open compartment. Albert spotted the Sandman and two elves assisting a tall skinny man wearing a San Diego Padres cap into one of the eggs.

"Hey, that guy's a grownup!" the boy blurted as a second pair of elves helped him off the walkway and led him to a dream egg. "He's a man. I thought the Enchanted Forest was for kids."

"It is." The familiar voice of the Sandman boomed. He appeared out of the darkness grinning wide, eyes glinting cat-like from the shadows of his cloak. "That's Eddie Driscoll, one of my helpers. I send him in every once in awhile to check up on that nasty old witch." He fluttered his cape. "Off he goes. Sweet dreams, friend." The cocoon whooshed shut, then the Sandman addressed his assistants. "All right you elves. Move quickly now. Hurry my young friend off to visit Hansel and Gretel."

A pretty girl-elf tightened her grip on Albert's elbow and exchanged smiles with the boy-elf at his other side.

"Come on, little man," the boy-elf said, helping him into a gleaming egg.

Albert settled back into the silken cloud and took a deep breath as the gel formed to his body like a soft giant hand. The girl-elf leaned into the cocoon and smiled. "Take care, and don't let the witch eat you for Halloween dinner." She stepped back. "Off you go." The cocoon hissed shut.

Nestled in his dream cradle, Albert smiled, feeling warm air brush his face like the gentle caress of a summer breeze. A humming sound followed, the egg seemed to rotate and he heard singing.

"The witches are waiting for you,

The witches are waiting for you,

They'll nibble your fingers and snack on your toes,

And fatten you up for stew."

Witches? More than one? The air turned cold and a chill danced over his back, raising his neck hairs. His heartbeat quickened. Gulping a deep breath, he held it like he did when he swam underwater. The humming grew louder until Albert felt as if something grabbed hold of him and pulled him spinning downward. Colored lights flashed. Blood rushed to his head and his skin tingled...

...cold, hard ground beneath his back.

"Wake up!" A girl's voice said. "Please wake up." Someone had hold of his shoulder, shaking him. "Wake up. Oh dear, hurry!"

He opened his eyes and blinked, trying to focus on the blurred face of his tormentor. "What's happening to me? Where am I?" He tried, but couldn't remember anything. A young girl bent over him, crystal blue eyes staring, a look of terror twisting her pretty face. "Hurry, for goodness sake." She tugged on his arm. "They're coming."

He blinked again, shook his head and looked around. He was in a small clearing, night sky above, a pale half moon hanging above the horizon. Shadowy trees and boulders surrounded them. "Where am I?

Who're you?"

"Gretel. Hurry. We're out of time. They're coming."

"Who?"

"The witches, silly."

Witches? Albert tried to concentrate, but couldn't even recall his name.

"Please hurry, they'll be here any second." The girl yanked him to his feet. "Hurry!"

He heard loud thrashing in the nearby woods.

Gretel caught her breath. "Too late! Hide!" She dragged him behind a pile of rocks. Crouching beside her, holding her hand, he squeezed with all his might. What was happening?

Someone stumbled into the clearing gasping for breath, then a shrill howl shattered the dark. A man's voice, wracked with terror. "Mama!" He shrieked. "Mama! For Christ sake, get me out of here. Can't run anymore. They have my shoes."

Gretel touched a finger to Albert's lips and shook her head.

"Mama! Mommy! For God's sake, hurry!" The man's voice cracked. "They're coming."

Something big crashed through the brush on the other side of the rock pile. Albert cringed, squeezing his eyes shut.

"Gotcha!"

Lightning flashed, thunder boomed and the man yelped in pain. Albert's heart thumped so hard he couldn't swallow. A scream caught in his throat.

"I got him, not you!" another voice screeched, louder than the first. "He's mine."

"Mine. Give him here!"

"Help, they're tearing me apart! Mama!" the man blubbered.

Cackling laughter sent waves of goose bumps up and down Albert's arms and legs, standing his hair on end.

"He won't need these shoes anymore," one of the witches squawked. Something sailed over Albert's head and landed in the brush behind him.

"Hold him still while I strip him." The witch croaked. "Let's see what we got."

Tearing cloth and the man's whimpering were the only sounds until one of the witches squawked. "Scrawny, ain't he?"

"Don't seem proper. Meat'll be tough and stringy."

"Ain't fair. We should have a nice plump, tender young boy for Halloween dinner." The witch sniffed several times. "Can't help feeling there's one around here somewhere."

Albert choked back a sob.

"Never mind. We better fatten up this bag of bones. Let's get him home."

"This can't be happening," the man whispered.

"Hold his hands while I hog-tie him. If he fights, bite off his ear. That usually calms 'em down." The witch grunted. "There, good'n tight. Lift him, see how meaty he is."

The man cried out.

"Hold him higher. That's better. Skinny son-of-a-bitch, ain't he? Look at these thighs. I can feel bone clean up to his asshole."

"How big're his nuts. Spread his legs, give 'em a squeeze."

The man grunted and screamed. "Gaaaaaah!"

"Ain't much here."

"I'll cook 'em up anyway. Bathe them tender little treats in buttermilk, slather 'em in egg and drag 'em through cracker crumbs." She cackled. "He'll hear his nuts sizzlin' before he knows they're gone."

"You're makin' me drool," the other witch said.

"Mama!" the man sobbed. "For God's sake, help me!"

Behind the rocks, Gretel leaned closer, her lips barely touching Albert's ear. A wisp of blonde hair brushed his cheek, silky, like a cobweb. "Soon as they drag him off," she whispered, "we'll run in the other direction. I left a trail of bread crumbs leading home. We'll follow them."

"Shouldn't we try to save him?" Albert whispered.

"Too late."

He heard a loud crack, like somebody biting hard candy.

"My toe," the man howled.

The witch slurped and chomped. "Not much meat."

A second crunch and another ear piercing scream.

"I ain't waiting no longer, let me at him!" the other witch said.

"No! Not my fingers. Mama! Mama!" the man mewled as the crunching started anew.

Albert jammed his fingers into his ears, but couldn't shut out the sounds of cracking and loud chewing, or the man's frenzied screams.

CHAPTER TWENTY FOUR

S everal stories beneath DreamLand's long lines of excited children and countless dream travelers, Hodge Michaels hurried through the dimly lit Hall of Dreams, increasing his pace as he entered the Gallery of Angels. He swallowed hard, remembering PermaDreaming children with smiling, expectant faces and the utopian plans he once had for the future. Now they were nothing more than broken dreams reflected in the long curving wall of picture frames.

Slowing as he approached a darkened section of the mirrored inner corridor, he took a deep breath and used his key card to open the door marked:

LIMITED ACCESS AREA

A hush of cool air brushed his face as he entered. Looking around, he saw a shadowy network of wires and tubes snaking out of receptacles, twisting across the ceiling, down walls and dangling from brackets like the remnants of an abandoned web.

The slumber room, once occupied by twenty peaceful PermaDreamers, had now become the private hospital ward for the living remains of the acrimonious, wild-eyed son of Ollie Daggett. Occupying the only remaining bed at the far end of the dimly lit chamber, Chazz lay still, a pile of emaciated flesh, locked in a never ending nightmare.

Hodge moved slowly through the flickering shadows cast by

changing displays and winking readouts until he recognized the petite, curvy backside of Rita Cariño hovering over the waxy figure, grumbling as she tried to shove a limp wobbly arm into the sleeve of the same bulky leather jacket Chazz wore a year ago. In response to Ollie's orders, his son would welcome his party guests wearing his favorite wardrobe.

Hodge stopped behind her, watching in silent admiration, awed by her professionalism. In spite of her distaste for the Daggetts, which she had no qualms about vocalizing, she gave Chazz her full attention when it came to his well being. Hodge realized that if faced with the same situation, he would be incapable of mustering the same compassion. "Hi, Rita," he said.

She jumped, dropping Chazz like a hot rock. Her hand flew to her chest. "Hodge! Jesus, if people don't stop startling me!"

"Sorry, sorry."

Rita brushed dark hair from her eyes. "I feel like a damned mortician dressing him. Can you can give me a hand?"

"A hand? My hand?" The thought of touching Chazz filled Hodge's stomach with butterflies. He backed away. "What do you want me to do?"

"Hold his head."

"His head?"

She grabbed Hodge by the sleeve and pulled him to the bed. "Morgan insists that I shave it."

Hodge placed his hands behind his back. "I can't help. I only planned to take a look at Chazz before I joined Ollie. Now, I'm sorry I did." He rolled his eyes. "Christ, he looks worse than I expected."

"His condition worsens every day. The past few weeks have been the most debilitating. Hold him while I shave his head." Hodge didn't move.

"At least, take him by the shoulders! Please. I've never shaved a man's head. I can't do it alone. It keeps flopping around." She lifted Chazz by the arm, then permitted him to slump to a sitting position. His head lolled forward. "Just hold him steady."

Hodge removed his hands from his pockets. "I'm afraid I'll let him slide. Christ, what if we slit his throat? What'll I tell Ollie?"

"Sit him up straight. Grab his armpits."

"Armpits?" The sour taste of bile clawed at Hodge's throat. "They're probably all sweaty. I'll – I'll take his hands."

"Whatever, just hold him steady." She placed a tissue on Hodge's shoulder. "In case he drools."

Hodge swallowed hard. If Chazz drooled on him, he would vomit for sure. He reached out, dreading the feel of the flaccid, yellow skin that would surely peel off if he grasped too firmly. He pleaded with his eyes, hoping for a reprieve, but saw only purpose in Rita's inflexible gaze. Gathering every bit of will, he took hold of Chazz's cold, bony, tattooed hands and lifted him upright, avoiding the snaking tubes and wires that tethered him to Morpheus.

Rita placed a towel around Chazz's neck. "All set?"

"Go ahead, shave him. Hurry." Holding the arms straight out, Hodge looked away, cringing.

"Be done in a sec." Rita spread a dab of green gel on Chazz's scalp, dampened her hands and worked it into a lather, then scraped at his pulpous skin with a disposable razor, making sure she reached every part before wiping the remaining vestige of shaving cream from the pale white dome. "There, all done."

Hodge lowered Chazz to the pillow and stared at him for an awkward moment, then backed away, unable to take his eyes off the bulbous head that lolled to the side and the pasty tongue sticking from the corner of his mouth.

With a swab, Rita coaxed the tongue into Chazz's open mouth, wiped saliva from his chin, and arranged a pillow beneath his head.

"I'm leaving now. See you at the party." Hodge backed away, moving fast, thankful for being unable to understand her muttered reply.

He arrived at Daggett's suite feeling small and weak. Ollie waited on the other side of the door, anxious to ask questions about Chazz. Hodge played out countless scenarios in his mind, wondering how Ollie would react when he laid eyes on his son. Nothing he envisioned offered any comfort. Nothing he could possibly say would prepare Ollie for the shock of seeing Chazz.

He toyed with the idea of not warning Ollie, remembering how Ollie had exploded while negotiating with the French and Japanese for PermaDream sites. How would the big man react when he discovered that Hodge had sent him the same video over and over again, praying for the miracle, deliberately avoiding the fact that Chazz had become an inanimate vegetable? Hodge didn't want to face it alone. He wanted the others to be present when Ollie made the discovery. They all had to share in the blame.

His stomach tightened and his feet felt cold and sweaty. He took a deep breath, but couldn't seem to fill his lungs. The time for thinking had passed. He steeled himself and knocked.

CHAPTER TWENTY FIVE

R ita stood by Chazz's bed listening to the pulsing tones from the console and the tiny squeaks and steady whoosh of the air conditioner; the clinical sounds of Morpheus controlling the release of nutrients and medication into the veins of Chazz Daggett while keeping tabs on his environment.

Chazz lay motionless, dressed in jeans, a dark tee shirt, leather jacket and boots. Except for the I.V.s and wires coming from his sleeves, he had the waxen look of a hairless corpse awaiting interment. Skeletal fingers fanned across atrophied thighs matched the talons of the withered tattooed eagles on the back of each hand. His only sign of life was the twitching of his closed eyes. If Rita's mother still lived, she would insist that Chazz had been cursed with *ultima patalejos*, the dance of death, inside his head.

Rita longed for Mama's gentle touch, assuring her, warming her. She switched off the bedside lamp and blinked as flickering console lights sent shadow patterns skittering up and down the walls and across the high ceiling.

The air conditioner felt too cold.

A shiver passed through her. She brushed her bare arms, aware of her racing heart, then looked over her shoulder. Nothing. Backing away from the hideous, ashen-faced figure on the bed, she hastened to the corner desk and snatched Morgan's sweater from the arm of his chair. Draping it over her shoulders, she snuggled into the cashmere softness. Warm and fuzzy, like the aura of its owner.

Feeling more at ease with a wider space between Chazz and herself, Rita peered at the desk clock. Seven fifteen. Almost two long, lonely hours until the others arrived. She sighed. A lousy situation to be in on a rainy autumn night, baby-sitting Chazz Daggett, waiting for the shit to hit the fan.

Hodge had really screwed this one up. He should have dealt with Chazz's frightening deterioration as soon as it began. When Ollie ordered life support to be maintained, he should have gone straight to Cancun and put it on the line, but nobody questioned Ollie's orders, especially Hodge, and tonight the big cabron would realize the results of his mandate. Tonight, the father would see his son for the first time in a year.

A high-pitched beep pierced the silence. Fever alarm. Rita dashed to the pulsing monitor beside the bed and tapped a waveform, silencing the ear splitting shriek. Chazz Daggett's body temp flashed digital red. 104. Rising fast. Following Morgan's instructions, she packed Chazz in Cold-Gel to combat the accelerating temperature, an operation performed by the nursing staff thousands of times over the past year.

A fly buzzed her ear and landed on the pillow. She brushed it away.

The console beeped. Body temperature, 106. Beneath pale blue lids, Chazz's eyeballs twitched faster. Perspiration streamed down his pallid face. The fly returned, lighting on his shoulder.

Without lowering her gaze, Rita reached for Morgan's newspaper on the bed stand and raised it, prepared to strike. The fly flew off in an arc and landed on the tip of Chazz's nose.

"Vanished?"

"I swear, one second it was on his nose, then it was gone."

"It probably flew off." Lorenzo brushed past Rita and stopped at the foot of the bed. "No wonder you were confused." He waved. "All these shadows."

"I'm not confused. I was staring right at it." Rita felt a twinge of irritation at his disbelief. "It didn't fly off. It faded away."

He sighed. "Why'd you call me? You know how busy I am."

"Morgan's gone, Hodge is with Ollie and I couldn't locate Denise, Jack, or Cheryl. Who was I supposed to call? This isn't the kind of thing that happens every day."

Lorenzo studied her, his handsome features expressionless.

"And stop looking at me like I'm crazy!" she snapped.

"Hey, calm down." He moved closer. "Let's brighten it up in here. This place is enough to give anyone the creeps with him lying there like that."

He switched on the bedside lamp and peered down at the pale still figure on the bed. "Look at that kisser. No wonder you leave the room so dark. He gets uglier every time I see him." He moved closer, squinting. "Christ, did you put makeup on him?"

"I didn't think it was noticeable," Rita said. "I was trying to give him a little color."

"How come he's so sweaty?"

"Fever just broke. His temperature returned to normal. For him anyway."

"How high did it go?"

"107, like always."

"Jesus." Lorenzo shook his head. "His brain cells must be screaming for help."

"This should've ended long ago."

"Yeah." Lorenzo grinned and patted Rita on the hand. "I'll stick around for a while. See if your fly shows up again."

His hand on hers felt warm and electric. She forced herself to remain composed as they sat together in the pool of light beside the bed. She felt safe with him here. No matter what happened, he had a way of keeping things under control, unlike Hodge whose presence gave her the opposite feeling. Lorenzo picked the newspaper off the floor and tossed it onto the bed stand. "Let's not mention this to Hodge," he said as if reading her mind. "He's carrying a big enough load. That girl with the fake rat bite is driving the poor guy nuts."

"Just when things were going so well."

"She claims to be a teenager, but Denise saw her on Hodge's office monitor. Says she's at least fifty, judging by her hands."

Rita felt her insides grow hot. Denise had been with Lorenzo while she shaved Chazz's head. She drew Morgan's sweater tighter around her. Denise should pay a little attention to Hodge for a change, instead of sniffing around Lorenzo. "Denise was with you?"

"Helping out in the lab."

"While Hodge faces Ollie?"

"Screw Hodge. Facing Ollie Daggett is his occupation of choice."

"Denise should support him."

Lorenzo shrugged and fell silent.

"There are times when a man needs a woman to stand by him..." As soon as she uttered the words, Rita knew by his sorrowful look that she had reminded him of his ex-wife. Damn it! A lump formed in her throat. She wanted to touch him and apologize for hurting him, but she also had the damnedest urge to kick him in the backside and tell him to get on with his life. "Sorry."

"That's okay." After a moment of silence, he said softly, "Guess you guys are tired of seeing me moping around all the time."

Startled, Rita could only reply, "Moping? You? I hadn't noticed."

"I'm tired of it too." He shook his head. "The conversation always shifts into high gear when Lorenzo shows up. I'm aware of the rules by now. Above all, keep it light. Sports or movies are ideal topics and anything pertaining to work, but for God's sake, don't ever mention women. He'll bleed all over the rug."

Rita squelched a giggle. Lorenzo had hit the nail square on the head. "You're exaggerating."

"You know it's true. It just happened again. You mentioned a caring woman and I dove straight into the dumpster."

Rita's heart fluttered. Could he be sending her a signal? Should she let him know she received it? She felt like a high school cheerleader, tongue-tied after being smiled at by the quarterback.

He'd appreciate a home cooked meal, she thought. If only she knew how to cook. Must be something. Steak? That's it! Anyone can cook steak. A big fat porterhouse, fried to a turn. Or is it roasted? No matter, she'd buy a cookbook. Tossed salad, garlic bread, a chilled bottle of wine, soft jazz and candlelight. Feeling in control, she looked straight into his dark eyes. "Lorenzo, how would you like to..."

"Hold it!" He raised a hand, silencing her. "Someone's coming."

The tapping of high heels echoed from the outer corridor. "Denise," he muttered glancing at the doorway.

Rita's heart sank as Denise rushed in, red-faced. "Renz, I'm so glad I found you." She hurried toward them. "I wouldn't have disturbed you if it wasn't important. I know how busy you are." She leaned on his shoulder and peered at Chazz. "Yech. Having a problem with your patient, Rita?"

"Chazz and I are fine. I was just chatting with Renz." Rita offered a starchy smile. "What's your problem?"

Denise stepped in front of her and touched the back of Lorenzo's hand. "It's Eddie, he's investigating Hansel and Gretel and they can't open his pod."

"Goddamn him," Lorenzo snapped. "Screwing around again. I just warned him about that." He stood. "Are we in communication with the jerk? Is he awake?"

"There's some tapping and he seems to be saying something, but it's muffled."

"Couldn't you do anything?"

"I tried everything I knew. I'm no expert."

"Emergency procedures?"

"Every one triggered automatically, but nothing happened. It acts like the escape system's locked out."

"Goddamn Eddie!" Lorenzo said. "Where's Jack?"

"At a political rally in Ocean Beach. Doesn't answer his cell phone. Someone's gone after him."

"Great!" Rita pictured an irate Jack Scanlon, drenched in sweat, his big ears a bright crimson, standing on a chair screaming about political correctness. "That'll take all night."

Denise snorted. "It isn't like Eddie's trapped in space you know. He's right upstairs for God's sake. Worst case, somebody pries him out with a crowbar and ruins one of Hodge's precious capsules."

Rita felt a professional concern for Eddie. "The oxygen's working, isn't it?" she asked. "Can he breathe?"

Denise rolled her eyes. "Of course. The door's stuck, that's all. Come on, Rita, Eddie's a big boy. Somebody even heard him call out a time or two." "Probably shouting for Mama," Lorenzo said.

Rita stood. "Eddie must be plenty scared."

"Serves the creep right," Denise said. "Maybe now, he'll change his attitude." She smiled at Rita. "He gives everybody such a bad time. Especially Renz."

Rita furrowed her brow. "Poor Renz."

Frowning, Lorenzo asked, "Hodge still with Ollie?"

Denise nodded. "The Kings are in the counting house, counting their money."

Angered by her contemptuous attitude, Rita couldn't stop herself from coming to Hodge's defense. "He's talking to Ollie because today is Chazz's birthday."

"I know, I know," Denise said. "And there's a party being planned for the little guy. Hodge and Ollie must be having a hell of a time trying to figure out which flavor of ice cream to serve." A flickering smile teased her lips. "I wouldn't miss this for anything."

Rita considered hitting her with a bedpan for mocking Hodge in front of Lorenzo until the horsefly buzzed her ear and landed on Chazz's forehead. "Lorenzo," she whispered. "On his head."

"I see it. Don't move." Cupping his hand, he eased closer to the bed.

"What's that fly doing down here anyway?" Denise asked, pinning Rita with her stare. "Isn't this supposed to be a controlled environment?"

Lorenzo snatched the fly off Chazz's forehead. "See that hand speed?" He held his closed fist under the lamplight, palm down. "And now, folks, I am about to take this mysterious creature to the men's room and make it disappear forever, then I'm off for Hansel and Gretel to do the same thing with Eddie."

As Lorenzo spoke, the horsefly materialized through the back of his hand, fanned its wings, rubbed its forelegs, and disappeared.

"Jesus Christ!" Denise said. "How the hell did you do that? Did you see it, Rita?"

"Twice," Rita replied, feeling smug over seeing Lorenzo's jaw drop, but managing a straight face.

Lorenzo opened his fist and studied his empty palm, then spoke as if in a trance. "Son-of-a-bitch passed clean through my hand and disappeared."

CHAPTER TWENTY SIX

H odge's sweaty palm slipped as he turned the cool metal of the shiny knob. He paused, then pushed open the door and entered Ollie Daggett's reception area, stopping when he heard the whirring sound of two motion- sensored cameras; same as in Cancun.

Wiggling his fingers in a self conscious attempt at a wave, he waited in clammy silence. After a long sweaty moment, the inner door opened.

Hodge's stomach flip-flopped. Drying his hands on his pants, he took a deep, shaky breath and stepped through the doorway into Ollie's inner sanctum. The familiar blast of frigid air hit him like ice water.

"Close it!" The big man's voice rumbled like the bellow of a bull, but his thick liver colored lips barely moved when he spoke. "Come on, come on! Shut the door!" He drummed club-like fingers on his desk. "You'll let in all the frigging hot air."

Before Hodge could react, Ollie slapped a button on his desk and the door closed, locking with a hollow click. A crawling sensation fingered the back of Hodge's neck as he stepped out of his shoes; the all too familiar tingle of vulnerability at being alone with Ollie. Unable to shake the corpselike image of Chazz waiting for them down in PermaDream, Hodge groped for words.

Ollie reached beneath his desk and removed a package the size of a wristwatch box wrapped in colorful paper, tied with a red satin ribbon.

Hodge winced. This year's birthday present. Looks like Ollie bought his kid a Rolex. Great! Chazz can wear it around his neck. "Know what this is, Hodge?" Hodge didn't dare reply.

"You'll see later. At the party."

Hodge smiled, feeling like an ingratiating fool. "It'll be a wonderful birthday party, Ollie."

"Your big-shot doctor's been faxing me memos, bitching about pulling the plug on my kid. It's my kid, not his. If I don't visit him, that's nobody's business but mine." He sniffed several times, then leaned forward and lowered his voice. "I took a risk coming up here. The American cops get hold of me and drag me across the border, I won't see Chazz or anybody for a long time. Besides, if Chazz doesn't move and he can't talk, what the hell does he need with me? I might as well stay safe at my villa and look at this." He pointed to a framed eight-by-ten of Chazz taken a year ago, soon after he slipped into the coma. "Sleeping like a baby," he muttered.

Hodge's stomach tightened. Soon, Ollie would know the truth.

"Anyway, hospitals give me the creeps."

"Rest assured, your son receives the best care available." Hodge flashed on the withered face of Emily Fulbright and blurted, "Could something have been wrong with Chazz before the dream?"

Ollie glared. "You suggesting my kid has a disease?"

"Of course not. Not a disease, just *something*."

"If he got something, he got it here." Ollie cleared his throat, snorted and swallowed. "Chazzy's a healthy kid. Still strong and handsome. And he gets his vitamins every day, so he'll stay that way until we can wake him up." He addressed the photograph. "We're going to have nothing but fun when you wake up, ain't that right, Chazz?"

Hodge felt as if he had swallowed an electric eel. Soon Ollie would see the chilling results of last year's birthday gift and realize that Hodge had concealed the truth. "Doctor Jackson will never give up. He's one of the top medical men in the country. I swear he..."

"Hasn't been able to bring my Chazz back."

"He's consulted with specialists from all over the world." Hodge felt himself sinking into a verbal quagmire. "And worked on a number of therapies that have shown a lot of promise."

"With no results."

"Yet." Hodge bit down hard, wishing he had kept his mouth shut. Again, he had failed to come up with the proper response. The more he said, the more he needed to account for, and Ollie seemed ready to pounce on every front. Damned if he spoke. Damned if he didn't.

Ollie tented his arms and rested his chin on knotted fingers. "You don't have the slightest idea why you're here, do you?"

Hodge saw an opportunity to initiate a calm, sensible discussion. Perhaps after plying Ollie with common sense and logic, he would broach the subject of his son's condition. He lowered his voice, choosing every word with care. "Of course I do. You're concerned about your son's well-being and you want some reassurance. And rightfully so. After all, it's been a year and you want to know that Chazz is receiving the best care money can buy. I promise you, he is. I can't tell you why he's not responding, but by God, we're doing our damnedest and we'll never quit. Never. The important thing is, the boy's alive." Hodge flashed the "thumbs-up" sign with both hands. "Chazz is alive, Ollie."

"Shut up, you mealy-mouthed asshole!" Ollie snarled.

Hodge cringed, stifled by the menace in Daggett's voice.

"This is it! No more bullshit! I want to see my son walking through that door." He lowered his voice to a harsh whisper. "I want to hear my Chazzy's voice again. I want to see him eat his birthday cake."

"We're doing everything we can." Hodge's voice sounded weak and small. "Really, we're trying."

Ollie's unblinking pig eyes pinned Hodge for a long uneasy moment, then his facial muscles relaxed. "Hey, what the hell. We'll discuss this later. Right?"

"Right."

"First we eat, then we shit. Right?"

"Right."

Ollie waved his hand in a dismissive gesture. His voice and expression became friendly again. "It's party time, Hodge. Today's a new beginning."

"*Carpe diem*," Hodge said.

"Yeah, seize that motherfucker." Ollie rubbed his palms. "Daddy's throwing Chazzy a party for his birthday and he's getting a cake and a special present. He held up the box. We'll make this birthday the best ever."

"We sure will."

"I'll be there at nine." Ollie looked past Hodge and nodded toward the door, then pulled a fresh cigar from his humidor.

Like always, Hodge had not been invited to sit.

CHAPTER TWENTY SEVEN

L ittle Albert held his breath until he felt his lungs would explode, then released it with barely a whoosh. He felt sick to his stomach. From far away, agonized screams pierced the dark silence of the forest. "No, don't squeeze me there anymore. It hurts!"

"Kitchie, kitchee koo, we're going to make a stew," one of the witches croaked.

The other said, "After we eat the meat off your bones, we'll sit you in the front yard and let the ravens pick 'em clean."

Gretel leaned forward, whispering, "The man's being taken to their house. They'll fatten him up for Halloween dinner. No noise little boy. Not a sound. Witches hear real good. Wait here." She tiptoed away.

Far off in the darkness, the man shrieked again. "Mama!" Crouched behind the boulders, Albert silently mouthed the word, "Mama," then sat still, trying to remember.

Something moved in the brush. Crouching lower, he drew his neck into his collar and squeezed his eyes shut until someone grabbed his arm. "One of them is coming back." Gretel pulled him to his feet. "If she catches us she'll take you with them. Hurry! My breadcrumb trail will lead us home."

A dark shadow rose above the pine shrubs. Gretel gasped and grabbed his hand. A witch leaped over a bush and landed in front of them, blocking their retreat. "Playing hide-and-seek, are we?" She towered above them, grinning wide, showing crooked teeth. "Got yourself a nice fat fellow, eh?" She licked her lips. Her nostrils quivered and veins pulsed at her temples. She pointed to the ground at her feet. "Get over here, boy!" Her eyes bulged. "Now!"

"No."

"No?" The witch seemed to grow taller. "You dare tell me no? Brazen little toad, ain't you?" She moved closer, eyeing Albert's fingertips. "Plenty of sweet meat on them young bones." Gretel tightened her grip.

"C'mere, sweetie," the witch cooed, spewing a foul stink into the boy's face. "Plump little lad like you shouldn't be out after dark." Her voice beckoned, this time soft and sweet. "Come home with me, little boy. I'll make you a nice hot cup of cocoa." She fingered a string of drool off her pointy chin and wiped it on her shawl, then glared at Gretel. "Turn the son of a bitch loose," she rasped.

"No." Gretel backed away, pulling Albert with her.

"I said, turn him loose!" The witch moved closer, her eyes glinting crystal green in the moonlight. She grabbed at Albert's shirt, but Gretel yanked him away. "Run, boy, run!" she said, racing into the woods.

Albert bolted, his legs pumping as fast as he could. Branches snapped and twigs raked his face as he ran through the forest. Sweat soaked his shirt. His lungs burned. Behind them, thunder boomed as the witch crashed through the brush. Her angry shrieks stabbed the night. "Give him here! Give him here!"

Gretel stopped where a trail of white led into a deeper section of woods. "My breadcrumbs. Quickly, little boy. Our cottage is enchanted. The ugly witch can't touch you there. Run!"

The forest floor shimmered silver in the moonlight as they raced along the winding breadcrumb trail through dark woods and across grassy valleys. Albert tailed Gretel around piles of boulders, through ankle deep swamps and past dark eyed caves worn into craggy rock cliff faces until Gretel dragged him into a clearing, where a dirt road fronted the edge of the woods. "Look, little boy. Home."

Albert's heart thudded like a velvet drum. A white picket fence traced a pebbled path to the front door of a thatched roof cottage. The windows glowed orange. Smoke puffed from the chimney. In a nearby thicket, a nightingale warbled. Behind them in the dark woods, twigs snapped and branches cracked.

"I want that boy," the witch bellowed.

"Hurry little boy, hurry!" Gretel shouted over her shoulder.

When they reached the front door, the witch raged out of the woods waving her arms and gnashing her teeth. She swooped down the path.

Gretel grabbed the doorknob.

Albert held his breath as the witch closed in.

"Mother!" Gretel rattled the knob and pounded the door. "Mother, open up!"

The witch stopped, spreading her arms wide. Thunder cracked. Lightning splintered a front yard tree.

"Mother, open the door! Hurry, Mother, hurry," Gretel screamed again.

Snarling, the witch pounced. Her clawed hand raked at Albert's face. He jerked his head back, dodging the sharp nails. The witch circled, licking her teeth, snarling. Another swipe. Albert dove into the dirt. The crone's sleeve brushed his face as he scrambled to his feet, backpedaling.

The door flew open, carpeting the ground with pumpkin colored light. Gretel grabbed him and they tumbled through the open doorway, rolling on the wood floor, gasping for breath. The door slammed behind them.

"Gretel honey, are you all right?" A blonde woman smiled down. Same pretty face as Gretel, same nose, same blue eyes.

"Yes, Mother, I'm all right. I brought this little boy with me. Those ugly witches wanted to eat him."

"Good girl." The woman kissed Gretel's forehead.

Gretel blushed and squeezed Albert's hand. He gulped, trying to catch his breath. "They—they wanted—to take me home with them."

"Nobody likes them." Gretel's mother patted his cheek and smiled. Her touch felt warm, stirring memories. A snarling, wart covered face appeared at the window, tongue flopping like a dying brown snake. Silver eyes glinting with crimson hatred, the witch clawed at the pane and hammered on the jamb, but her shrieks and pounding couldn't be heard inside the cottage.

"Why can't we hear her?" Albert asked.

Gretel's mother crossed to the window. "This is an enchanted cottage. Those ugly witches aren't welcome here. They can't come in." She closed the curtain.

"Once upon a time, long, long ago, Mother cast a magic spell over our cottage," Gretel said.

"A spell? Your mother cast a real spell?"

Gretel and her mother exchanged glances, then the tall blonde woman grabbed him by the throat and lifted him off the ground as if he weighed nothing. Chips of green light flickered in her blue eyes as she croaked, "Get the feeding cage, Gretel. Hurry, this boy's plenty lively. Oooooh, see how he kicks." She tore off his clothes and held him up by his ankles. "He'll be a delicious Halloween dinner, once we fatten him up. Just right for the two of us."

"I tricked him, didn't I, Mother?"

"Sure did, hon. He never suspected."

Giggling, Gretel skipped into the pantry.

Her mother cackled. "Boys never learn do they? Not every witch is ugly."

CHAPTER TWENTY EIGHT

Hodge stepped off his private elevator, crossed to his desk and switched on the lamp. Emily Fulbright's picture filled the flat screen on his desktop alongside the small circle of light that highlighted his emerald eyed statuette of the Sandman. He studied her youthful smiling countenance. So lovely. So sweet. He could almost smell the beauty soap.

Picking up the remote control, he pointed it toward the 72 inch central monitor and scanned the employee records file, calling up the video of Emily's initial employment interview.

A youthful, smiling face framed by blonde hair brightened the giant screen. In a tissue-paper-thin-voice, Emily Fulbright chatted about her love for children. Hodge glanced at his watch. Less than an hour until party time. Morg would return soon with some answers. Aiming the remote, he blanked out the monitor, picked up the phone and punched in Morgan's cell number. After a series of beeps, a computer-voice said, "Your call cannot be completed at this time. Please try again later. Your call can not be..." He hung up.

Morg must have switched his cell phone off while tending to the Fulbright kid. Probably didn't want to be disturbed. Just as well. That was Morg, the touch of a small town doctor, making rounds by daylight and leaping out of bed for emergencies at all hours of the night. Morgan believed that a doctor acquired a better feel for a patient in the home environment. Hodge looked at the blank screen, wondering what sort of environment Emily Fulbright called "home".

The elevator door opened and Denise rushed in. "Problem, Hodge," she said, her voice prickling with needles of urgency.

His hand flew to the control panel on his desk to brighten the lighting. "What now?"

"Eddie Driscoll's trapped in a dream capsule."

"Oh, terrific." Hodge grabbed the remote and turned on the monitors. "If he's damaged that piece of equipment..." The screens sequenced through the DreamLand facility. Denise snatched the control from him and aimed it. The 72 inch screen flashed to life. He recognized the Hansel and Gretel dream room. She switched to wide angle. Work lights had been turned on. Pods stood open.

Hodge frowned. "I don't get it." He loosened his tie. "What's going on?"

"I don't see Lorenzo?" she said. "He should be there."

He plopped down on the sofa. "How the hell did this happen?"

"Lorenzo's trying to find out." Denise sat beside him, smoothing her skirt over her thighs and crossing her legs. "He's certain Eddie did something to cause it."

"Goddamn Eddie!" With Ollie Daggett in town, another display of stupidity from Driscoll will only make things worse. "How the hell could he screw things up from inside the capsule?"

"Lorenzo's trying to find out."

"He better do something fast." Hodge felt sweaty. He switched on the air conditioner and a gentle breeze whispered through the room. "Don't tell me we have another Chazz Daggett on our hands. That's all we need. Two of them down in PermaDream rotting away."

"Easy, Hodge." Denise patted his knee. "Eddie's wide awake with plenty of oxygen. He's banging on the wall of the pod, shouting. They sent someone to run down Jack Scanlon."

"Good." Hodge noticed a second closed cocoon. "Who the hell's in the other pod?"

"Damned if I know. Look, there's Lorenzo." Denise uncrossed her legs and leaned forward. "Now, we'll get some answers."

They watched Lorenzo and Rita circle Eddie's pod. Rita tapped on the opalescent skin and knelt to listen with her stethoscope, then Lorenzo took a turn with it while running his hand over the seams before they joined the half dozen technicians huddled by the opened console. A burly Mexican man clutching a crowbar joined the group. Hodge activated his speaker phone and autodialed Lorenzo.

Lorenzo fumbled in the pocket of his lab coat and pulled out his cell phone. "Yeah?"

"Tell that man he's not to use the crowbar unless I personally issue the order."

Lorenzo looked up and stepped toward the camera, his face filling most of the screen as the scene played out behind him. "Calm down, Hodge, it's strictly for emergency."

"Tell him! There's no emergency unless I say so." Hodge reinforced his instructions the way Ollie Daggett always did. "One of those damn pods is worth more than he'll earn in a lifetime."

Denise cleared her throat and poured a glass of water.

Hodge nodded toward Lorenzo's image on the screen. "Why is the other pod closed?"

Lorenzo glanced toward the second cocoon and lowered his voice. "There's a kid in there."

Denise gasped.

"A kid. Oh God." Hodge's heartbeat quickened. He rose halfway, then sat again. "How?"

"Search me."

"Who is it?" Denise asked.

Lorenzo looked at his IPad. "Albert Moffit."

"How old?"

"Nine."

Hodge said, "We'll tell the parents we blew a fuse and give the kid a summer pass. I don't want any problems. Not tonight."

Denise stood. "Is the boy communicating?"

"Not verbally," Lorenzo replied, "but he's breathing. Every so often, he stops, then starts again." He shrugged. "Rita figures he's still asleep."

Hodge covered the mouthpiece and turned to Denise. "Let's not panic. I don't want to tear off that door unless we have to. Let him dream until Jack shows up."

Denise continued to stare at the screen. "That could take a while."

"So what? The little guy's having the time of his life. Why wake him up to sit in the dark. Suppose he panics and starts screaming?" He returned his attention to Hansel and Gretel and uncovered the mouthpiece. "Let him sleep, Lorenzo."

"Okay, for now." Lorenzo looked over his shoulder, then moved closer to the camera. He lowered his voice. "What're your thoughts on the fly?"

"The what?"

"He doesn't know, Lorenzo," Denise said. "I didn't tell him."

Hodge stood and began to pace. "Somebody tell me, before I take charge of the damned investigation."

"Better have a talk in private." Lorenzo motioned for Rita to join him. "We're coming up."

"I think Rita should stay down there and keep an eye on things," Denise said.

Lorenzo smiled and slipped his arm around Rita. "No sense wasting a fine mind. We'll need her input."

Denise didn't reply.

Hodge disconnected and sighed, staring at the screen. "Y'know, Rita, I envy that kid, sound asleep, dancing around with those happy witches and pigging out on gingerbread, while we're going through hell."

CHAPTER TWENTY NINE

"Here's the boy cage, Mother." Gretel backed into the room dragging a wire cage about three feet square. Bolts of pain shot through Albert's back and fire bit into his wrists when Gretel's mother took hold of the rope binding his hands and feet and yanked him into the air.

Jamming him into the cage, she adjusted his legs, then grabbed his hair and yanked his head through a square in the top, securing his neck in the opening with a leather collar. She cut the rope, leaving Albert scant room to sit with his feet pressed against a small doorway in the front of the cage and his head poking through the tiny opening.

"There. When he's not being fed, we can slide the boy cage out back with the pigs so he won't be underfoot." She filled a mixing bowl with a gray, pasty mixture. "Bulgar wheat, mashed kidney beans and plenty of lard'll stretch out that stomach real good. We'll force-feed him every hour for the first two or three weeks. Then we only have to feed him five or six times a day until Halloween. I have a feeling we'll need a bigger cage real soon."

"Hooray for Halloween!" Gretel jumped up and down. "Can we sit the skeleton in the front yard?"

"If you're a good girl and scrape all the meat off the bones." Her mother shook a finger at the little girl. "You remember what happened last year when you were sloppy."

Gretel pouted and stared at the floor. "Buzzards ruined it."

"That's right."

"I'll be a good girl mother. I'll clean them good. Honest."

"Promise?"

Gretel nodded quickly. "All right."

The little girl brightened and clapped her hands. "Wheeeeee. I love the holidays."

"Me too," her mother said, voice sharp with excitement. "Let's shove a bowl or two of this down his throat right now."

Albert sobbed. Cramps knotted his legs and arms. His shoulders ached from being crammed into the unyielding cage. Gretel peered down, eyes twinkling. "Hi, hungry little boy." She turned to her mother. "Think I'll name it Fatty."

"You'll do no such thing." Gretel's mother tied on a ruffled white apron. "I don't like you naming the Halloween boy." She unrolled a long rubber tube and attached it to a funnel. "You're too sentimental." Dipping into a bucket, she removed a glob of lard. "Naming them only causes you to think of them as pets." She spread the lard, sliding the full length of the tube back and forth between a loosely clenched hand. "Boys are not pets dear, they're food." She frowned. "Promise to eat Halloween dinner if I permit you to name this one?"

"I'll eat, mother. I promise. Oh, please."

"Well, okay, you can call it Fatty."

"Hoooooray! Can I be in charge of feeding Fatty?"

Her mother's perfect teeth gleamed when she smiled and her blue eyes sparkled. "It's quite a responsibility. You have to keep that belly skin tight as a drum."

"I'll learn, Mother. I'll do exactly what you say." Gretel jumped up and down, her bright eyes wide like diamonds. "Please, please, teach me how to feed Fatty."

"Oh, all right."

"Wheeeee." Gretel did a cartwheel.

Her mother's crisp flowered housedress swished as she crossed the room to the caged boy. The tube, with its attached funnel dangled from her greasy hand. "First thing, be sure your tube is coated with lard so it slides real good.

Albert vowed to keep his mouth shut no matter what.

"Pull that head back, so the throat's nice and straight. Like this!" Gretel's mother grabbed his hair and snapped his head back so he faced the ceiling. Hot tears burned his eyes. She poked greasy fingers into his mouth, smearing lard across his clenched teeth. Albert gagged and she tightened her grip on his hair, holding the back of his head against the cage. "This one's a fighter, all right." She handed Gretel the tube. "Take over, honey. Lard up those lips."

Gretel wiped the tube across Albert's mouth and chin. "I slide it down his throat as soon as he opens up, right, Mother?"

"Uh, huh."

Albert's lips quivered. They would never make him open his mouth. Never.

"Want me to hold his nose shut?" Mother asked.

"I'll do it." Giggling, Gretel pinched Albert's nostrils.

"Tighter, honey, squeeze tighter."

Gretel squeezed so hard she grunted. Albert held his breath, clenching his teeth until his jaw ached.

Gretel's mother laughed. "Boys are such stubborn little creatures. If you're ever in a hurry, don't waste time, shove red pepper up its nose. That mouth'll stay open for a long time."

Gretel giggled. "Look, look, he's rolling his eyes."

"Be ready with the feeding tube. He'll open up any second now. Once you get it in, leave it in his gullet. It'll be easier than jamming it in every hour."

Gretel giggled again. "I like the way the Halloween boy snorts and his eyes pop open when it slides down his throat. It makes me laugh," she tittered.

"Traditions, traditions, traditions." Her mother chuckled. "They leave behind so many warm memories. Silly little girl, I love you." She kissed Gretel on the cheek.

Gretel giggled. "Come on, Fatty-watty, open up." She tweaked Albert's nose.

Tears streamed down his cheeks. His head throbbed and his chest ached. Couldn't hold out much longer.

"Hurry Fatty, hurry." Gretel's eyes narrowed. "Open up, you!" She jabbed at his mouth with the greased tube.

"Not too rough. You'll bruise the lip meat. Be patient." Fiery green sparks seemed to dance in Gretel's periwinkle eyes.

Albert's stomach churned and blood pounded at his temples. He needed air. He opened his mouth fast to gulp down a breath. "Now Gretel!"

Gretel pushed the tube past his teeth into his mouth.

"Beautiful," her mother cackled. "Now, hold it steady and pay close attention. This is the tricky part."

Gretel released Albert's nostrils.

"I'll hold his head back," her mother said. "You wiggle the tube back and forth and work it into his belly. Take your time, Fatty isn't going anywhere. Once the tube's in his belly and the funnel's sticking out of his mouth..."

"I know." Gretel held up a long wooden rod. "Ram in the feed."

"We have to fill that stomach until it's about to burst and keep it that way. On Halloween Eve, we'll have pate de foix gras and plenty of crisp stomach skin."

An icy knot twisted deep inside Albert followed by a sparkling surge of relief. His memory had returned.

This wasn't really happening. He was in DreamLand. Sound asleep. He could wake up any time. What was the escape word? Albert forced himself to concentrate, trying to remember.

"Can I have a rose bud before I start the feeding?" Gretel asked.

"Just one, sweetie. Chew it up real good."

"Okay."

The escape word danced out of Albert's reach like a kite on the wind, then he remembered. His pulse quickened. When he spoke the word, he would awaken and hurry home to his family.

The door at his feet opened.

Small, hot hands grasped his ankle and yanked his foot through the opening. "I'm eating one of the big ones, Mother." Tiny fingers grabbed his big toe and fanned it away from the others.

The tube in little Albert's mouth prevented him from screaming.

CHAPTER THIRTY

Hodge folded his arms, leaned on his desk and smiled. "I'm not buying into this disappearing fly bullshit."

"I said the same thing at first," Lorenzo said. "But, it's not bullshit."

Rita put her hands on her hips and frowned. "Nobody's going to tell me I didn't see what I know I saw. That fly disappeared. I saw it twice."

Hodge couldn't believe this was happening. Between Ollie Daggett, Emily Fulbright and the broken pods, he felt his whole life being ripped apart. Now this! "C'mon, guys, this isn't like you, going off half-cocked over simple hallucinations."

"We all saw it," Denise said.

Hodge held up a finger. "You think you saw it. Hey, being in PermaDream with Chazz is enough to tilt anyone's wheel."

Rita looked away.

Denise rolled her eyes.

Lorenzo held out his fist. "That fly came through the back of my hand."

"Calm down, Lorenzo," Hodge soothed. "Calm down."

"Okay, forget the fly. How about the girl with the rat problem?" Lorenzo nodded at the big screen where the two gleaming pods remained sealed under work lights, awaiting the arrival of Jack Scanlon. "And, how about that?"

"Coincidence and imagination!" Hodge squared his shoulders and forced fire into his voice. "Emily Fulbright's a nut and Eddie Driscoll screwed up the capsule release mechanism. That's all. With Ollie Daggett in town, you people are feeling pressure. Hell, everyone's worked up. It's perfectly understandable."

"Not to me." Lorenzo softened his tone. "Something's wrong here, Hodge. Let's shut Morpheus down and give everything a good going over. I'll do a complete diagnostic."

Hodge raised his hands. "Oh, sure! I'll send everybody home and tell Ollie Daggett I closed DreamLand because someone saw a fly disappear." He looked toward the elevator, wondering what the hell could be keeping Morgan.

"Rita, if Morgan's late, you'll have to field Ollie's medical questions."

"Great," she said between gritted teeth. "Just what I need."

"You'll do fine." Hodge glanced at the telephone. "Cheryl should be in on this. We can use another cool rational mind around here."

"She's working at home," Denise said. "Suppose Eddie had nothing to do with the dream pods locking up?"

"Forget it." Hodge checked his Rolex. "Jesus, thirty minutes until the party. Where the hell is Jack? He'll pop open those pods in a heartbeat." He made a calming gesture with both hands. "Let's all maintain our cool. Everything's under control. He snatched up the telephone. "I'm calling Cheryl."

CHAPTER THIRTY ONE

Morgan stumbled down the stairs and staggered out the front door into the empty street. His legs wobbled as he forced himself to run to the car through the pouring rain. Wracked by a coughing spasm, he leaned against a fender and doubled over choking for air, then he straightened, tore open his collar, snapped his head back and closed his eyes. The cold rain smelled sweet and felt clean on his face. Tossing his medical bag on the seat, he slid behind the wheel, started the car, and pulled away from the curb. At a stop sign, he lowered the window for fresh air. Country music and harsh laughter drifted from a neighborhood bar.

He drove a few blocks to the 805 freeway and crossed the Mexican border at San Ysidro. Once clear of the border congestion, he pressed down on the accelerator and made his way south to the four lane Ensenada toll road. Turning the wipers on, he flicked the high beams and watched silver raindrops glisten in the headlights and splatter like crystal insects against the windshield.

He turned off the toll road and continued south along the narrow coast road that curved and ascended rugged cliffs. The fog shrouded trees resembled woolly black shadows. He stopped at one of his favorite thinking places, a large barren field at the cliff's edge. He often came here on breezy afternoons to watch hang gliders drift like gulls over the beach hundreds of feet below. Tonight, the rain swept field ended in murky gloom.

Morgan dreaded breaking the news to the others, but they needed to know. Reaching into his medical bag, he fumbled for the cellphone. Hodge answered on the first ring.

"It's me," Morgan croaked. His hand shook. He spoke slowly, trying to steady his voice. "I just left Emily Fulbright's apartment."

"Hold it." Hodge lowered his voice. "I'm moving away from the others so I can talk. Okay, I'm at my desk. What the hell's taking so long? I tried to call you."

"I'm in the car," Morgan gasped. "At the TJ Gliderport."

"What the hell are you doing there? It's almost party time. Did you forget?"

Morgan closed his eyes. His head ached and he felt thick-tongued. "The Fulbright girl. She's – she's..."

"Never mind her. Get back here fast. Everyone's going nuts. Lorenzo's here. He wants to shut down Morpheus."

"He's right! Something's gone wrong. Close it down."

"Oh sure, just like that!" Hodge's voice tightened. "For God's sake, Morgan, Ollie Daggett's here. There are thousands of people waiting to..."

"Stop arguing with me! Jesus Christ, man, I just left Emily Fulbright." Morgan paused, feeling sick to his stomach. Tears stung his eyes. "I can't handle this, Hodge. I'm hurting so bad."

Morgan told Hodge about taking the elevator to the top floor, and how he stood in the dark hallway outside her apartment. "I didn't know it at the time, but Emily had smashed the light bulb. She was waiting in the dark to make sure I was alone and the man I claimed to be." He choked out the words. "Couldn't see a lick. Followed her into the apartment. Smelled like rotting garbage. No light at all. I told her I couldn't see to examine her. Said I had to switch on a lamp. She refused."

Morgan blinked back tears, fighting to draw a deep breath. The wind gusted, blowing cold rain through the open car window. "We sat in her dark, foul-smelling living room. She wouldn't let me near her. I kept explaining how the nervous system can break down, told her I had medication to calm her. Figured I could at least get her to turn on some lights. I was still thinking she could have a Progeroid disorder, and I wanted to see her face." He shuddered, recalling the moment when Emily finally consented to light a lamp. "She turned on the lights and proved us all wrong," he whispered.

"What?"

Morgan's mouth went dry. He tugged at his collar and muttered, "Beady eyes. Long, yellow teeth." He sobbed. "And she —she – she..."

"What the hell are you saying?"

Morgan lowered his voice, speaking between clenched teeth. "She had a tail."

"You're talking like a fool," Hodge croaked.

Morgan spoke in a monotone. "Found something in her kitchen. Fed it to her in warm milk before I left."

"What was it?"

"Rat poison."

Silence, then Hodge gasped. "You killed her?"

"I'm a murderer, Hodge."

"God, Morg."

"Listen. Tell Lorenzo I'm convinced there's some kind of bizarre crossover aberration affecting Morpheus. I think it's a computer virus capable of infecting humans."

"Computer virus? For Christ's sake, Morg, now you're talking like a nut."

"Don't think about it. Don't waste time. Just tell Lorenzo. And Cheryl. And close that place down. God only knows what will happen next."

Hodge didn't respond.

Tears flooded Morgan's eyes and streamed down his cheeks. "I murdered Emily Fulbright," he rasped. "I took a life!" His heart slammed in his chest as if trying to break through his rib cage. "God forgive me!"

Throwing the car into drive, he stomped on the gas pedal. The motor roared and the wheels spit mud and pebbles as the car skidded sideways, then straightened and raced toward the black nothingness at the cliff's edge. As it launched into space, Morgan clutched the wheel, holding his foot to the accelerator, praying aloud. "Our Father, who art in Heaven..."

CHAPTER THIRTY TWO

Unable to speak and afraid to think, Hodge squeezed the silent telephone to his ear and listened, praying to hear Morgan's voice again. This couldn't be. Not Morgan. Jesus, his friend, Morgan.

"Something wrong, Hodge?"

Denise's husky voice at his shoulder jolted him. Had she overheard?

"Who's on the phone?"

Thank God. She hadn't heard a thing. Above all, he needed to be calm.

Denise shook his arm. "Is anyone on the phone?"

Hodge pulled away and waved for her to be still. He heard an electronic chirping sound, then the recorded voice. "Your party is not answering at this time. Please try again later..."

Across the atrium, the crack of light bordering the drapes disappeared. Oh Jesus, Ollie had turned out his lights. Party time.

Tiny sparks pinwheeled before Hodge's eyes as he glanced at Denise and the others. Telling them about Morg now would serve no purpose. They would leave him to face Ollie alone. He decided to wait. After the party he would sit everyone down and break the news.

He felt cold and sweaty. His voice quivered as he spoke over the recording. "Okay, Morgan, I'll see to it. Drive carefully." Slowly, Hodge clicked off and lowered the phone. He faced the others, unsure of what to say, but aware that he had to deliver an Academy Award performance. Words poured from him like an actor reading from a script. "That was Morgan. Everything's under control."

167

"Will he make it back in time?" Denise asked.

"He's going to be delayed with the Fulbright girl. He's counting on Rita to handle the medical details with Ollie."

"Dammit," Rita muttered.

"I'll go with you," Lorenzo said.

"Me too." Denise stood beside him.

"We're all going," Hodge said. "First, let's contact Hansel and Gretel. I want to be notified as soon as Jack Scanlon shows up."

"Lorenzo better do that." Denise took the phone and handed it to Lorenzo. "You go on ahead, Rita. Ollie's on his way. Wouldn't want him to see Chazz without someone there who knows what's going on."

"We'll be down in a minute," Hodge said.

"Hopefully before Daggett shows up," Lorenzo added.

"All right, all right!" Scowling, Rita headed for the elevator.

"Deal with Ollie, Rita," Hodge called after her. "He respects you. You're the medical expert. I can't help. I know nothing about medicine, everybody knows that."

As the elevator doors closed behind Rita, Hodge muttered, "She knows I can't help."

Part of him felt detached, as if observing his actions through a glass ceiling, watching his lips move, unable to stop the lies from flowing. "Morgan gave the Fulbright girl a sedative. Poor kid. She's suffering some kind of genetic disorder. Had a nervous breakdown because of it. Jesus, it never fails. Everything happens at once." He shrugged. "Oh well, at least it's genetic." Hodge paced back and forth while Lorenzo spoke on the phone.

"Everything'll be fine, you'll see. In a few hours DreamLand will be closed, then, we'll get to the bottom of this."

Lorenzo hung up, grabbed Denise by the arm and headed for the elevator. "I just spoke with Jack. He's picking up Cheryl and heading here. Let's go."

"All right!" Hodge forced a smile and clapped his hands together, feeling like a cheerleader for a losing team. "We have a party to attend."

CHAPTER THIRTY THREE

Rita thought of ghosts as she stood in the dark corridor peering through the mirrored glass into the huge shadowy PermaDream facility. The comatose form of Chazz Daggett reposed in a far corner, where red, green, blue, and amber L.E.D.'s pulsed in time to beeps, giving testimony to his pitiful existence. She listened, thinking she might hear the buzz of the horsefly, but all was silent, save for the sibilant hiss of air conditioning and the monotonous beep of life support.

Her skin crawled at the thought of facing the crude, foul-mouthed, Ollie Daggett again. If only Morgan would show up. He would know how to handle that creep.

She felt a puff of air. Somewhere in the gloomy passageway someone had opened a door. Rita glanced over her shoulder, listening, longing to be someplace else, preferably some place with bright lights, loud music, and laughter.

She heard footsteps and raspy breathing, then caught a whiff of cigar smoke.

Daggett!

Pressing her forehead to the cool glass and shielding her eyes with cupped hands, she watched the PermaDream door slide open. A hairy hand grasped the jamb, then Ollie Daggett's ham-sized head appeared in the doorway, brow furrowed, unlit cigar stump pressed between thick, bloated lips. "Hey!" he bellowed, glassy pig-eyes glittering in the reflected light from the bedside console.

Rita held her breath as Ollie stepped into the room carrying a cake box that barely covered his open palm.

"Anybody here?"

Rita crossed herself and whispered the prayer her mother had taught her when she was a little girl. "Keep me safe, keep me well, bless me with thy spirit, dear Jesus."

"It's time for the fucking party," Ollie roared. "Where the hell is everybody?"

She crossed herself again while he stepped closer to Chazz, then dedication overcame fear and she found herself hurrying to the open door. Better to stay close. Ollie looked to be heart attack type AAA and he was about to receive the shock of his life.

Unaware of her presence, the big man craned his neck toward the bed at the far end of the long room. Rita barely heard him whisper, "Chazzy boy, wake up, Daddy's here."

Afraid to breathe, she stood still, waiting.

"Surprise Chazz," he whispered. "Happy Birthday." Ollie moved forward, then stopped as if he had slammed into a glass wall. "Chazz," he cried, backing away. "Jesus, what'd they do to you, boy? What'd they do?" His massive body trembled.

Rita eased toward him and reached out to touch his elbow, speaking softly. "Mister Daggett."

Ollie whirled toward her, eyes wide, arms outstretched in an expression of helplessness. His lips moved in silent speech while his teeth still clamped tight to the cigar butt. His sweaty face contorted with rage.

Icy fear held Rita immobile. "Don't touch me!" she warned.

"Look at Chazzy!" He grabbed her sleeve and dragged her to the bed. "Look at my kid." He bent closer to Chazz. His shoulders slumped. His voice cracked. "Jesus, he looks like you starved him to death."

Rita remained silent, listening to Ollie's ragged breathing, then she came to life inside. "Let go!" she snapped, yanking her arm away. "I had nothing to do with this."

"You were supposed to feed him, give him vitamins," Ollie rasped.

"He's fed intravenously," Rita said, brushing her sleeve. "This isn't a health resort, you know. Your son's lucky to be alive."

"Hodge sent me video-disks. Chazzy looked great."

"He's been at this weight for months," Rita said, her rising temper gathering energy with each passing moment. "If you'd have visited him once in a while, you'd know these things."

"You shut up!" Ollie threw the cake box, smearing the mirrored wall with frosting and crumbs. "Don't preach to me, bitch! What I do is none of your business." He towered over her, his big face inches from hers. "Where's that spook doctor anyway? You're a waste of time."

"Doctor Jackson has been delayed," she fired back. "An emergency." In spite of her anger, Rita felt pity for Ollie. Morgan would want her to show compassion. "I realize this is a shock. I'm sorry."

"Save the bullshit." Ollie balled his fists. "Who's the asshole who painted my kid to look like a fucking drag queen?"

"I'm the asshole!" Rita snapped, her voice tight with sudden fury. "I put a little makeup on him so he wouldn't look so awful when you saw him for the first time. I'm also the asshole who washed him, shaved his head, and dressed him in that stupid costume for your asinine party. I even changed his stinking diapers."

Ollie shook his fist. "You made my kid look like a goddamn fruit."

"Don't shake your fist in my face," she snapped. "I'm not afraid of you."

Ollie threw his cigar to the floor. "We'll see about that, sweetheart."

The lights came up around them. "Here we are." Lorenzo strode in followed by Denise and Hodge. He eyed the cake oozing down the glass wall. "Started the party without us, huh?"

Ollie scowled as Lorenzo approached. "Great, the class clown is here."

Lorenzo stopped beside Rita and eyed Chazz. "Speaking of class, when do we sing Happy Birthday?"

"Lorenzo's only trying to lighten things up," Hodge said quickly. "After all, this is a party. Hey, good news, guys, Jack Scanlon's on his way. I told him to pick up Cheryl. They know more about this than I do."

"You said Chazz was okay, Hodge. You sent me videos."

"I thought Morgan could ... I thought we..." Hodge backed away. "I'm sorry."

Ollie's anger seemed to drain from him like water through a sieve and his eyes glistened with tears. His voice sounded weak and strained. "I kept my part of the deal. Stayed out of the way. Kept the cash flowing. Never once turned you down." He turned to Chazz. "Jesus, my kid looks like a scarecrow. Your famous doctor ain't even here to tell me what's going on."

"Rita's here," Hodge said. "She can tell you."

"We already talked," Ollie said. "I'm tired of that cold chile pepper." He squared his shoulders. "You've been jerking me around for a year, Hodge. Look at my son." He shook his head. "Tonight, we try something Ollie believes in." He stuck his hand into his coat pocket, produced a small brightly wrapped package. "Happy birthday, Chazzy," he cooed, untying the satin ribbon. He tore away the colorful paper, opened the box and withdrew a gleaming syringe with a vial of amber liquid on its tip.

Nobody moved as he stroked his son's forehead. "Everything'll be okay." The tender smile on Ollie's face would have done the Virgin Mother proud, but the words he whispered came straight from the belly of hell. "Tonight, Daddy's going to wake you."

Rita rushed toward him. "You don't think you're going to..."

"Of course not!" Ollie faced her, holding the syringe flat on his palm. "You are! Straight into the blood stream, little sister. Take it. Hook him up."

She stopped and backed up holding her hands at her side. "I will not!"

"Sure you will." Ollie's other hand dropped into his pocket and came out holding a nickel plated thirty-eight.

Rita froze, determined to match Ollie's glare. From the corner of her eye, she saw Lorenzo ease to the side. Careful, Lorenzo. Careful.

"I can't give an untested drug to your son," she said. "I have no idea what the dosage should be."

"Every drop," Ollie snapped. "You're wasting time."

"I don't even know what it is."

"Methamphinephrine-G," Ollie growled. "Straight from the lab. Stimulates the shit out of rats and monkeys. It's untested on humans." He nodded toward Chazz. "Until tonight."

"I can't do it," Rita said. "I won't!"

"Move!" Ollie cocked the pistol. "Life doesn't mean shit to me without Chazz." He aimed the gun at Rita's head. "I swear, we'll all die tonight."

Lorenzo edged closer. Rita held her breath. A few more steps.

With a sudden flick of his wrist, Ollie aimed the thirty-eight at Lorenzo's chest.

Lorenzo stopped. "Easy, man. I only want to help."

"Back up, handsome," Ollie said. "I don't need any bullshit from you."

"I'll give him the medicine," Lorenzo said.

"You? What do you know?"

"I've helped before."

"So I should trust you?"

Lorenzo shrugged. "Forget trust. Try logic. Rita doesn't have the heart for this. Your son means nothing to me. Chazz brought this on himself. I give him the shot and he dies, it's on you. He lives and he's out of here. Either way, I don't have to look at him any more. Come on, Ollie, keep your gun on me while I do it."

Ollie snorted. "Who the fuck're you, Humphrey Bogart?" He glanced at the others. "This jerk thinks he's in a Goddamned movie. Okay, Bogie, you asked for it." He placed the syringe on the bed beside Chazz. "Do it!"

As Lorenzo picked up the syringe, Ollie grabbed his wrist and pressed the gun barrel to his ear. "Do it right movie star, or your face'll be all over the wall."

Lorenzo tilted the syringe and drew the amber liquid into the cylinder, then pulled the vial off the end and pressed the plunger, firing a spurt from the needle's tip. Grabbing at the IV tube, he followed the smaller conduit jutting from its side and pressed the tip of the needle to the red cap.

Sweat poured down Ollie's face. He stepped back, still pointing the gun at Lorenzo's head. "Do it!"

Holding Ollie's gaze, Lorenzo pressed the plunger, watching in silence as the amber liquid left the cylinder, wound through the tube, and entered Chazz Daggett's blood stream.

A high-pitched electronic squeal fractured the silence. Chazz twitched and the monitor flashed, its red glow streaking across the mirrored walls, reflecting in Ollie Daggett's small eyes. "What the hell is that?"

"Fever alarm!" Rita rushed to the console and tapped at a waveform on the touch screen. The high-pitched beep continued. She tapped it again. "Dammit, I can't turn it off."

"Temperature's already 104," Denise called from another monitor.

Rita pulled open the bedside refrigeration unit, unrolled a Cold-Gel blanket and tossed it to Lorenzo. "Cover him!"

Lorenzo tucked the cover under Chazz's chin and pressed the sides tight against him.

"Stop that racket!" Ollie waved the thirty-eight, then aimed it at the flashing monitor. "I'll put a bullet in it. I mean it."

"106!" Denise said. "He's burning up."

Rita slapped at the touch screen. "I feel so damned helpless."

"The cut-off switch, where is it?" Lorenzo opened the console and peered inside.

"108," Denise said.

"It's never gone that high before," Rita added.

The alarm wavered, sputtered, and died, leaving silence. Lorenzo straightened, holding up a fingernail clipper.

Ollie lowered the pistol and mopped his brow. "What the hell was that all about?"

"His temperature is erratic," Rita said.

Ollie looked past her, wide eyed and ashen faced, except for his pink cheeks. He backed away, pointing toward the bed. "Jesus Christ, his face!"

Oozing red sores peppered Chazz Daggett's sweat-soaked head. A bright red spot appeared on his cheek, formed a blister and broke, leaving a circle of raw flesh which quickly turned pink, then disappeared. Another blister appeared on his nose.

Rita shook her head. "I don't understand."

"It's this Goddamn thing." Ollie yanked the Cold-Gel blanket off Chazz and tossed it away. "Get it the hell out of here."

"Temperature's 105," Denise said.

"Going down, thank God." Rita stared at Chazz her eyes wide in disbelief.

"What's happening to him?" Lorenzo asked.

"I don't know." Rita leaned closer. "Those lesions look like burns. Look, they heal in seconds." A red spot appeared on Chazz's lip. Another on his twitching eyelid.

Lorenzo turned to Hodge. "Look, they're all over the back of his hands too."

"Where the hell is Morgan?" Rita asked.

"With Emily Fulbright, dammit!" Hodge snapped.

"Get him on the phone," Lorenzo said.

"No!" The blood drained from Hodge's face. "Rita can handle things. Morgan's too busy right now."

"What the hell's wrong with you, Hodge? We need help." Lorenzo pulled out his mini-phone and flipped it open. "I'm calling him."

"Wait!" Hodge held up his hand. "You don't understand. Morgan turned his cell phone off."

Ollie pushed past Lorenzo, grabbed Hodge by the throat and bent him over a desk with the pistol to his head. "Do something, motherfucker."

"Look!" Denise cried out, backing away, her voice trembling. "Chazz."

Ollie peered over his shoulder at the bed. "Jesus Christ!"

"Jesus, he's moving," Hodge said in a hoarse whisper.

"It worked." Ollie gulped. "The shot worked. Look at his hands."

Chazz's bony fingers quivered, making hollow thudding sounds as they tapped his leather jacketed ribs, then he pressed his palms together over his heart.

"Looks like he's praying," Lorenzo muttered.

"Or pleading." Denise moved closer to Lorenzo.

Rita stared in disbelief. "Sweet Jesus, he's waking up." She crossed herself.

"Stand back," Ollie shouted. "Give the kid room to breathe."

Chazz shivered and moaned. His bony head bounced up and down, teeth clicking like castanets. His shoulders shook and his arms jerked, sending wires and tubes flying. He went limp, then stiffened again and again as if jolted by a series of electric shocks before his body collapsed. His face went slack, then his eyes popped wide open.

"He's awake," Denise whispered.

"Chazzy," Ollie croaked, moving closer to the bed. "Happy birthday, son. It's Daddy."

Chazz stared at the ceiling, eyebrows raised, nostrils flared, a look of unfocused terror gleaming in his pale blue eyes.

"Talk to me, Chazzy boy," Ollie said.

Chazz's lips opened and closed like a dying carp's.

"Come on, talk to Daddy. Say it. Daddy."

Chazz raised to a sitting position. His head wobbled and his face contorted as if he had eaten something bad. "Dah!" he croaked in a half whisper.

"He said it. He said it! Say it again. Daddy."

Chazz twisted his body, until his feet hung off the bed. "Dah!" His massive head fell forward, then snapped to the side, tongue lolling from his mouth. "Dah!" Spittle flew from Chazz's painted lips as he struggled to his feet. "Stay there, Chazz. Sit down again." Ollie backed away, glaring at Lorenzo. "Do something. I can't stand seeing him like this!"

"Sorry," Lorenzo said.

Chazz stumbled forward, arms outstretched. His legs gave way and he dropped to his knees with a thud.

"Back to bed, Chazz, back to bed!" Ollie ordered. "Do something for him, you bastards. I swear, you'll all die."

Chazz groaned. Drool ran from the corner of his mouth and his head shook like the plastic dog in the back window of Rita's car. He stood again, his face twisting into something between a grin and a frown. "Dah!" He tottered toward Ollie, like a giant marionette. "Dah!"

Ollie's nose wrinkled and his chin trembled. His eyes brimmed with tears. "Chazzy," he whispered. "My Chazzy. I love you, sonny boy. Daddy loves you." He raised the gun.

Rita heard a deafening crack and saw blood and brain spray the wall behind Chazz. A quarter-sized hole bloomed in the center of his forehead. The younger Daggett stiffened and fell backward, toppling like a tree. His lips moved wordlessly, even after hitting the ground.

Lorenzo pulled Rita to the floor behind the nurses' desk. "Quiet," he whispered, holding her tight. The caustic smell of gunpowder permeated the air, burning her nose. Rita held still. What now? Had Hodge and Denise taken cover or were they facing Ollie's wrath alone? Would he make good on his threat and execute everyone? She closed her eyes and prayed. Dear God, let them be safe. Please God, protect us all. Please.

Another shot exploded in front of the desk. Rita squeezed her eyes shut. Hodge? Denise? She opened her eyes as Ollie Daggett hit the floor, his glassy pig eyes inches from hers, the top of his head a jagged crown of shattered skull spilling gray matter that had been his brain.

CHAPTER THIRTY FOUR

Cheryl felt better after laying down the law to Eddie Driscoll. Later, she'd confront him and reinforce her promises in no uncertain terms. No one must ever find out about her foolish dalliance with the dream Lorenzo. Her career would be ruined.

The sound of someone pounding on the door startled her before the gruff voice hit her like a bullet. "Open up, Cheryl!"

Jack!

"Open up!"

She imagined him standing on the balcony, stark naked, slapping the cat-o-nine tails against his palm, hell-fury seething in his green-flecked eyes. Her mouth worked from side to side. Could her mind still be playing tricks? Too much time had passed for a delayed post synaptic response, unless she was indeed in the middle of some kind of hallucinatory flashback.

"Cheryl." Jack's voice sounded as if his lips were pressed to the door crack. "If you're okay, let me know, because I'm about to break down this door."

"All right, all right." The door wouldn't stop him. Not in this ungodly dream. Cheryl crossed the room, threw it open, scrunched her eyes shut and stood trembling and vulnerable. Jack grabbed her shoulder. His touch sent a silent scream knifing through her.

"You could've answered the phone. Damn near wore out my redial on the way over here." After a pause, his gruff tone softened. "Hey, Cheryl, you look awful. Jesus, what the hell's wrong?"

She opened her eyes to see a fully dressed Jack.

Backing away, she breathed hard, as if a cold hand had taken hold of her heart and squeezed, pumping ice through her veins. "What do you want?"

"Big problem at DreamLand. They rousted me out of a meeting. Tried to call you too. Asked me to stop by and get you. Let's go."

Her mind exploded in a flurry of shame, confusion, and worst of all, fear. "Jack?" She lowered her hands and stammered, "Are you – are you – really Jack?"

He raised an eyebrow. "No, I'm fucking Woodrow Wilson." He held out his arms. "Hey, Cheryl, don't go crapping out on me. They need us at DreamLand. That dip-shit, Eddie got himself trapped in a Hansel and Gretel dream pod."

"Trapped?"

"Pods won't open. Some kid's trapped too. Lorenzo's panicking." Jack snorted. "Software people can't handle emergencies. He's already screaming about hardware failure. Come on Cheryl. Get dressed. They need us to bail them out."

Cheryl searched his dark eyes for the telltale glimmer of green sparks and found none. Thank God, the real Jack. Tears streamed down her cheeks as she ran to him and fell into his arms.

"What the hell's gotten into you?"

His warmth and the softness of his flannel shirt comforted her. "Just hold me a minute," she whispered. "I'm scared."

He patted her back. "It's okay. We're in this together."

Cheryl's lips trembled as she tried to smile. Something wrong with the pods. A puzzle to unravel. Questions to be answered. A problem she could sink her teeth and her mind into. Eddie's trapped himself in a pod. The circle is small, Eddie Driscoll, she thought.

Jack squeezed her shoulders and held her at arm's length, his eyes searching hers. "It won't take us long to figure out what's wrong. Nothing's changed. Like always, it's you and me against those half-wits. With me?" Smiling through the spate of unanswered questions, bruises, and tingling pain, Cheryl took a deep breath and permitted her mind to settle. "Let's go."

CHAPTER THIRTY FIVE

The concussion from the gunshots rang in Rita's ears and the acrid stench of gunpowder burned her sinuses. Ollie Daggett lay on his back, the shattered remains of his huge head inches from her face. His remaining eyeball stared toward the ceiling and a thin stream of smoke curled from his nostrils. In spite of Rita's experience as an intern in the gore soaked UCSD trauma center, the grisly sight shocked her. She turned away, gagging.

Lorenzo whispered in her ear. "You okay?"

She nodded, battling to regain her composure. "I'm okay."

"Omigod! Their heads," Hodge croaked from somewhere nearby. "Look at their heads!"

Rita forced herself to speak in a cool detached voice, the hallmark of her latter days at the trauma center. "I'm coming, Hodge." She started to rise.

Lorenzo held her back. "Wait." His dark eyes locked with hers, his expression offering more respect than shock. "You're terrific, Rita." He took her hand and squeezed as they rose together.

Gun smoke hung in the air like wisps of tattered gray lace. Hodge and Denise stood by the edge of the console where the shadows began.

Denise sobbed, ashen-faced, eyes glazed and out of focus. A smoking Beretta dangled from her hand. She huddled behind Hodge, mumbling, "I had to. I had to. He was going to murder us."

"It's all right. It's all right." Hodge's voice faltered as he stared at the bodies. "You saved our lives," he whispered. "It all happened so fast. Jesus Christ, their heads." He turned away and leaned over the console, trying to catch his breath.

Chazz lay on his back, foot-to-foot with his father, mouth open, eyes bulging, face frozen in an expression of perpetual surprise. A scarlet rosette bloomed in the middle of his forehead, like a ubiquitous third eye. A thin red line oozed from it, trickling down his cheek into the dark pool beneath his head.

Lorenzo eased up beside Denise and gently relieved her of the pistol. "Where the hell did you get this thing?"

"I bought it when we moved to Mexico," she said, her voice trembling. "I never thought I'd..."

Lorenzo pocketed the Beretta. "I'll lock this up for the police." He yanked sheets and blankets from the bed. "Better cover the Daggetts."

"Wait." Rita hurried to the bodies. "I'd better check their vitals."

"This is a crime scene," Lorenzo said. "Don't touch anything else."

She pushed past him, not wanting to ruin their prospective romance, but determined to stand her ground. Kneeling beside Chazz, she reached for his bony wrist. "This'll only take a moment."

"For Christ sake, Rita, their brains are all over the floor."

In spite of the obvious she checked their pulses. When she finished, she stood. "They're dead."

"No kidding."

"Don't be sarcastic," she said, speaking softly. "The Federales would be bitching all night, knowing there was a medical person who failed to check the victims for vitals. Rita had learned long ago that police investigators on both sides of the border could be incredibly anal when it came to determining time of death. She checked her watch. "It's ten-fifteen."

"Okay, okay. Let's go," Lorenzo said.

"Do we have to leave them there like that?" Hodge asked in a shaky voice. "On the floor?"

"Why not?" Lorenzo covered the corpses. "They're dead. To hell with them. Eddie and the kid are still alive. Let's get them out of the pods." He pulled out his cell-phone. "I'm calling Morgan. If we ever needed him..."

"Forget it," Hodge said. "I told you, his phone is dead." He slipped his arm around Denise. "We'll meet Morgan in my office. You two find Jack and Cheryl and get Eddie and the Moffit boy out of those pods."

Rita felt a twinge of compassion as she studied Hodge's pale pinched face. Nothing but a scared kid trying hard to be a man. She touched his shoulder. "I know how rough this has been on you."

He shrugged her off. "I can handle it." He licked his lips. "Keep me posted Lorenzo."

Lorenzo slipped the cell-phone back into his pocket. "Okay, Hodge, you're the boss."

"Stay in touch through visual and audio."

"Will do."

"I'm still in control," Hodge muttered to Denise as he guided her around the shrouded corpses on the blood soaked floor.

Rita watched them leave, then exchanged glances with Lorenzo. "I thought we were finished," she said hugging herself. "Daggett would've killed us. Denise saved our lives."

"Guess so."

"Poor Hodge. Did you see his eyes?"

"Screw Hodge. It's been a lousy day for all of us." Lorenzo pulled her to him and slipped an arm around her. "C'mon, we have to open those pods. Let's get Eddie and the kid out, then we'll hold Hodge's hand."

Feeling as if she had literally been taken under his wing, Rita allowed Lorenzo to lead her away from the cold tile and mirrored glass of PermaDream, leaving the Daggetts stretched out on the floor. The secret would soon become public knowledge and everybody with a pimple on their nose would file a lawsuit. Unable to stop shivering, she snuggled closer to Lorenzo's warmth.

They hurried through the corridor around the structure's inner circumference. As they passed the Gallery of Angels, Rita felt a pang for little Albert Moffit, remembering the children who had dreamed their final moments in the arms of Morpheus. Brave little people who left behind a world of pain and suffering for a few moments of bliss in one of Lorenzo's dream worlds before slipping over to the other side.

Albert Moffit had no cancer, disease, or any other life diminishing death sentence. He was a healthy boy who deserved the chance to enjoy a full and productive life. She looked up at Lorenzo, knowing he shared her thoughts. The grim look on his face reflected his concern. Rita vowed to do her best to free Albert from the dream pod and bring him back to the real world, safe and sound.

Lorenzo continued holding her as they rode the elevator up to the main level. Without a word, he gave her one last squeeze before the door opened, then removed his arm from her waist and hurried down the empty corridor behind Storybook Land.

As they approached the rear entrance the ceiling lights went out and the night lights came on. "Looks like Hodge finally took my advice and shut the place down," Lorenzo growled. "About time."

Rita opened the door to the rear entrance of the Enchanted Forest. "Let's go. Albert needs you."

"And I need Eddie out of that pod so I can fire him."

CHAPTER THIRTY SIX

Guards escorted stragglers from the DreamLand lobby, security doors closed, motion sensors activated, and pastel light panels darkened a section at a time, spiraling around the atrium perimeter from top to bottom like falling dominos. The muted glow of emergency exit signs cast ghost-like shadows in darkened hallways.

In Hodge's office, Denise Moore's computerized voice emanated from a speaker. "It is ten-thirty. DreamLand is closed. Full power remains in the executive suite, Storybook Land, and the research and development section. All exits are secure. Automated pass-key access activated. There are fourteen people on the premises. Twelve on lobby level. Two on level five."

A bead of perspiration ran down the nape of Hodge's neck when the music died on the other side of the glass in the darkened atrium. He turned from the window, wondering if he would ever hear it again.

Denise slumped on the sofa, hollow-eyed, staring straight ahead, looking fragile and haggard. "Sixteen," she muttered.

"What?"

"Sixteen people in the building. The sensors didn't recognize the Daggetts."

"They won't. They're heat and motion sensors." Hodge pointed the remote at the bank of monitors on his office wall. The dim lighting of PermaDream filled the big screen. "There they are. Cold and still." The two blood spattered corpses lay on the floor, foot to foot, the sheets and blankets beside them.

"Oh, Jesus." Denise lowered her eyes and turned away. "Didn't Lorenzo cover them?"

"Thought he did. Guess he changed his mind. Doesn't surprise me. He was being a pain in the ass about leaving the crime scene intact." Hodge pointed the remote and switched cameras. A pair of klieg lights whitewashed the normally soft shadows and twinkling lights of Storybook Land, highlighting the shimmering opalescence of the two tightly sealed dream capsules. Multicolored cables spilled from the base of each pod like the innards of a gutted fish. "See?" Hodge waved the remote. "I can run the whole damned show from right here."

"When are you calling the police?" Denise asked. "I'd like to get this over with."

"Soon." Hodge pondered telling her about Morgan, but decided to hold off. Denise had just taken a life. Besides, Hodge was unable to even think about his friend without choking up. "I'll call the cops after they free the kid and get him the hell out of here. It won't take long now." He nodded toward the display. "Lorenzo and Rita are figuring things out already."

Rita stood at the console peering over Lorenzo's shoulder. As he tapped at a touch pad, a hi-speed sequence of screens flashed by. Rita recognized the leafy path through the Enchanted Forest where the witch had chased her during the only dream trip she had ever taken. Unwilling to relive her uneasiness, she turned away and faced a group of technicians huddled over one of the consoles checking test equipment, probes, and wires.

A young, blonde woman nodded. "Hi, Rita. Need something?"

"How about setting me up with some of those respiration sensors we used in the trials. I want to monitor the pods."

"Give me twenty minutes. I'll tie them in to the COM ports."

Jack's voice boomed from the doorway. "Can't you people do anything without us?"

Cheryl pushed past Jack and went straight to the sealed pods. Rita felt a slight lessening of tension knowing they had arrived. "We have a big problem here," she said.

"It better be big," Jack snorted. "I left a major political rally."

"Too bad," Lorenzo said. "What'll the, 'California Asshole Party' do without their poster boy?"

Despite the tension, Rita bit down hard to keep from laughing.

Jack's ears reddened. Muttering to himself about the mental frailties of software developers, he elbowed a technician aside and joined Cheryl at the pods, checking waveforms on a signal analyzer. "Nine out of ten times, we find out it's the goddamned software." He grabbed a probe and prodded a circuit. "If you ask me, Lorenzo's little toady played with one bit too many."

"Let's check the pre-amps," Cheryl said.

Jack grunted agreement as she read off test points and voltages from a diagram.

Lorenzo studied the screen in front of him, then looked up at Rita. "Maybe something *is* wrong with the program. Better run a virus check."

"Doesn't Morpheus do regular scans?"

"We upload virus signatures every day, but that doesn't guarantee something new hasn't slipped in. These things can move fast. I'll run a scan, then do a parity check with our last backup. If everything looks kosher, we'll look at the pod release sequence to see why it's not triggering."

Lorenzo worked the touch pad, nodding as the screen in front of him flashed a series of messages:

CHECKING MEMORY FOR VIRUSES

NO VIRUSES FOUND

CHECKING ROOT STRUCTURE AND EXECUTABLES

NO VIRUSES FOUND

STARTING FULL DATA SCAN

"Here we go," he said.

A flashing red horizontal bar graph popped up on the screen and incremented from left to right. Above it, a percentage number increased, showing how much of the scan had completed. When the graph reached ninety seven percent, it stopped and beeped. A new message flashed.

*THE FOLLOWING FILES ARE OPEN

AND CANNOT BE SCANNED.*

PLEASE CLOSE FILES TO COMPLETE.

"What the hell is this?" A list of files scrolled down the screen, most of them under the Hansel and Gretel subdirectory, some under Pied Piper and a few under Cheryl's development subdirectory.

"Hey, Cheryl," Lorenzo called out. "Some of your development files are open."

"What?" Cheryl's hand flew to her throat and her eyes grew wide, as if she'd been struck. "What – what do you mean?" Her face reddened. "What are you doing, nosing around in my private files?"

"Take it easy. You left some folders open in your subdirectory, that's all. I'm doing a virus scan. Can't check them until they're shut down. Okay to close them?"

She let out a sigh. "By all means."

He shook his head. "Everybody else has programs open, I'm shutting them down too."

"Close them all," Cheryl said.

Lorenzo tapped keys while the Hansel and Gretel, Pied Piper, and Cheryl's development subdirectory files blipped off the screen. A message flashed.

NINETY-NINE PERCENT COMPLETE

"Ninety-nine? What now?" Lorenzo clicked on the last unopened journal file. Instead of closing, the word processing module kicked in, opening a document titled, "Jackson Diary.Doc."

"What's this?" Rita asked.

"One of Morgan's files. Must've hit the wrong key." Lorenzo moved to hit the close button until the word "virus" seemed to leap out of the text. "Virus?" Lorenzo leaned closer to the screen.

"It's dated October 18 at ten PM."

"Last night."

Together, they read Morgan's diary entry.

Once again, I'm alone in the dark, with Chazz and Morpheus, puzzling over the bizarre medical condition that continues to ravage my unfortunate young patient. I've exhausted every possible avenue of research I can think of and now find myself resorting to what some would term "whimsy."

The only counsel I have is that which I have come to think of as the language of Morpheus; the rhythm of his beeps, the pulse of his indicators and the softer presences, like the click of a thermostat and the hum of the air conditioning. As I sit here night after night in my puzzlement, I have only the cold dry breath of Morpheus whispering secrets in my ear.

After spending so much time down here, I became aware of subtle changes in the patterns of Morpheus. At first, I blamed it on an overactive imagination, but I soon found myself able to predict when Chazz would experience a fever crisis. Following this line of thought, I worked out a formula based on computer generated DNA replication that allowed me to forecast the occurrence of these attacks. (See file, "Jackson Med.Doc")

Morpheus actually supplied the answer when I did a compare between the replication of known mutating virus strains that attack humans and the computer generated model supplied by Morpheus. The patterns match. I'm not sure what this means and I'm far from sharing this with anyone, lest they think I've gone off the deep end.

Still, I have to wonder, could Morpheus have somehow integrated the pattern and propagated the virus that's infecting Chazz? What if by some bizarre fluke, this virus did in fact exist? Suppose it's a damned mutation that crossed over, rewriting its own DNA faster than any analysis I have been able to devise.

"Jesus Christ." Lorenzo shook his head. "A virus moving so fast, it defies detection." He whistled. "That's a stretch even for this screwball place."

Rita felt her heart pick up a beat. Morgan suspected Morpheus of somehow propagating the virus that infected Chazz Daggett. She shivered. "A crossover virus. What a frightening thought."

A frown creased Lorenzo's face. "A mutant strain transmitted through dreams. After seeing your fly disappear and everything else that's happened, I'm ready to believe anything." He eyed the pods. "We better break Eddie out first. He's our virus expert. Hell, he collects the damned things."

"Sensors are on line," Rita's friend called out.

CHAPTER THIRTY SEVEN

Spotlights mounted on the back of a Rosarita Beach Emergencia Jeep illuminated the boulder strewn sand at the foot of the tall cliffs south of the village. The bright lights assimilated color from the surroundings and cast eerie shadows on the rocks.

A BMW lay upside down between two large boulders, partly submerged in the ebbing tide. Men in yellow slickers aimed flashlights through shattered windows while a pair of scuba divers walked into the surf carrying flashlights. The man on the driver's side called out, in Spanish, "One negro male dead in here!"

The other man faced the red and blue flashing in the mist at the top of the cliff. Cupping his hand over a radio mouthpiece, he squinted into the falling rain and rasped, "No survivors. One body."

The speaker squawked and a man's voice replied, "Tow truck and ambulance are on the way from Rosarita."

"He's well dressed," the man on the driver's side said.

"Probably a doctor," the other man replied from the rear of the car. "It has California vanity plates, DREAMDOC." He looked up. "Here they come." Headlights rounded a bend and colored strobes exploded like fireworks, illuminating the fog and rain as the caravan drove along the beach toward the death scene.

CHAPTER THIRTY EIGHT

The ringing signal purred like a cat.

"Answer it, Lorenzo," Hodge grumbled, staring owl-eyed at the big screen. "Answer." He turned to Denise. "Look at them, standing around yakking. What the hell is this, a cocktail party?" He shouted at the screen, "Hey, Lorenzo, answer the Goddamned phone!"

"Hang up, Hodge." Denise spoke quietly, her voice hoarse and weak. "Lorenzo will call when he needs you."

Hodge glared at the monitor, fists clenched. "I'm in charge, dammit!" Fear had left him weak-kneed with a shaky stomach, but the brief eruption of anger helped balance his emotional scale.

"You should be down there with them."

"I can handle things fine from here."

"Then let Lorenzo and the others do their job," Denise said in a voice devoid of emotion.

Hodge faced Denise, planning to reassure her, but the pain in her eyes silenced him. He sighed and disconnected the speakerphone.

She patted the sofa. "Sit here. We'll watch."

Hodge slumped beside her and took her hand. "I want the kid out of here before the cops start snooping around," he said. "Let's not give them any reason to poke their noses anywhere they don't need to be. God knows it'll be bad enough trying to answer questions about Chazz and Ollie." His stomach twisted into cold knots when he thought about Emily Fulbright and Morgan. "I'm calling Lorenzo again."

Denise pulled her hand away. Her voice took on a cold edge. "Leave Lorenzo alone, Hodge. The man is doing his job."

"I'll call if I want," Hodge snapped. He eyed the speakerphone, but didn't move to touch it.

Denise fell silent, her smoke-gray eyes open wide, seemingly absorbed by the activity at the pods. Hodge tried to organize his thoughts. That crazy bastard Ollie had left him holding the bag. In his final words, Morgan spoke of feeding rat poison to an abhorrence he believed to be a mutation of Emily Fulbright. Hodge dreaded telling *that* story to the Federales. How the hell could he explain the Fulbright girl to some hard-nosed Mexican detective?

How could an innocent fairy tale dream with friendly rats have caused such horror? Millions of people had safely dream-traveled over the past year. Morgan truly believed some weird mutating crossover virus had infected both Morpheus and Chazz. Jesus, suppose he was right? Could the damned thing be spreading? Hodge glanced at the two gleaming pods on the big screen.

Impossible, yet he couldn't deny the anguish in his friend's voice as he described long whiskers, yellow teeth, a tail, and finally the rat poison. The pain of killing a living creature had been intolerable to Morgan the healer.

Hodge choked back a sob. His head ached and his lungs felt shriveled. The memory of Morgan's final prayer ripped at his mind. "I'm burning up!" he said. "Can't sit still!" He pushed off the sofa only to totter on spongy legs, wanting to pace, but fearful of stumbling. Denise sat, glued to the giant monitor, brow furrowed, her mouth a thin tense line.

Just a short time ago, she had killed to save all their lives. No telling how she would react to the news of Morgan's suicide. Sweet, gentle Denise, already pale and shaken since the Daggett killings, needed careful handling. He wouldn't tell her about Morg until they were all together.

"Hodge," she said in a flat voice. "Listen to me, Hodge." She continued to stare at the monitor, her voice showing no emotion. "We can turn this thing around. A smart public relations campaign can overcome any ill effects from the Daggett flap."

"What are you talking about?"

"How's this? Chazz picked up some off-the-wall disease on one of his sex trips and was comatose for a year. When Ollie finally visited and got a look at his son, he couldn't take the shock. He murdered his own son and threatened to kill us all. I shot in self defense. You and the others witnessed everything. All we have to do is convince Lorenzo and Rita."

Hodge listened in stunned silence. How could she sound so cool after killing someone?

"There's a positive side to this, Hodge," she said. "We can move back to the States and start over. PermaDream can be a reality. It's what we all want. What we wanted all along."

"No." Hodge shook his head. "We have to stay in Mexico. Ollie said..."

"Ollie's dead." She stared at him, her eyes flat and expressionless as she continued to map out her campaign. "There's even compassion here. We give the story some pathos and semi-humanize those two animals."

"Good Lord, that's the last thing I ..."

"Open your eyes, Hodge," she cut in. "*You're* the man now. No more Ollie to order you around. If you move fast, we can jump across the border and deal legitimately with the United States government. I can help. I have friends. They'll protect us. We can forget this DreamLand crap."

"For Christ's sake, Denise, do you think Ollie left me everything in his will? There are other things to consider. I suppose the PLC'll roll over for us and stand by the border blowing farewell kisses? They'd track me down. There are things you aren't aware of. Dreadful things. Something's wrong with Morpheus."

The desk speaker pulsed and Denise's computerized voice announced, *"Motion sensor activated. There are fifteen people in the building. Two on level five. Twelve in Hansel and Gretel section. One on Z level."*

"Z level?" Hodge felt a tingle ripple across his scalp. "Who the hell's on Z level? There's no one there..." His tongue turned to lead when he saw the terror in Denise's eyes, her frightened gaze fixed on the monitor behind him.

"Chazz is gone," she whispered.

CHAPTER THIRTY NINE

Virus? Cheryl blinked. Had she heard right? A chill tickled her spine followed by a surge of panic. Her dream! She called out the final test points to Jack as if speaking through a fog. A virus? Could it be possible?

When they finished, Jack looked up from the signal analyzer until he found Rita. "Anything?"

Seated at the station beside Lorenzo, Rita tapped keys, accessing the feed from the respiration monitors to the two sealed pods. "Coming up now."

Confused about her own experience and more than apprehensive over little Albert's safety, Cheryl hurried to the console and stood uneasily behind Rita, watching a series of screens flash by. "Did you say something about a virus?" she asked.

"Morgan did. In his notes."

A waveform representing Albert Moffit's breathing crawled across the top of the screen. "Respiration's erratic," Rita muttered. "Seventy five to ninety. He pauses occasionally. Seems to be swallowing."

"Or gulping for air." Jack checked a readout beneath the pod. "Oxygen level's steady. I don't get it."

Lorenzo hunched in front of his monitor staring at a screen full of text. "Jesus, this is a load."

Cheryl touched his shoulder. "Where are Morgan's notes about the virus?" She hoped he couldn't hear the tremor in her voice.

He pushed back from the console, pointing to the monitor and Morgan's diary entry. "Right here."

Cheryl read Morgan's words, her mind spinning faster with each passing line.

Computer generated DNA replication. Matching patterns between known mutating viruses that attack humans and a model generated by Morpheus.

A crossover virus? Fascinating. If anyone else at DreamLand proposed such a theory, she would have dismissed it, but Morgan was a methodical man of science. He would never theorize in so a light a vein. Her heart rose into her throat. If Morgan's theory were correct...

Cheryl touched the back of her neck. A computer virus infecting her brain stem? The thought made her legs go weak. She peered at Jack out of the corner of her eye. What next? One glaring fact clawed at her mind. Eddie Driscoll had modified her dream sequence. Had he deliberately infected her with a virus?

After more clicks from the keyboard, Eddie's respiration pulsed across the bottom of the monitor. "Respiration's 140!" Rita called out.

"Contact Hodge," Cheryl said.

"Never mind him," Jack cut in. "We can deal with it. Hey Alejandro," he shouted.

A burly, dark-haired Mexican stepped from behind Eddie's pod brandishing a crowbar.

"Stay close, Alejandro," Lorenzo said. "In case we need a computer override." He snatched the phone from the console. "To hell with Hodge, I'm calling Morgan. I need to find out what this diary is all about." He punched in a number, listened for a moment, then frowned. "Same damned recording. Guess he is off line."

"This isn't like Morgan." Rita eyed the monitor as she spoke. "He always keeps in close touch. I know he was concerned about Emily Fulbright. Maybe he discovered something."

"Let's crack the eggs and be done with it," Jack said.

"Be cool, Jack," Lorenzo said. "I'll check the escape sequence. If there's nothing wrong with the pods, there's no sense destroying them."

"Now you sound like Hodge," Jack snorted.

"Eddie's respiration is creeping up," Rita said. "Hurry!"

"Shit!" Lorenzo's fingers flew across the keys. Line after line of code flashed across the screen. "Come on, come on, where are you?" he muttered.

On Rita's screen, Eddie's waveform increased in frequency. A red numerical readout pulsed across the bottom.

RESPIRATION 170

"Climbing faster," she said.

Sweat broke out on Lorenzo's forehead as he banged away at the keyboard like a demented concert pianist, sending code racing across the monitor. "Everything I touch is a dead end."

"Respiration one-seventy-five."

Jack came from the pod area and stood beside Cheryl, his eyes darting from Rita's display to Lorenzo's and back again. "Look at them fucking numbers."

"One-eighty," Rita said. "Do something," she shouted. "Eddie's hyperventilating."

"Alejandro!" Jack bellowed.

The big Mexican stood in front of the pod, white-knuckling the crowbar.

"The hell with Alejandro." Lorenzo sprung from his chair and headed for the door. "I'm pulling the plug."

"Hey, come back!" Jack hurried after him, shouting, "You can't do that. You don't know how."

"I'll figure it out." Lorenzo lowered his head and kept going.

Still following, Jack turned to Cheryl. "Hey, tell this asshole that you don't just pull the plug on Morpheus."

Lorenzo wheeled and shoved Jack into the wall. "One more word out of you and I'll pull your plug!" He cocked his fist.

Jack shut his eyes and swallowed hard.

"He's right, Lorenzo." Cheryl touched his arm, trying to calm him with reason. "Morpheus has never been shut down. We can deactivate him, but we have to move one step at a time. Please, Lorenzo."

Lorenzo sighed, released Jack and lowered his fist. "What's step number one?"

"Eddie stopped breathing!" Rita shouted.

"That's it! Here's step number one, Lorenzo. I tear off the fucking door." Jack skittered around Lorenzo and grabbed the crowbar from Alejandro. Waving it like a baseball bat, he raced for Eddie's pod. Lorenzo made no move to stop him.

Jack forced the end of the crowbar into the seam near the bottom of the pod. Cursing and grunting, he pried back and forth until the metal edges groaned and the steady strobe of the LED's faltered. Holding the pry end of the crowbar in both hands, he jammed it into the seam again and again, denting the edges as he pounded at the unyielding metal, until he poked through. A puff of sweet-smelling smoke billowed up out of the crack.

Jack sniffed. "What's this? Smells like a Texas barbecue. Alejandro, get your ass over here. Give me a hand."

Cheryl followed Rita and Lorenzo to the pod while Alejandro worked the crowbar. Massive muscles rippled beneath his tee-shirt as he pried at the widening seam.

Jack pulled at the exposed gap, then yanked his hand back. "Shit!" A thin line of crimson widened across his palm into a dripping ribbon. "Son of a bitch." He shook off the blood and grabbed the metal again, grimacing as he pulled. Veins popped out on his neck and his face purpled. Lorenzo shouldered in beside him, pulling at the widening gash.

Inch by inch, the door peeled back and slowly screeched open.

A fluttering sound came from inside and a dark, shadowy mass filled the jagged opening.

"What the hell is that?" Jack shouted, backing away.

"Some kind of bird," Lorenzo said.

"A vulture," Rita gasped. "It's a vulture."

Cheryl watched the winged black creature leave the pod, spread shiny black wings, and flap upward, vanishing in a cloud of smoke.

"Damned if Hodge can call *that* a hallucination," Lorenzo muttered. "Get Eddie out of there fast!" He poked his head inside the capsule, then stiffened. "Jesus Christ." He stepped aside, joining the others in ashen-faced silence.

Cheryl peered through the ruptured portal, then covered her mouth, gagging from the odor of cooked flesh. Taking hold of Jack's sleeve, she stood in stunned silence, transfixed by the grisly horror inside the battered pod.

Stringy bits of ragged flesh hung from charred rib bones and pieces of gray gristle clung to the joints of a skewed skeleton. A scorched San Diego Padres cap contrasted with the chalky white bone of Eddie Driscoll's skull. His grimacing rictus, with its double row of gleaming teeth seemed to mock her.

Cheryl gasped as the jawbone came unhinged and dangled from one side of the skull, connected by a glistening strand of tendon.

CHAPTER FORTY

Hodge studied the big central wall screen. Who could be moving around on Z level? What happened to Chazz's body? The video camera scanned PermaDream on wide angle, showing blinking lights, flickering screens and the dangling mass of cables and I.V. tubes; Chazz's former lifeline to Morpheus. Ollie lay on the floor where they had left him, a dark puddle by his feet, marking the spot where they last saw his son's corpse.

"Look!" Hodge pointed a trembling finger. "The blood trail leads away from Ollie. Through the doorway."

Denise rose and moved closer to the screen. "Someone dragged Chazz out of PermaDream."

"Who?"

"Had to be Morgan. Probably couldn't stand to see the two of them on the floor like that. As much as he detested Chazz, he worked hard trying to cure him." She let out a long sigh. "Morgan must be down there."

"No!" Hodge realized he couldn't keep Morg's death a secret any longer. "It isn't Morgan." His voice faltered. "Couldn't be."

"How can you be so sure?"

Hodge closed his eyes and took a deep breath, then surprised himself by answering in a steely voice. "Morgan's dead."

Denise faced him, an incredulous look on her face.

Words spilled out of him. "He killed himself. I was on the phone with him when he did it. He drove off the cliff on the old Ensenada road. He was – he was praying."

Her shoulders began to shake, then tears came, followed by staccato sobs. She swayed, looking as if she were about to crumple. When Hodge tried to touch her she pulled away.

"I tried to tell you," he said, "but I couldn't bring myself to say anything. The others don't know."

"I can't believe it," she whispered. "Morgan. Dead. A good man, dedicated to easing suffering and making the pain of death bearable for others taking his own life? Doesn't make sense."

Hodge told her about Morgan's house call to Emily Fulbright and their chilling final conversation. Denise listened in silence, tears streaming down her cheeks. At the end she buried her face in her hands and cried.

Hodge shook his head. "This whole rat thing bothers me. I still don't buy it."

"You don't buy it?" Denise looked up with red teary eyes. "Jesus Christ, Hodge, Morgan is dead! You saw the Fulbright girl. We told you about the fly." She clicked Hansel and Gretel onto the large screen and pointed without looking. "Two people are trapped down there and you don't buy it?" Her voice sharpened. "What the hell's wrong with you?"

Hodge felt thick-tongued and panicky. Icy needles of fear pierced his heart at the prospect of being grilled by stubborn Federales in the back room of some filthy Mexican jail. He had no answers. No telling what they might do. He had heard of beatings. Torture. "Let's get out of here before time runs out." He touched her cheek. "Guatemala, Nicaragua, South America. Name it."

"Are you insane?" She turned away. "I'm going back to the States. Alone."

"Don't say that. Don't think it. Please." Hodge moistened his lips as he struggled to catch his breath. "You know how I feel about you. You led me to believe we'd..."

"Not now, Hodge. For Christ's sake, not now."

"Now is when we need each other."

She glared at him. "What the hell does it take to turn you off?"

"I'm in love with you, Denise." Tears stung his eyes. "My world is ending. My heart is breaking."

"Take it like a man." She turned away.

Hodge had never expected this from her. With a trembling hand, he splashed several inches of brandy into a tumbler and drained the glass.

It felt warm and soothing. He poured another.

The desk speaker pulsed. "Motion sensor activated. There are fifteen people in the building. Two on level five. Twelve in Storybook Land. One on Z level, entering the North Tower elevator."

Hodge's heart leaped. "North Tower? That's us." His attention went to the monitor. He punched the remote, isolating the interior of the North Tower elevator that led to the reception area down the hall from his office.

The screen was dark.

He downed another drink. "Whoever's down there must have disconnected the emergency light."

CHAPTER FORTY ONE

At the top of the rain swept cliff, the detective frowned as she separated the soggy contents of the wallet. "Morgan Jackson. Chief Physician at DreamLand." She turned to the driver. "Guess he lived on the premises."

Her compadre, seated behind the wheel raised an eyebrow. "I didn't know anybody lived at DreamLand."

"Apparently, Jackson did. It's listed as his home address on the driver's license."

"*Ay Cavrone,*" the driver muttered, inserting the ignition key.

"It says Hodge Michaels is to be notified in case of emergency." She reached for the phone and punched in the number. "I'll make sure he's there. It's late. No sense wasting a trip."

After several rings, a man answered. "Hodge Michaels speaking."

"Sorry," the detective said, in English. Wrong number." She disconnected and fastened her seat belt. "He's there, let's go."

CHAPTER FORTY TWO

H odge stared at the receiver as if in a trance before hanging up. "Who was that?" Denise asked in a hushed tone.

"Wrong number."

"I can't deal with this." She stood. "I'm leaving."

"Please. Stay with me."

She crossed to his private elevator and thumbed the button. Nothing happened. "Great, your elevator's dead."

"Dead?" He reached around her and tried it, unable to fathom why it didn't work. He had personally programmed Morpheus to never shut down power to his private elevator.

A buzzing noise caught his attention. Frowning, he did a slow pan of his office. The lights remained on and stable, but the bank of monitors lining the wall flickered, pulsing images from different parts of DreamLand in random patterns across the screens. The large central display showed the Hansel and Gretel pods moving in jerky stop-start frames interspersed with white, static filled screens.

"What the hell's happening?" He clicked the remote. The long hallway leading from his office door to the reception area elevator popped onto the big screen.

"I'm out of here," Denise said. "I'll take the stairs."

"Wait." Hodge reached out and took her arm, stopping her. "You can't leave now."

"I can't?" She pulled away and something exploded against the side of Hodge's head with a brilliant flash. On his knees and unable to think clearly, his world flickered in and out. His head throbbed. He tried to

201

stand, but fell onto his back, tasting blood. His nose felt mushy and his right eye blurred. He opened his left eye and saw Denise standing over him holding the blood-spattered statuette of the Sandman, poised to strike again. "You son of a bitch!" she snarled.

Pain shot through Hodge's jaw. His lip felt numb and swollen. "Don't," he mumbled through broken teeth, trying to raise his arms in defense. His muscles wouldn't respond. Only his leg twitched. "Not again. Please."

"Shut up." Denise rolled her eyes. "You and Daggett destroyed everything we worked for. I never planned on hurting you, Hodge, but you've become money-crazy, just like that murdering scum."

"No! No!" he mumbled, slurring his words. "It's never been proven that he murdered anyone."

"Ollie Daggett killed the Manzur family," she said, her voice rising to a quavering pitch. "And God knows how many other innocent people. I've studied his file. Congressman Manzur was my uncle. He put me through school. Got me a job with the FDA."

The FDA? Denise? Of all the unreal moments Hodge had experienced in the last few hours, this one seemed the most dreamlike.

"I was working under cover for the FDA when I went to your father's lecture, then I began to believe in him. My uncle asked me to stay on when he caught wind of Daggett's involvement."

Each word hit Hodge like a sledge hammer, pounding deeper and deeper into his soul. He never even had a chance. She didn't love him. Never did. Never would. His throat tightened and his already blurry vision grew cloudy with tears.

She glared down at him, her face a tight mask of contempt. "You're a spineless coward," she said evenly. "You didn't have the balls to stand up to Ollie Daggett a year ago and you weren't man enough tonight." Hatred flashed in her eyes. "Do you know what it's like to snuff out a life? Can you possibly imagine it?" She shifted her grip on the Sandman statuette, grasping it tighter.

Hodge wanted to beg her not to hit him again. His mouth moved, but he couldn't speak. Finally, he managed to say, "Please, let me live."

She smiled, then her look turned hard. "You made it easy for me to kill that murdering scumbag by insisting that I show up at that goddamned party. Killing Ollie was a piece of cake, no pun intended. Hell, I even got Chazz as a bonus. Now Morgan's gone, one of the most decent human beings I ever met. Because you shuffled around, whining, while Daggett buried PermaDream. Why should you live?"

Her words ripped into Hodge's heart. Couldn't she see that he was under pressure? Ollie didn't leave him any choice. Ollie had all the money. "Try to understand," he muttered. "My hands were tied."

"You're sniveling again, Hodge." Her voice rose again to a higher pitch. "You let that bastard turn PermaDream into a carnival. You sold us out to a murderer. I'll never forgive you for that."

"But everyone agreed."

"The others fell in line like sheep. Even big-mouthed Jack, but not me. No way."

"What do you mean?"

She faced him, eyes wide, nostrils flared in anger. "Did you think I'd let that pig, Chazz, get his jollies wallowing in sick fantasies while others had to suffer? You didn't give a damn. You sat back and allowed the Daggetts to prostitute Morpheus. I'm the one who took action."

"What kind of action?"

"I'm responsible for Chazz Daggett's coma and his year long nightmare. He deserved every miserable second of it."

"What are you saying?"

"I had help, but the idea was mine. We knew about Freedom Hart and his hot tar and wanted to extend the dream for an extra hour or so. Teach the pervert a lesson and change his filthy mind about taking recreational dreams."

Hodge gasped. "You tinkered with Chazz's dream?"

She nodded. "Now, Morpheus has a virus. Had it for a year."

"Then, you caused Emily Fulbright to..."

"It was unintentional."

"You knew of the danger to the public. Never said a word. Millions could have been affected."

She nodded, barely moving her head.

"Good Lord, Morgan..."

"Oh no you don't, you gutless bastard. You knuckled under to Daggett. You're not blaming Morgan's death on us."

"You and who else? Lorenzo?"

"I wish." She smiled.

"Who?"

"Eddie Driscoll. It's his virus, Hodge. One of Eddie's pets." Her voice went flat. "He swore to me that it wouldn't spread to the rest of the system, and it seemed that he was right, until Emily. Now, it looks like it's out of control."

"Oh, Jesus." Hodge choked back a groan as his world crumbled.

"I tried to share my secret with Lorenzo," she said, "but he's not interested in anything I have to say. He will, once we're back in our own country. Once Rita's gone." The central screen fluttered and the pod area came into view. "There she is, the little bitch."

Hodge groaned.

Denise raised the bloody statuette of the Sandman. "Lie still, Hodge. Don't move your head. You won't know what hit you."

CHAPTER FORTY THREE

A sick hollow feeling gnawed at the pit of Rita's stomach. The cloud of smoke that had been the buzzard hung in the still air. She gagged from the sickly-sweet smell of roasted meat and turned away from the carnage that had been Eddie Driscoll, focusing on the straight line that moments before had undulated with the breath of his life. Little Albert Moffit's respiration pulsed across the bottom of the screen, rapid and jerky.

If they broke open the pod, would he incinerate like Eddie? Nothing could be predicted. Chazz Daggett's coma, the fly, and Emily Fulbright, a possible Progeroid disorder who believed she was turning into a rat. Only Morgan knew the answer to that one. Now the death of the Daggetts and Eddie Driscoll. All connected to Morpheus.

She looked up at the hollow-eyed skeleton and shuddered at the memory of her only computer dream. A witch had chased her, trying to turn her into a worm. Everything had seemed so real. Eddie had laughed off her fears. Now Eddie and Chazz offered proof that things in the dream world could become reality in the physical world. She studied Albert's erratic breathing, then faced Jack. "Can we save him?"

"We better try." Jack started toward Albert's pod. "Let's get him out."

"Wait," Rita heard herself saying. "We're not sure what'll happen if we open it. As long as his breathing's okay let's try to come up with another solution."

Jack frowned. "Jesus, Rita, you sound like Hodge. Look at Driscoll.

You want another solution like that?"

"This thing is so unpredictable we can't be sure. We might have hurt Eddie by forcing it."

"You said he stopped breathing."

"Sure, he stopped breathing, but who expected this?" She nodded at the incinerated skeleton.

Lorenzo cleared his throat. "We don't have a clue about what's happening here. We need more info."

Jack stared at the floor shaking his head. "You think we burned him?"

Lorenzo hung his head and shrugged. "No limits on this one, man."

"Keep trying," Rita moved closer, linking her arm with Lorenzo's. "If Albert's breathing gets any worse, I'll give you the high sign."

"Look for alternatives," Cheryl added. "Don't give up."

Jack clenched the blood spotted gauze Cheryl had bandaged to his palm. "Say the word and I'll crack the son-of-a-bitch like an egg."

"Cross-check the sub-routines Lorenzo," Cheryl said. "There has to be something."

"There's something, all right," Lorenzo growled. "Some monster virus I can't eradicate. Hell, I can't even locate it. Any time a piece of infected code is executed, or a program is written to memory, the damned thing spreads." "The only alternative is a complete shutdown," Jack said.

Lorenzo nodded. "And fast. Let's do it." "We need Hodge," Jack said.

"What the hell for?"

"He wrote the shutdown sequence. He and Morgan are the only ones with the password."

"There's a series of backup systems and auto switching power routers along the way," Cheryl added. "Pull all the plugs and it won't miss a beat. Morpheus can last eight hours, totally self sufficient."

"Anything can happen in eight hours." Lorenzo sighed. "That limits our options. I better go upstairs and deal with Hodge. Don't worry, I'll get the password out of him, then I'll hit Z-level and shut down Morpheus."

"We'll stand by here in case the egg needs to be cracked," Cheryl said.

"I'll tell you this right now." Jack jerked his thumb back over his shoulder. "That little shit in the egg gets in any deeper, we're gonna hatch him."

"Lorenzo smiled over his shoulder as he left. "You do that."

"Stand by." Rita looked up from the screen. "Breathing's faster, more erratic."

"Hey Alejandro!" Jack called out.

Torn between her fear of killing him by opening the pod or watching his life get sucked away by Morpheus, Rita studied Albert's respiration. The waveform of the little boy's breath suddenly spiked. "Open it, guys," she snapped. "Looks like he's choking."

Alejandro jammed the pry bar into the seam near the back of the pod and yanked, gashing the pod's luminescent skin.

"Come on, come on," Jack shouted as Alejandro made another try. This time he pushed the bar deeper, grunted, and leaned on the crowbar.

The LED's blinked out and the pod door screeched open an inch.

Rita's screen went dark. She hurried to the pod, holding her breath, expecting smoke, but seeing none.

Jack grabbed with his good hand and tugged on the door. "Hang on little guy, we're coming."

Cheryl squeezed in beside Alejandro. Together they pulled, slowly forcing the door all the way open. "My God," she gasped. "Look at him."

Rita pushed the big Mexican aside. "What is it?"

Little Albert writhed up and down with his hands behind his back and his feet crossed at the ankles as if bound. His head bobbed and his lips and throat worked convulsively like an owl swallowing a mouse. His stomach had bloated to the size of a basketball, popping his shirt buttons and stretching the skin of his belly to the limits. It looked smooth, tight, and shiny in the glare of the kliegs.

CHAPTER FORTY FOUR

P ain ripped away the cloak of unconsciousness and raged like lightning between Hodge's ears. He heard a far away beep followed by a series of soft tones, like somebody noodling on a marimba from the bottom of a deep well.

Squinting with his good eye, he saw Denise pressing a cell phone to her ear. "Rita, this is Denise," she said. "Hodge needs your help. Meet us at the Z-level-ProtoLab."

Hodge trembled, desperate to shout a warning. His effort brought little more than a hiss.

Denise didn't seem to notice. Her voice crackled with urgency. "Little Albert's life is in your hands. You have to go into the Hansel and Gretel dream, find him, hold him tight and say, Mama. It's our only chance to save him."

On screen Rita shook her head and spoke rapidly.

"Take another look at what's left of Eddie," Denise said. "If we don't rescue Albert, the same thing could happen to him." Rita eyed the pods. Her shoulders slumped.

"The only reason we've asked you is because Morgan insisted. You're the medical person. What? No. He's still with the Fulbright girl. He can't get back in time and he's afraid for the boy's life. He doesn't want anyone else going in but you because you're the only one with an understanding of his physical condition." She nodded quickly. "Don't worry, sweetie, we'll be with you all the way. Ease away from the others," Denise said, lowering her voice. "If you get there first, don't wait. Get into the pod. Every second counts," she said in a dry whisper, while isolating the ProtoLab on the big central screen.

Two half-finished pods lay open, with mazes of wires, sensors, and electronics spilling from them. A third fully functional pod sat upright, its front hatch gaping like an accepting mouth. "It's already programmed for Hansel and Gretel," Denise said. "Close the door and activate the dream. Hodge and I are on our way. Hurry!" She disconnected.

Hodge choked back a sob as he watched Rita slip away. His heart sank. Nobody saw her leave. A flush of anger surged through him and he tried to stand. Move, damn it, move. His limbs barely twitched.

Through a fuzzy halo, Hodge spotted Rita on the big monitor. In the ProtoLab already.

Denise rinsed off the bloodied statuette, dried it with a bar towel and returned it to the desk.

Hodge closed his sighted eye. If she looked in his direction, he wanted to appear dead. Once she left he would do his best to warn the others. He held his breath, listening as she hurried for the door. As soon as it closed, he opened his swelling good eye as far as he could. Soon he wouldn't be able to see at all. Better act fast.

"Motion sensor activated. There are fifteen people in the building. Two on level five. Twelve in Storybook land. One in the North Tower elevator."

Propelled by fear, he struggled, and with great effort, rolled onto his stomach. Had to warn Rita. Weak from pain, sickened by the warm salty taste of blood, he tried to stand, but had no feeling in his legs. On the monitor, he saw Rita settle into the pod. His heart raced. Almost out of time.

The remote control sat on the floor inches away. Pain lanced his shoulder as he reached out, straining every muscle. His arm appeared to grow longer as if stretching halfway across the room. Closer. Closer. Finally, his fingertips touched it and he pulled it to him.

Now to contact whoever the hell was on the North Tower elevator at the end of the hallway and send them back to warn Rita. Willing himself past the pain, Hodge thumbed the remote and activated the North Tower elevator videocam.

Still dark.

Out of patience, he clicked on the intercom. "You, in the elevator, this is Hodge Michaels. I'm in my office. I've been injured. We have an emergency. I need your help. Can you hear me?"

Silence.

"Can you hear me?"

From the darkness, a voice croaked, "Dah!"

CHAPTER FORTY FIVE

Hodge lay in agony on his office floor trying to pull his thoughts together. Chazz in the North tower elevator? Impossible. Four people had seen Ollie fire the .38 straight into his son's forehead. Chazz stiffened and fell like a tree, gushing blood and brains. No doubt about it, Chazz was dead. "Dah!"

Hodge flinched as the harsh voice cleaved the stillness. Unconsciousness threatened to envelop him, but he battled back, trying to compel unresponsive limbs to obey.

Hodge's stiff bloody fingers slipped as he fumbled with the remote, trying to press the proper buttons. He managed to shuffle the images on the wall until the corridor leading from the reception area to his office appeared on the big center screen. He watched Denise push at the locked staircase door, then run back to the reception desk to tug at the drawers, probably hoping to find a key card. Hodge felt a glimmer of satisfaction at her disappointment. The drawers had also been locked. Standing orders from him.

The voice from his desk speaker said, "The North Tower elevator bearing one passenger is at level five."

Denise must have heard it over the hall speakers, because she hurried back down the long hallway toward Hodge's office. Halfway there she stopped and nibbled on a fingernail, seemingly deep in thought.

Hodge blinked away a trickle of blood from the cut above his eye and smiled through the pain. What now, Denise? Figuring out a new story to tell? A bigger lie?

Soon she would discover the identity of the lone elevator passenger. Maybe Ollie's birthday injection did the job. Maybe it was the sudden fever that raged as the untested medication entered his vein. Perhaps the same damned thing that caused Emily Fulbright's deformity had infected Chazz. Whatever the cause, Denise was about to discover that Chazz Daggett lived, bullet hole and all.

The elevator door opened behind her.

Denise stood immobile, lips puckered, brow furrowed. Hodge snickered. That's it, baby. Think up a good alibi. Something clever to say to the newcomer.

Behind her, something stirred in the darkened elevator at the end of the hall.

In spite of the pain thundering through Hodge's head, he felt a compelling sense of euphoria watching the monitor, aware of his heartbeat thumping against his windpipe.

Chazz Daggett staggered out of the shadows, scrawny arms sticking from the sleeves of his blood spattered leather jacket. His huge bony head wobbled back and forth, barely supported by his reed-like neck. Reddish-purple blood congealed around the gaping hole between his eyes. A toothless grimace contorted his pallid face.

Like a mouse oblivious to the reality of a stalking snake, Denise stood with her back to the elevator. Unaware of his presence, she preened, running slender fingers through her dark hair. Hodge tensed. That's it, Denise. You look perfect. Now, turn around. Fixing a concerned frown on her face, she wet her lips like a model about to pose for a photograph and turned.

Hodge couldn't hear her scream, but he could see that it was a real tight-fisted head-shaker. Part of him wished he could hear her pleading as Chazz groped for her face, his eyes looking in two directions, his flaccid tongue snaking back and forth.

Denise backed away until she snagged her heel in the carpet and fell, flailing her arms. Chazz lurched toward her, stumbling from wall to wall like a careening bumper car, arms outstretched, skeletal fingers twitching.

Hodge giggled as she scrambled to her feet and limped toward the office door. When her fingers reached for the door, Hodge pressed the button, triggering the electronic lock, smiling as it clicked into place.

Denise's features filled the huge screen, her face contorted, glistening with sweat. Hodge held his breath. The knob jiggled. Tears streamed from her eyes. He snickered as she opened her mouth in another vein-popping, silent scream.

When she pounded on the thick door, Hodge barely heard it.

A tattooed hand reached around and grabbed her face. Long, bony fingers slid into her mouth and poked up her nostrils. Her eyes popped open wider as the other hand took her throat.

Chazz pulled Denise away from the door and dragged her back down the hallway. The last thing Hodge saw before the door closed was her feet, still kicking.

He turned off the monitor. The screen flickered and went dark. He lay still, breathing deep and ragged, listening intently. She must have made plenty of noise, but he hadn't heard a thing. What a job of soundproofing. Hodge smiled. He'd gladly recommend the acoustical firm anytime.

CHAPTER FORTY SIX

A whirring hum stirred Hodge from his stupor, then Lorenzo's breathless voice crackled over the speaker. "I'm on my way up in your private elevator. Finally got the damned thing started. Intercom's intermittent. Circuits are going nuts all over the building."

Hodge felt a wave of relief. If Lorenzo hurried, he could stop Rita from entering the pod. Squinting with his half-opened good eye, Hodge struggled to bring the intercom numbers on his remote control into focus, but saw only tiny lights twinkling in front of him.

He heard his private elevator door whoosh open. Lorenzo ran toward him, his footsteps stopping short when he came close. His eyes grew wide and the blood drained from his face.

If Hodge had any doubts about the extent of his injuries, Lorenzo's shocked expression assured him he had been seriously hurt. Hodge struggled to tell him about Rita, but his swollen tongue filled his mouth like a hot towel, making him gag. The walls appeared to be melting and the floor beneath him felt like a water bed. "I'm hurt, Lorenzo." His temples throbbed when he spoke and the lights swirled inside his head like fiery bees. "Blacking out. Can hardly see you."

Lorenzo knelt beside him, his head bobbing like a balloon on a string. His voice sounded tinny and seemed to come from another room. "Jesus, Hodge. Your face is all busted up. Who the hell did this?" He looked around. "Where's Denise?"

Hodge barely managed a whispered reply. "With Chazz."

Lorenzo sighed. "C'mon, Hodge, pull it together. We need you, buddy."

"I'm okay. I'm in control here." Gritting his broken teeth, Hodge swallowed the fresh trickle of copper that drained into the back of his throat. "Hurry. Rita is ... Rita is..." His mind blanked. He tried again. "I'm in ... I'm in..."

"You're in control, Hodge." Lorenzo spoke in a calm, steady voice as he wet a bar towel and wiped Hodge's face. "I have to shut down Morpheus. I need the password."

"No, no, listen. Rita. Hurry."

"Hodge." Lorenzo said. "Pay attention, man! There's some kind of virus affecting Morpheus."

Virus? The word riveted Hodge. He thought hard about it.

"It's like nothing we've ever seen. The damned thing seems to have crossed over."

Something flashed in Hodge's mind, then words and names came like shooting stars. "Denise did it. Denise and Eddie Driscoll."

Lorenzo sighed. "Jesus, Hodge, pay attention. We have to shut down Morpheus. Give me the password." He switched on the monitors. Starting with the top left of the bank, images filled the screens. "Don't waste time. Look."

He scanned the monitors, pausing at a close-up of Eddie Driscoll's remains, then he lingered on little Albert with his convulsing mouth, bobbing head, and bloated stomach.

"Why is the boy doing that?" Hodge heard himself saying. "I don't like that gulping. Do something. Wake him up."

Lorenzo shook his head. "He's trapped in a dream. Take another look at Eddie. I'm trying to shut down Morpheus before the same thing happens to the kid. We're out of time. I need the password."

Hodge lay motionless, his mind racing haphazardly. He tried to pull his thoughts together, but unanchored words and detached images drifted through his mind like dust motes in a sunbeam. Ollie Daggett's snarling face. A smiling Morgan. Denise, the night they met, looking sweet and sexy. Then, through a milky haze, he pictured Chazz dragging her down the hallway and smiled until he heard his dad's voice saying, "PermaDream will live. That's all that matters."

Lorenzo grabbed Hodge's shoulders and shouted in his ear, "The password! Give me the password!"

Hodge's vision cleared. He caught his breath as he remembered Rita planning to enter a dream world she might never escape from. "Rita," he croaked, barely holding on to the thought. "ProtoLab. Going into Hansel and Gretel. To rescue the kid."

Lorenzo straightened and his gaze flashed to the Hansel and Gretel screen. He stabbed at the loudspeaker switch. "Jack!"

"What the fuck?" Jack jumped back from Eddie Driscoll's pod. "Scared the shit outta me."

"Where's Rita?"

"Right over..." Jack looked around. "She was here a minute ago." He shrugged. "I don't know where the hell she went."

"She's going into the Hansel and Gretel dream to try and save the kid."

"Holy shit!"

"I'm heading for the ProtoLab."

"Go, man. We'll watch out for the little guy." Jack turned to Cheryl. "Rita's in trouble."

Lorenzo clicked off.

Hodge grunted. With bloody fingers, he tapped at the remote, reshuffling screens. Pain crashed through his head with every beat of his heart and his vision clouded at the edges as if he were looking through a hairy pipe. Finally, the ProtoLab view moved from the small monitor to the big screen.

Rita stood by the pod looking pale and shaken, brow furrowed, the corners of her mouth turned down.

"Poor kid. Scared to death." Lorenzo fumbled at the console, jabbing at the intercom button. "Rita. Rita!" He turned to Hodge. "Z-level intercom's out." He started for the elevator.

"Wait," Hodge said. "The password."

Lorenzo stopped short. "Hurry, man, hurry."

Hodge felt tingly as he tried to remember. His vision dimmed. He would never stay conscious if he remained on the floor. "Get me up. Help me, Lorenzo. My desk."

After giving the password to Lorenzo, Hodge sat in his darkened office, slumped at his desk, squinting at the monitors, watching Lorenzo bolt from his private elevator on Z level to the North Tower elevator. Ahead of him, the elevator door opened, then almost closed until something blocked it and it opened again.

Lorenzo slowed to a trot, then stopped. Hodge zoomed the camera in on a close up. Denise's arm flopped back and forth on the floor in time to the opening and closing of the sliding door.

Lorenzo held the door open and peered into the elevator, then kneeled and lifted the limp arm. After holding it and checking for a pulse, he gently set it down inside the car. He stood, took several deep breaths, then rushed down the Z-level corridor to the ProtoLab.

The elevator door closed.

Hodge's stomach lurched. Should have warned Lorenzo. Chazz Daggett was probably somewhere on Z-Level.

CHAPTER FORTY SEVEN

Jack wheeled a portable console to Albert's pod and braked it beside Cheryl.

"We're in trouble, Jack," she said, wide-eyed behind her thick-lensed glasses.

"I've been saying that since the day Hodge got us tangled up with that piece of shit, Ollie Daggett." He shook his head. "We've been following that nut like a pack of trained apes. Even you, the big shot brain authority."

"Please." Cheryl grabbed his arm, wanting him to understand. "I'm convinced we acted properly, Jack. It's our work that's important. DreamLand would be here with or without us. At least we managed to keep things on a family level. No telling what would've happened with Ollie Daggett in complete control. Who knows what sort of sick, perverse, X-rated dreams we'd..." Their eyes met and Cheryl's cheeks burned. She turned away. "Hodge is having a bad time dealing with this."

"Screw Hodge." Jack pointed to the opened pod where little Albert Moffit gulped and breathed in short jerky spasms. "This little dude's in trouble and until we bail him out, Hodge doesn't matter. We can't turn our backs on an innocent kid to hold that asshole's hand." He patted her arm. "Help me get this thing going."

Battling waves of panic, Cheryl reached for the keypad. "Okay, plug him in."

Sweat dripped from Jack's brow as he kneeled by the pod and hooked a cable to one of the ports. He stood and flicked several switches. "Here goes." The monitor blinked to life, flashing details of its power cycling self test.

Cheryl fingered the keys. A sharp-peaked waveform of Albert's respiration appeared on screen. "No change."

CHAPTER FORTY EIGHT

Rita studied the ProtoLab console. After her first experience in the Enchanted Forest, she had vowed to never enter a computer generated dream again, but things at DreamLand had veered out of control and a small boy had been placed in danger. The sight of Eddie Driscoll's charred bones in the opened pod haunted her. Nobody deserved to die in such an ungodly fashion. She vowed to prevent anything so horrible from happening to little Albert.

Something crackled and sparked. The overhead lights sputtered, casting shadows before glowing steady again. She caught her breath. What if something went wrong? She clenched her fists until her palms hurt. No time to think now. She had to try in spite of the danger. Flexing her fingers, she tapped out a stream of data.

A hum filled the air followed by a series of clicks. The activation lights on the egg flashed red and blue. Denise's computerized voice spoke from a console speaker.

"Program departure time and enter pod."

Keying in a ten second delay, Rita slipped into the contoured seat and settled back, waiting for Morpheus to take her to the shadowy place where human fancy and machine became one. She had to stay alert and aware at all costs. During Lorenzo's demonstration, she had become so involved, she forgot she was dreaming. Couldn't risk that now. Tonight she needed to remember.

Once inside the dream, she would move quickly, find Albert, grab his hand and shout the escape word at the top of her lungs. With luck, it would only take a few seconds, real time.

She heard footsteps running toward the lab and Lorenzo calling her name.

"Rita, stop! There's a virus!"

She leaned forward to intercept the sequence, but the capsule door whooshed shut, swallowing her in darkness. A virus? She breathed deep, trying to calm herself. Her hand went to the silver angel at her throat. Lorenzo's birthday angel. She silently mouthed his name. She had to set aside any fears and concentrate on rescuing Albert.

She felt a chill as the huge drooling witch from her previous dream came forth from the back of her mind, clicking rotten teeth, reaching for her with dirty green fingernails. The image faded as Rita spiraled downward through ethereal gloom, into a land of verdant hills and fertile green valleys pocketed with early morning fog...

CHAPTER FORTY NINE

Jack drew up a chair for Cheryl and sat on the edge of another. "Now, we wait." He drummed his fingertips on the console. "This'll drive me nuts. Dial up the ProtoLab. Let's stay with Lorenzo."

Cheryl pulled the monitor closer, rested a hand on Albert's shoulder, and split the screen, keeping his respiration pulsing across the top while she brought up a view of the ProtoLab on the bottom. "There it is." Onscreen, she watched Lorenzo rush into the lab, stopping when he saw the closed pod.

"Jesus, he's too late," Jack whispered, his face pale and drawn. "Rita's already inside."

Lorenzo placed a hand on the surface of the closed cocoon as if feeling a child's forehead for fever. Closing his eyes, he pressed an ear to the pod's metallic skin. His lips moved as he whispered. When he opened his eyes, he looked drawn and haggard.

Jack thumbed the intercom. "Hey Lorenzo, we're with you, buddy. Anything Cheryl and I can do, let us know. Hey, Lorenzo, we're standing by. Got that?"

Lorenzo didn't respond.

"Z-level's out," Cheryl said. She pressed several buttons. "The whole intercom's dead." As she spoke, the lights flickered. "Goddamned Morpheus," Jack said. "All we can do is watch."

"I feel so helpless."

On screen, Lorenzo stepped to the console and started typing on the keyboard. A moment later, overhead lights and panel indicators flashed in unison. Lorenzo stepped back and Denise's computerized voice echoed throughout every room and hallway of DreamLand. "Sixty seconds until system shutdown."

KEN REETH & MATTHEW J. PALLAMARY

CHAPTER FIFTY

Cold, gray dawn. Cobblestones, wet and glistening. Tiny houses with thatched roofs. No chimney smoke, no breeze, no sound; an empty stage, awaiting the curtain. Rita felt a chill. This was not the Enchanted Forest of Hansel and Gretel. Instead, she stood in the Hamelin village square. She would know it anywhere. Lorenzo had shown her countless renderings of Pied Piper Land and Hodge often boasted of personally creating the horde of friendly rats.

Rats!

Terror simmered in the pit of her stomach at the thought of the hairy, beady-eyed creatures. In the fairy tale, Hamelin had been infested with filthy rodents and the Pied Piper came to lure them to their doom with music.

She glanced over her shoulder at the empty square. Something strange in the morning air. A feeling? A whisper? A sense of movement?

After a moment of chilly gray silence, a faint, shimmering sound prickled the nape of her neck and drifted to her like an ethereal breeze. Music?

A haunting melody ruffled the purple dawn, stirring long forgotten feelings. A rush of elation coursed through her like the air-time at the top of a roller coaster in that brief moment when you raise your arms and lift off the seat before taking the big drop.

She laughed, tilted her head and listened, trying to remember the name of the song or where she heard it, but it fluttered beyond her thoughts like the pretty butterflies she had tried and failed to catch in her childhood. The profundity of the melody intensified with each note. Music seemed to surge through her veins. Another delicious shudder wracked her as a shadow moved from the mouth of an alley and the Pied Piper stepped into the square.

Her heart leaped at the sight of the tall, handsome, blond man, wearing skin tight forest green cloth and matching suede boots. A long scarlet feather highlighted the silver band of his pointed hat. She eyed his trim waist, wide shoulders and silver-blue eyes as he pranced around with his flute pressed to his lips. Rita sighed. Such an elegant figure. Such haunting music.

Somewhere, in the back of her thoughts she realized she had something important to do. While her logical mind puzzled over her reactions, her emotions abandoned themselves to the song. The mysterious music had taken hold and she no longer cared. Swaying with the rhythm, she allowed the Piper's music to rush through her like a swollen stream, compelling her to tap her feet and snap her fingers.

"I won't dance," she shouted, trying to regain control of her movements. "I won't." Even as she protested, her feet shuffled and pranced like a marionette. "No, no, I have something important to do. Something important." If she could only remember.

Smiling, nodding and waving her arms, she yielded to the music, circling the village square, following the Piper, clicking her heels and strutting to the wonderful melody. Faster and faster, she danced, spinning, twirling, unable to stop.

She heard a rustling sound and spied movement in the shadows. A shiver caressed her like a clammy hand and a seething, squealing horde of rats swarmed into the square, scurrying from between buildings, creeping out of sewers and skittering through doorways and windows. One chubby gray rat with a cold pink tail brushed her bare legs, making her skin crawl. She wanted to scream and run away, but she could only nod and dance.

As the Piper played, the rodents followed, snapping, biting, and scratching in a wild scramble to be first in line. Rita's heartbeat pulsed with the music, quickening as the tempo increased, slowing when it slowed. The impulse to follow made her dance with wild abandon, despite the rats, yet beneath the exhilaration, she realized something had gone wrong.

She giggled. What could possibly be wrong with dancing to the Piper's tune? She burst out laughing from sheer joy, performed a pirouette and twirled across the square. Huge hairy rats with wet noses darted behind and around her legs, turning the square into a writhing mass of wet fur and long cold tails.

Rita tripped along behind the choreographed multitude as the undulating procession left the square moving in waltz time, following the tall blond musician across a stone bridge and down a forest path toward Hamelin Gorge, where sheer granite cliffs plunged three thousand feet to a rock studded river bank.

Like a burst of sunlight in a shuttered room, she remembered her mission. Albert. She had to rescue little Albert. "Mama," she shouted.

The music stopped, but Rita couldn't. She shouted again and her voice echoed like a church bell in the still morning air. The Piper faced her, lowering his flute. She didn't know when he had changed, but he wore a red flannel shirt. Just like...

Grandpa smiled at her. Looking down at his stomach she saw frenzied movement beneath his shirt. She looked away and saw that the multitude had stopped dancing. As one, they turned to stare, then parted, leaving a path for Rita to toe-dance to the lip of the gorge.

For the briefest moment, her *abuelito's* eyes glittered green. The spectral image of her grandfather flickered and faded like the picture on a suddenly darkened television before she danced off the edge.

CHAPTER FIFTY ONE

"There are fourteen people in the building. One on level five. Ten in Storybook Land. Three on Z level"

Propped up at his desk, Hodge thumbed the remote, switching monitors until a wide shot of the ProtoLab filled the big screen. Grim-faced, Lorenzo stood in front of the closed operational pod as if hypnotized by its flashing, multi-colored parade of lights.

Hodge glanced at a smaller monitor, past the pod containing Eddie's remains, fascinated by the bizarre form, posture, and behavior of little Albert Moffit. What could Rita be experiencing in her dream? He swallowed hard. What would Lorenzo find when he opened her cocoon?

Jumping at the sound of a loud pop, Hodge watched the central monitor flicker and pulse. The pale-skinned, sickly, flat-chested image of Emily Fulbright filled the giant screen. His stomach lurched. "Oh, Jesus, no!" He punched the remote again and again, trying to make her go away, but the screen wouldn't blank. "Oh, Jesus, oh Jesus," he whined.

Clutching her sweater at the neck, Emily's beady eyes darted into every corner of his office. "Light bothers me, Mister Michaels," she piped in a thin, watery voice. "Hurts my eyes." She dabbed at the inner corners of her eyes with her fingertips. Her tiny pink tongue flicked at dry, cracked lips. Suddenly, she leaned forward, stuck her head out of the screen and shouted in a deep, raspy man's voice, "Turn off the fucking light!"

Panic clawed at Hodge's insides. If only he could run.

"Leave me alone," he whispered. "Please."

Emily glared at him. "*You* did this." She wiggled her nose and pulled back her upper lip, exposing long, yellow incisors. "You and your vicious rats."

No." Hodge winked blood from his all but closed eye. "My rats are friendly."

"Liar!" she shrieked. A foul odor permeated the air. Her mouth stretched into a hairy snout and her ears grew long and pointy. "I'll get you for this." Her eyes blurred into shiny black marbles.

"No, no, don't," Hodge pleaded.

The huge rat leaped from the screen, its eyes glinting green.

Hodge's world went dark. "Jesus, I can't see," he whimpered as pain ripped through his head. He heard Emily's long tail swishing as she crossed the floor, coming closer.

"This isn't fair," he mumbled. "I created lovable rats."

CHAPTER FIFTY TWO

Rita hurtled down through a maelstrom of darkness, plunging into frigid water, swirling like a leaf being sucked into a huge drain. She held her breath as brilliant bubbles of emerald phosphorescence boiled around her. Far above on the glittering silver surface, the amorphous reflection of the sky grew hazy.

Her lungs felt like balloons stretched to the breaking point. Propelled by sheer panic, she flailed her arms and legs, struggling to reverse her descent. Desperate for air, she kicked and clawed at the seething water.

As if by magic, the churning bubbles changed direction. Stroking against the raging current, she pulled herself up toward the distant hazy light where dusky spots swirled among sparkling bubbles. Every part of her wanted to exhale and take a deep breath, but Rita forced the thought from her mind, thinking only of the blessed air she longed to pull into her lungs. As she neared the surface, the dark spots whirled closer.

She gulped when her head broke the surface. Air. Sweet air, delicious, fresh air.

Something wet and hairy brushed her cheek. Looking up, she saw thousands of rats tumbling off the jagged cliff, screeching and twitching as they hit the water. Hundreds floated on the swells, tiny legs and long tails dangling. Others scratched at her clothing. One clawed at her hair. Another scrambled onto her head. She screamed, grabbed its cold, slippery tail and threw it as far as she could. A furry head surfaced in front of her, snapping at her face, eyes glinting, yellow teeth clicking, jaws working frantically. Terrified rats clung to her shoulders. Her teeth chattered as she slapped at the fat furry bodies.

The dark chaotic waters whirled in the opposite direction, drawing her away from the cliff and the mass of squealing rats. Again, she swam with all her might, fighting the pull of what she thought of as a giant hand, but the roiling water sucked her under and she plunged downward, like a stone spinning into blackness.

CHAPTER FIFTY THREE

Unable to see, Hodge held his breath and listened.

The half human monstrosity crossed the room, coming toward him, brushing the carpet with its tail, sniffing as it passed his ear. The creature's foul, icy breath made him gag.

Again, Denise's computerized voice filled the room. "Fifty-five seconds until system shutdown."

At his shoulder, a sudden high-pitched, inhuman squeal sent shivers rippling down his spine.

"Fifty seconds until system shutdown." "Please don't bite me," he whimpered.

CHAPTER FIFTY FOUR

"Less than fifty seconds, Cheryl. Let's get him out of there!"

"We can't, Jack. Not yet."

"Dammit, we're in the middle of a countdown. Morpheus is going to dump everything."

"If we pull him out, we may damage his brain."

"At least he'll still have a fucking brain. Suppose he's unconscious when the power goes off? It'll be lights out for sure, that's what. Lights out for Albert."

"We have to give him every possible second."

"You're pushing it."

"Forty seconds until system shutdown."

CHAPTER FIFTY FIVE

Hodge heard a sniffing sound. Something cold and wet touched the back of his neck sending chills cascading across his scalp like tiny scrambling claws.

"Thirty-five seconds until system shutdown."

He felt a vague sense of something tugging at his lifeless left arm. "Don't eat me," he muttered. "For God's sake, don't eat me."

CHAPTER FIFTY SIX

"Thirty seconds until system shutdown. Pod release sequence activated." Little Albert sobbed. Tears streamed from his eyes.

"Screw this," Jack growled. "I waited long enough." He leaned into Albert's pod. "Give me a hand, Cheryl. This kid's a porker. My back ain't what it used to be."

Cheryl hurried to the other side of the pod.

"Automatic locking and motion sensors are now inoperative."

She glanced at the screen. Lorenzo knelt in front of the prototype pod. Jack grabbed her shoulder. "Look. Behind him. What the hell is that?"

In the shadowed doorway, light glinted off the bald head of a dark hulking form.

Cheryl gasped.

"Ain't this the topper?" Jack muttered.

They watched in silent horror as Chazz Daggett wobbled into the lab, his huge head bobbing above his shoulders like a spectral balloon. Cheryl pounded the intercom button. "Lorenzo, behind you. Lorenzo!"

"No use." Jack's voice broke as he said, "Intercom's still dead."

On screen, Lorenzo stared at the blinking lights like a man in religious awe. Chazz lumbered closer, arms outstretched, fingers twitching, the shriveled eagle tattoos on the back of each hand flailing the air like withered bats.

"Twenty seconds until system shutdown."

CHAPTER FIFTY SEVEN

R ita slowed as if sinking into a pile of warm eiderdown, then bounced to an easy stop. Flat on her back, she stared up at a rough hewn ceiling. Brilliant sunlight streamed through an open window. Outside, silver dewdrops shimmered on red roses and a pair of bushy-tailed squirrels chattered, concealed by the leafy boughs of a sugar maple. She had obviously fallen into somebody's cozy featherbed. Whose?

A woman's cheerful voice from the next room startled her. "Sweetie pie."

A reply came from somewhere outside the window. "I'm in the shed with Fatty."

Something familiar about the voice.

"Open the cage and chase him outside. I'm ready for him."

"Yes, Mother."

Rita slipped out of bed, looked out the window and saw Gretel, the girl from her early dream, peering into a wooden shed. Good. A friend.

Tiptoeing to the door, she opened it far enough to peek through the crack. Across the room, a statuesque blonde woman stood by a cutting board, her back to Rita. "Don't dawdle, dear," she chirped. "I'm starved." Accompanied by the whisk of a blade against whetstone, she burst out singing in a glistening soprano.

"Did you ever think, when the hearse goes by,
that one of these days you're going to die.
They shut you up in a wooden box,

and cover you over with dirt and rocks."

Gretel shouted, "Oh, Mother, that's my favorite holiday song." She joined in, from the yard, singing at the top of her voice. "The worms crawl in, the worms crawl out, into your nostrils and out of your mouth. Cage is open, Mother," Gretel said.

"Be right there, hon. Bring him out to the butcher block."

Gretel grunted. "Ooooh, Fatty's so heavy he can barely move."

"I'm coming." The mother turned from the counter, startling Rita with a head-on look at her outlandish outfit. Black mini-dress, matching headband, orange stockings and patent leather knee boots. She wore green eye shadow, unnaturally long eyelashes and pumpkin colored lipstick. Tying a blood-spattered butcher's apron around her waist, she ran her thumb across the edge of a glistening blade.

Rita studied the warm, cozy kitchen. Gretel's home? Yes. Her mother was about to butcher a holiday turkey. Surely they could help her locate little Albert before time ran out.

A loud squawk startled her and a shadow fell across the floor.

She jumped back and saw a large raven perched on the window sill, blotting out the roses. It leaned into the room, beak open, wings partly unfurled, making a hissing sound deep in its throat. Something about the dark creature reminded Rita of the giant witch who wanted to turn her into a worm. "Shoo!" She whispered, waving her arms. "Go away!"

The bird remained frozen like an ebony statue. Behind her the door creaked open all the way.

Rita turned.

Gretel's mother stood in the doorway, scrutinizing her with shiny green eyes. "It's about time. We didn't think you were going to make it, Rita."

I'm dreaming. It's only a dream. Rita backed away, repeating the phrase to herself. Only a dream. Only a dream. "No time to waste. Have to find the witch's house. A little boy is lost."

The woman entered the bedroom. "Chubby little boy?"

Rita's heart swelled. "Have you seen him?"

"Maybe."

"Gretel knows me. Hurry. She'll know where he is. I helped her rescue Hansel from an ugly witch who wanted to turn me into a worm."

"Witches do that to girls around here." The woman shut the door. "Prettier the girl, the livelier the worm." The raven squawked again.

Gretel's mother shook her head. "Isn't he the greedy one? Always begging. Always hungry. Never satisfied. He wants his Halloween meal too." Snatching a shoe box-sized carton from the cupboard, she threw off the lid. Writhing sounds and shrill squeals came from the open container. The squawking bird spread its wings and raced back and forth on the window sill.

"Aaaaah, here's a nice fat one." The woman reached inside and pulled out what looked to be a squirming pink snake, about a foot long and as thick as a broomstick. Its tail wriggled from the bottom of her closed fist, slapping against her arm.

Rita gagged when she saw a tiny human head at the other end with long stringy hair and a girl's face, pinched and twisted in horror. Faint shrieks streamed from the creature's quivering mouth. "Help me! Help me!"

With a laugh, Gretel's mother tossed the abomination to the shiny-eyed bird. The raven snatched it from the air and flew to a fence post where it tilted its head and devoured the screaming morsel in one gulp.

Gretel's mother smiled at Rita. "Next."

CHAPTER FIFTY EIGHT

TEN SECONDS UNTIL SYSTEM SHUTDOWN.

Cheryl winced as she watched the lights go out in the ProtoLab. She stared at the dark screen, holding her breath until the emergency lights flickered on, then she pulled Jack closer to the monitor in time to see the pod door open. Inside, Rita squirmed in the recliner, eyes shut tight, face contorted in terror.

Cheryl said, "She's trapped in the dream."

"At least she's alive." Jack stared at the screen. "Heads up, Lorenzo!"

Chazz Daggett careened around the end of the console, reaching for Lorenzo. His boot tangled in a clump of wire and he stumbled forward, knocking over a chair. Lorenzo looked back, then deliberately turned away from Chazz to reach for Rita's hand. To Cheryl, the unfolding scene looked like a surreal silent movie. Lorenzo put his head closer to Rita and closed his eyes. His lips kept moving, as if in prayer.

Chazz stumbled to his feet.

Jack grabbed Albert's hand, shouting, "Grab the kid! Grab the kid!"

Cheryl's heart sank when she realized time had run out.

"Five seconds until system shutdown."

Leaning into the pod, she grabbed little Albert's other hand and squeezed.

CHAPTER FIFTY NINE

Rita backed away from Gretel's mother, trembling like an aspen leaf. "Witches. Both of you!"

From its perch on the fencepost the raven shrieked, flapping shiny black wings.

Gretel's mother blocked the door. Rita heard pitiful screams and slithering sounds from inside the box. She backed away until her back touched the window jamb. "I don't want trouble," she said. "All I want is the boy."

"And all I want is you." Gretel's mother reached out. "Come here. You'll be the liveliest worm in the box."

Rita turned and dropped out the window, surprised to land on her feet. She ran across the huge yard screaming, "Albert! Albert Moffit!"

Behind her, Gretel's mother shrieked, "Come back here, you!"

Gretel stepped through the doorway of the shed, dressed in black from head to toe. "Happy Halloween, Rita," she beckoned.

Rita skidded to a stop.

"If you're looking for the boy, he's in there." She aimed a polished black thumbnail over her shoulder. He'll be right out."

Gretel's expression sent a shiver up Rita's spine. "Why should I believe you? You're a witch."

Gretel folded her hands behind her back and stuck out her chin. "Never said I wasn't."

Rita tried to see around her. "Is he really in there?"

Gretel stepped aside. "See for yourself."

Rita heard guttural sounds from inside the shed. A huge mound of naked, pale-gray flesh, topped by a patch of carrot colored hair

240

wobbled into the doorway, laboring to inhale through tiny nostrils, then exhaling with a whistling sound. Thick, puffy lips and two rows of teeth marked its gaping mouth.

"Albert," Rita gasped, tears welling in her eyes. "Sweet Jesus."

Through bulging slits in the oleaginous flesh, tiny glazed eyes pleaded for help as the creature groaned and lurched forward on toeless feet, grunting and squealing like a baby pig. Stumps that had once been fingers wiggled from between thick rolls of fat.

"So his name is Albert." Gretel giggled. "I call him Fatty. He's our Halloween dinner." Dinner!

Rita's stomach twisted into a knot as she recalled the sickening smell of burned meat and the blackened skeleton of Eddie Driscoll.

The raven spread huge black wings, flew off the fence and perched above the door, glaring down at her, its malevolent intelligence cutting to the core of her being.

"Gotcha!" An icy hand grabbed Rita's shoulder, sending a bolt of terror through her. The mother's voice croaked in her ear. "Look, little girl, the birdie's hungry again."

Rita recalled the terrified screams of the pink worm with the tiny human head and the look of horror on its little face as the rapacious creature gobbled her down. Fear flashed to anger. Rita balled her fist and fired a left hook at Gretel's mother. With a surprised grunt, the witch tumbled backward into the trunk of an oak. As dead leaves drifted to the ground, the disheveled beauty stumbled to her feet. Waving her arms and pointing at Rita, she chanted in a deep monotone.

Rita felt a dark presence envelop her like a giant fist, squeezing tighter with each utterance. Her mind reeled. Her arms and legs quivered and her limbs felt like rubber. The witch was changing her into a worm.

The bird squawked and the pressure of the grip relented for a beat. Rita dove forward and grabbed one of Albert's wiggling hands.

"Mama," she shouted.

...Rita felt as if she'd turned into steaming liquid, swirling through a tunnel and pouring out of a pipe. Her body felt solid and heavy as her shoulder slammed against a hard floor. Somebody landed on top of her and rolled off. She opened her eyes to Lorenzo kneeling over her, holding her hand, staring into her eyes. "Rita, are you awake? Talk to me."

"Thank God," she sobbed. "I'm okay. I'm safe." A sob caught in her throat as Chazz Daggett's face appeared over Lorenzo's shoulder. Before she could shout a warning, bony hands clawed at Lorenzo's collar and clamped around his neck. Chazz yanked him up, spun him like a doll and slammed him into the wall, clutching his throat.

"Dah!"

"Run, baby, run," Lorenzo croaked, punching ineffectively at Chazz's head. "Save yourself."

Rita scrambled to her feet and bolted for the door, stopping short when she spied a screwdriver on the console.

Lorenzo's eyes bulged as Chazz pressed his windpipe shut with skeletal thumbs. Lorenzo tugged at the rigid fingers, wheezing for breath until his knees buckled. His eyes rolled up into his head and his hands fell to his sides.

"Bastard." Rita plunged the screwdriver through Chazz's skinny neck. He stiffened and a wet gurgling sound bubbled up from him. His tongue shot from his gaping mouth in a silent scream. Eyes glittering green, he fell backward, crashing to the floor.

Denise's computer voice filled the room. "System shutdown complete."

Rita gasped as Chazz Daggett faded and disappeared, same as the fly.

Monitors, displays and readouts brightened, then faded to darkness and the lights went out all over DreamLand, shrouding the magical creation of Hodge Michaels under a dark blanket of silence.

CHAPTER SIXTY

Albert's plump distorted fingers twitched in Cheryl's hand, then felt bony. The pull of the boy's weight slackened as if someone holding the other end of a rope had let go, causing him to slip from her grasp. She stumbled backward, landing hard on her backside, stunned and disoriented by the sudden darkness. She heard Jack's curse as he fell, followed by the sound of the boy slipping back into the open pod.

Battery powered emergency lights winked on. Pushing herself up on her elbow, Cheryl saw a blinking and bewildered, normally proportioned Albert frowning out at her from the pod. In that moment, his vacant expression and open mouth convinced her that the boy's brain had been damaged.

Little Albert's face pinched into a scowl and his chubby lips puckered into a pout. "What're you gawking at, lady?"

Cheryl breathed a sigh of relief. He would be all right. "Lie still, young man."

"I didn't even dream. I want my money back."

Jack rolled onto his hands and knees, then stood. "Ain't this a kick in the head? The little shit wants a refund."

Albert glared at him. "I better get one, too, Mister. This place is a big, stupid rip-off. I was supposed to see witches. All I did was sleep." He climbed out of the pod and shook a finger at Jack. "I'm telling my dad. He's a lawyer."

"Don't sweat it kid, you'll get a refund," Jack said. "Take him to the snack bar, Alejandro."

243

As Alejandro led the boy away, Jack rolled his eyes and helped Cheryl to her feet. She allowed the momentum to carry her into his arms. The warmth of his hand and the strength of his body against her softness triggered an unexpected surge of arousal. She leaned her head against his chest, closed her eyes and took a deep breath.

"That was a close call." Jack pulled a handkerchief from his pocket to mop his brow. Something metallic hit the floor; a round shiny hoop the size of a poker chip.

Cheryl stared at it. "What in the world is that, Jack?"

His face split into a toothy smile as he picked it up, then tilted his head back, laughed and drew her closer. "Don't tell me you've never seen a nipple ring."

CHAPTER SIXTY ONE

"Is that you, Denise?" Hodge's voice crackled with urgency.

"Lie still, Mister Michaels," the woman detective said with only a trace of Spanish accent. She exchanged glances with her partner.

"Denise, it is you," Hodge wheezed. "Thank God. Listen carefully. Find Morgan – tell him – tell him he's right. Emily Fulbright has morphed into a rat."

The detective's stocky male partner turned to one of the ambulance attendants. "He secure?"

The attendant tugged at the dolly straps and nodded.

"Release me." Hodge struggled against the restraints. "I'm in charge here. People are depending on me. Turn me loose!"

Lorenzo let go of Rita's hand. "I'll get the door." He headed for the double exit doors holding a key card.

"I'll see to that, *señor.*" The detective held out her hand.

As Lorenzo handed over the card, Rita stepped up beside him, touched his shoulder and whispered to the detective, "Where are they taking Mister Michaels?"

"Across the border. Scripps Hospital."

"Liar. Don't believe her," Hodge muttered as they wheeled him out of the building. "She's putting me in the sewer. The rats are going to eat me."

They stood beneath the emergency light at the DreamLand exit. Cold Pacific mist and swirling fog shrouded the parking lot, empty, save for the police cars and ambulances at the exit doors.

"We'll see you at the hospital, Hodge," Rita said.

"Don't let them take me. Don't let the rats eat me." His whole body shook with sobs.

The lead attendant released the dolly's brake and pulled up his collar. "What a shitty night." They guided the litter bearing Hodge down the long ramp to the waiting ambulance. "And tomorrow's gonna be another lousy day."

"Maybe he's wrong," Lorenzo whispered, slipping his arm around Rita's waist. He pulled her close and kissed her cheek. "Maybe tomorrow'll be okay."

ABOUT THE AUTHORS

Ken Reeth (1932 – May 9, 2005) was a colorful and creative disc jockey well known to many hippies and rock music fans as **Brother Love**. *Brother Love's Underground* was a radio show in the late-60's that was dedicated to psychedelic and underground rock music. It originated from Pittsburgh radio station **WAMO-FM**, with Reeth being its psychedelic DJ and Emcee. It was also aired, via tape, on Dynamic Broadcasting which owned **WILD-AM** in Boston, **WUFO-AM** in Buffalo, and **WOAH** in Miami.

While working at **WAMO**, which had a soul and R&B format, Reeth got the idea to do a show promoting the growing psychedelic rock music scene, mostly based in San Francisco and Los Angeles. Like Tom Donahue, his west-coast counterpart, he was one of the first to introduce listeners to Iron Butterfly, Country Joe and the Fish, The Mothers of Invention, the early Doors, Jimi Hendrix, West Coast Pop Art Experimental Band, Vanilla Fudge and others. Although many of the artists on the show have been mainstays of classic rock stations for decades now, this was very adventurous radio programming at the time.

Ken was born in The Bronx and moved to Allentown, Pennsylvania when he was a teenager. He was part of a nightclub comedy team called Reeth & King and later became a morning radio duo on **WHOL** in Allentown and then on **WDRC** in Hartford, Connecticut. He went on to **WAMO** in Pittsburgh and later to Vice President of programming for Dynamic Broadcasting before moving on to Dynamic Broadcasting's **WLTO** station in Miami, Florida as manager. He left Pittsburgh in 1973 for the West Coast and bought **KKAR**, a country station in Pomona, where his on-air personality was **Romeo Jones**.

Ken was a multi-published member of ASCAP, the American Society of Composers, Authors and Publishers and wrote the lyrics to dozens of recorded songs, including the Rockabilly Hall of Fame classics, ***Rockin Billy***, ***Endless Love*** and ***Pity Me***, featured in the international award winning film, "**The Exiles**". He also served on the Board of Directors of the Academy of Country Music and garnered several **CLIO** awards for writing and producing radio commercials. During a highly successful thirty year radio career, Ken authored countless newspaper columns, promotion pieces, and hundreds of press releases.

A familiar voice to radio listeners in Pittsburgh, Boston, Miami and San Diego, Ken left a thriving radio career to nourish a lifelong hunger to write.

Matthew J. Pallamary's historical novel of first contact between shamans and Jesuits in 18th century South America, titled, *Land Without Evil*, was published in hard cover by Charles Publishing, and has received rave reviews along with a San Diego Book Award for mainstream fiction. It was chosen as a Reading Group Choices selection. *Land Without Evil* was also adapted into a full-length stage and sky show, co-written by Agent Red with Matt Pallamary, directed by Agent Red, and performed by Sky Candy, an Austin Texas aerial group. The making of the show was the subject of a PBS series, Arts in Context episode, which garnered an EMMY nomination. *Land Without Evil* is in development as a feature film.

His nonfiction book, *The Infinity Zone: A Transcendent Approach to Peak Performance* is a collaboration with professional tennis coach Paul Mayberry which offers a fascinating exploration of the phenomenon that occurs at the nexus of perfect form and motion, bringing balance, power, and coordination to physical and mental activities. *The Infinity Zone* took 1st place in the International Book Awards, Nonfiction, New Age category, and was a finalist in the San Diego Book Awards

His first book, a short story collection titled *The Small Dark Room*

Of The Soul was noted in The Year's Best Horror and Fantasy.

It's follow up *A Short Walk to the Other Side* was an International Book Award Finalist.

Dreamland, a novel about computer generated dreaming, written with Ken Reeth won an Independent e-Book Award in the Horror/Thriller category.

Matt's work has appeared in Oui, New Dimensions, The Iconoclast, Starbright, Infinity, Passport, The Short Story Digest, Redcat, The San Diego Writer's Monthly, Connotations, Phantasm, Essentially You, The Haven Journal, and many others. His fiction has been featured in The San Diego Union Tribune which he has also reviewed books for, and his work has been heard on KPBS-FM in San Diego, KUCI FM in Irvine, KX 93.5 in Laguna Beach, television Channel Three in Santa Barbara, and The Susan Cameron Block Show in Vancouver.

He has been a guest on the following nationally syndicated talk shows; Paul Rodriguez, In The Light with Michelle Whitedove, Susun Weed, Medicine Woman, Inner Journey with Greg Friedman, and Environmental Directions Radio series. Matt has also appeared on the following television shows; Bridging Heaven and Earth, Elyssa's Raw and Wild Food Show, Things That Matter, Literary Gumbo, Indie Authors TV, and ECONEWS. He has also been a frequent guest on numerous podcasts, among them, The Psychedelic Salon, and C-Realm.

He has taught fiction workshops at the Southern California Writers' Conference in San Diego, Palm Springs, and Los Angeles, and at the Santa Barbara Writers' Conference for twenty five years. He has also lectured at the Greater Los Angeles Writer's Conference, the Getting It Write conference in Oregon, the Saddleback Writers' Conference, the Rio Grande Writers' Seminar, the National Council of Teachers of English, The San Diego Writer's and Editor's Guild, The San Diego Book Publicists, The Pacific Institute for Professional Writing, and he has been a panelist at the World Fantasy Convention, Con-Dor, and Coppercon. He is presently Editor in Chief of Muse Harbor Publishing.

Matt also received the Man of the Year 2000 from San Diego Writer's

Monthly Magazine. His memoir *Spirit Matters*, which details his journeys to Peru, working with shamanic plant medicines took first place in the San Diego Book Awards Spiritual Book Category, and was an Award-Winning Finalist in the autobiography/memoir category of the National Best Book Awards, sponsored by USA Book News. *Spirit Matters* is also available as an audio book.

Matt frequently visits the jungles, mountains, and deserts of North, Central, and South America pursuing his studies of shamanism and ancient cultures.

WWW.MATTPALLAMARY.COM

BOOKS BY MATTHEW J. PALLAMARY

THE SMALL DARK ROOM OF THE SOUL

LAND WITHOUT EVIL

SPIRIT MATTERS

A SHORT WALK TO THE OTHER SIDE

THE INFINITY ZONE (WITH PAUL MAYBERRY)

CYBERCHRIST

EYE OF THE PREDATOR

NIGHT WHISPERS

PHANTASTIC FICTION